# FREEDOM BRIDGE

## A COLD WAR THRILLER

# ERIKA HOLZER

To men and women who share this common conviction:
Freedom is a right, universal and inalienable.

# HISTORICAL NOTE

President and Mrs. Ronald Reagan arrived in Berlin on June 12, 1987. At 2:00 P.M. the President appeared at the Brandenburg Gate behind two panes of bulletproof glass.

Roughly 45,000 people were in attendance, among them Chancellor Helmut Kohl, West Berlin mayor Eberhard Diepgen, and West German president Richard von Weizsacker.

"We welcome change and openness," Ronald Reagan declared, "for we believe that freedom and openness go together, that the advance of human liberty can only strengthen the cause of world peace. There is one sign the Soviets can make that would be unmistakable, that would advance dramatically the cause of freedom and peace. General Secretary Gorbachev, if you seek peace, if you seek prosperity for the Soviet Union and Eastern Europe, if you seek liberalization, come here to this gate."

President of the United States of America, Ronald W. Reagan, then spoke six words that ushered in the coming of a new era . . .

*Mr. Gorbachev, tear down this wall!*

# PREFACE

When the iconic prime-mover of the 1917 Bolshevik Revolution, Vladimir Ilyich Ulyanov Lenin, died, he left behind the political, economic, and cultural embodiment of soul-killing collectivism and the institutionalized statist force necessary to implement it.

Lenin's philosophical and political heirs, especially Josef Stalin, would carry Marxist-Leninist principles and programs to their logical extremes, leaving in the wake of their almost 80 years of power destroyed nations, tens of millions of corpses, and the moribund but never fully discredited killer viruses of collectivism and statism.

# CHAPTER 1

It was during the Soviet Union's collectivist-statist hell
that, in 1917, eighteen-year-old Anna Petrovsky married
fellow medical student, Yuri Glazov.

The next year, inspired by hatred of the Czar, grinding
poverty suffered by the lower classes and the peasants,
opposition to Russia's war with Germany, and influenced
by communist-socialist propaganda slogans such as
"Peace, Land, and Bread," Yuri Glazov decided to leave
medical school and join the Revolution.

That night, as he told Anna of his decision, she took a
step back and looked at him with luminous eyes. He stood
before her with the pride of a gladiator poised for battle,
she thought, with the dignity and flair of a centurion as he
flashed a smile of perfect teeth . . . like the sun coming out.

"I'm glad you approve of my decision," he said, the smile
reaching his eyes as he pulled her into his arms.

But by 1918, Anna had learned that her husband
had become a member of the Cheka, the dreaded secret
political police—later to become the GPU, the NKVD, and
by 1954, the KGB.

Yuri was a rising star, Anna thought bitterly as she recalled that moment of intimacy and candor soon after their son Aleksei had been born. Yuri had encouraged her to complete her medical studies. "Become a doctor for both of us," he told her. "I've lost my taste for medicine."

What he *hadn't* told her was that he'd acquired a taste for blood.

From then on, she was determined to keep her husband away from their son, Aleksei, but long hours of study and an exhausting schedule punctuated with exams left her with little time at home. She watched helplessly as her son—under his father's sometimes patient, sometimes boisterous tutelage—changed from a timid, introverted child into a self-centered bully.

Anna had vowed never to have another child. She'd lost that battle not once, but twice. Kiril, born in 1921, was conceived on a night when her usual deftness at putting her husband off with an excuse was met with unusual force fueled by vodka. Kolya, born the next year, was conceived under the same circumstances.

Though her pregnancies had been unwanted, Kiril and Kolya filled Anna's life with optimism. It was impossible not to feel that way in the presence of two such wholesome beings with their boundless energy and playful inquisitiveness. They had also inherited some of her Petrovsky genes—miniature mirrors of her face and each other's. Prominent cheek bones. Hair so thick and glossy she could never resist running her fingers through it, which caused them to erupt with giggles. Their eyes were the same dark brown as their hair, and she could tell that both boys would grow up to be tall and angular like her and her father before her.

Then one night in 1925, everyone's life changed. Anna had been working late at the hospital. When she returned to the spacious GPU-provided apartment she shared with Yuri, she opened the front door, heard him mutter something from the bedroom, and then a thunderous crash. Her drunken husband had fallen out of bed—again. Dropping her medical bag, she rushed into the bedroom to attend to the besotted man, not realizing her bag had popped open.

Understandably, the two young boys had been drawn to some of the items that spilled from her medical bag, but it was four-year-old Kolya who grabbed hold of a pair of scissors.

*Would she ever forget that scream? It had pierced her own heart even as Kolya punctured his chest with the scissors.*

As soon as Anna had slowed the bleeding, she closed Kiril inside the boys' bedroom, out of the reach of his father, and rushed Kolya to the hospital for x-rays. What they revealed was a mixed blessing.

The point of the scissors had lightly touched Kolya's heart, but had not pierced it. The only way his heart could be examined for further damage was by sawing through his sternum, and if Kolya's heart *did* need repair, Anna knew—as did her colleagues—that no one in the Soviet Union had the skills to perform such a difficult procedure. She would have to leave the country or Kolya would die.

When she returned home and confronted Yuri, he was hesitant—torn between GPU disapproval and remorse that his drunkenness had as good as pushed those scissors into his child's heart. With steely resolve and a mercilessness she hadn't known she possessed, Anna cut through her husband's indecision by using his own interrogation techniques against him. She played on his guilt until he capitulated.

Yuri Glazov had called in every favor owed him by his secret police colleagues, swearing on his life that Anna and the child would return to the Soviet Union.

When the time came for her to leave, Anna's "goodbye" was painfully brief. Aleksei was out somewhere with friends, so to see her off, there was only seven-year-old

Kiril and Anna's younger sister, Marissa, who promised to care for Kiril until Anna returned. As Anna bent down to embrace Kiril, her gold charm bracelet jangled. Dangling from it were a half-dozen miniature medical instruments. The child frantically tugged at one of them, not wanting his mother to leave, and it broke off and fell to the floor. Anna picked it up and pressed it into Kiril's hand. "It's called a *scalpel*, little one. Doctors use real ones," she said softly. "Grandfather Petrovsky was a doctor too. He had all these tiny instruments put on my bracelet the year I entered medical school. Will you do me a favor, Kiril? Will you keep the scalpel with you *always*? Until I get back?" she corrected herself as tears streamed down her face. "Take care of him until I return, Marissa," she pleaded as Kiril began to cry. "Promise me you'll protect him from his father."

\* \* \*

When the German doctors opened the four-year-old's chest in April, they were shocked to see that although the scissors had not punctured Kolya's heart, he suffered from a malfunction in his mitral valve which needed repair. As experienced as the German surgeons were, they were reluctant to attempt the operation. In 1923, Dr. Elliott Cutler of the Department of Surgery at Harvard Medical School had performed the world's first successful heart valve surgery on a 12-year-old girl with rheumatic mitral stenosis, but they knew the procedure had a ninety percent mortality rate. As Kolya lay on the operating table with his chest open and his little heart beating, Anna told the surgeons to go ahead. It was when Kolya was recuperating from the successful operation that Anna first considered not returning to the Soviet Union.

While waiting for Kolya to recover, Anna had come to

recognize the nature of the regime to which she would be sentencing her youngest son if she returned to the Soviet Union. Lenin and his Bolsheviks had done their work too well. Central planning, antithetical to the prosperity generated by a market economy, had become the means by which the state made all economic decisions. An agrarian country inhabited mainly by peasants was to become a nation of heavy industry, necessitating countless tons of coal, iron, and other natural resources to be torn from the earth by millions of slave laborers. Agriculture was to be collectivized, with private land ownership a relic of the past. Strict censorship prevailed. Police and intelligence agencies had unbridled power. There was no rule of law. And the Gulag—or worse—awaited enemies, and even friends, of the regime.

Anna knew her son Aleksei, completely under the sway of his father, was already lost to her. If she defected, Kiril would be cared for by an Enemy of the People, her sister Marissa. But if she went back, she would be sentencing Kolya to life in Lenin's hell. For the first time, she realized with a kind of quiet horror that she wouldn't only have to choose between family and freedom; she would be choosing between brothers. There were moments when she felt ready to die rather than make that choice—a choice no mother should have to make. It was one Anna would remember making every waking moment of her life, and often in her dreams.

What finally pushed her in one direction rather than the other was the knowledge that whatever she could do for Kiril if she did go back was infinitely less than what she could do for Kolya if she didn't.

The waiting had been hard. First in Berlin, when the Nazi Party had marched into Nuremberg. Then more waiting for her fears to diminish, to be replaced by a growing conviction that she was safe from the long arm of Soviet retribution.

Gradually, she felt free to accept the attentions of a young American physician—one of the surgeons who'd assisted in the operation that had saved Kolya's life. She waited with eagerness for him to complete the last days of a two-year fellowship program under the best heart surgeon in Germany. She waited with impatience for papers to come through which "proved" that she was a native-born German. For more papers that "documented" the American surgeon was the father of her German-born son. And finally, for American passports that permitted the three of them to set sail in November of 1927 from Bremen to the United States.

En route, the captain had married Anna "Petrovsky" to Dr. Max Brenner, giving her child a father and Anna a husband. It also gave her son a new name and the opportunity to live his life to the fullest in the freest country on earth.

# CHAPTER 2

For the first three weeks of Anna and Kolya's departure, Yuri Glazov had been able to placate his Cheka colleagues despite their insistent questions about when his wife and son would return—a task made more difficult by Anna's unwillingness to communicate with him. Glazov's excuses were plausible. The child's heart surgery was more complicated than originally diagnosed. Tests were needed. Finding the best surgeon took time. The doctor's operating schedule was overbooked. An operating theater had to be available. A judge's order was necessary for such a major operation. Financial arrangements had to be made. Serious cardiac complications had arisen. But as three weeks turned into two months, his excuses became more transparent, and he knew it.

He also knew that during the past two months, GPU agents in Berlin had kept their Moscow superiors abreast of the developments. So when he was informed, along with his superiors, that the operation had been performed but that recovery time for repairing Kolya's heart valve repair was lengthy, he celebrated by drinking himself into an alcoholic stupor and prevailed upon his widowed sister, Sofia Andreyev, to care for Aleksei.

Three more months passed, after which reports from the GPU agents in Berlin ceased. Yuri Glazov's drinking continued unabated, his mental and physical condition deteriorating so rapidly that Sofia took over the care, not only of Aleksei, but—despite the pleas of Marissa Petrovsky—of seven-year-old Kiril as well.

Glazov's GPU superior, Oleg Reznikov, had run out of patience, and Yuri Glazov's descent into physical and mental oblivion was the least of his problems. He issued orders to his GPU agents in Berlin to find out exactly what had happened to Yuri's wife and son.

The agents' inquiries, having taken a back seat to more pressing intelligence assignments, took another two months. Finally, fearing for their lives, they reported to Reznikov in December that Anna Glazov and her child, together with one of the boy's physicians, had the month before departed from Bremen for the United States—and that they had been married by the captain of the passenger ship *S.S. Stuttgart*.

Reznikov was apoplectic. Two citizens of the Soviet Union had defected to the United States despite the promises of a fellow GPU operative who had sworn on his life that his wife and child would return!

*On his life.*

If he were to save his own skin, Reznikov knew, he had to act quickly. He arranged for poison to be slipped into Glazov's vodka, followed by a bad fall that broke the poor fellow's neck. Since it was a way of life with Yuri—the drinking, the falls—Reznikov was confident an autopsy would be ruled out. It was.

As for the Glazov children—Aleksei, age eight and Kiril, three years younger—Reznikov came up with the perfect solution. The children would be raised by Yuri Glazov's widowed sister, Sofia, reliable long-term member of the

Communist Party.

Nor did the red-haired Marissa Petrovsky present a problem. Tainted by her sister's traitorous conduct, she would only need to be reminded that the State was omnipotent. That the Gulag awaited.

Oleg Reznikov was not without a sense of humor. In Anna Glazov's haste to defect with her German surgeon, she'd had no opportunity to divorce her husband. By arranging for Yuri's death, he thought drily, he had done Anna the great service of obliterating the stigma of bigamy.

His sister, Sofia Andreyev lived in Novogorod, an important historic city in the Soviet Union that lay between Moscow and St. Petersburg. Using a stubby finger to push his wire-rimmed glasses up his nose, Reznikov decided that henceforth the surname of both children would be Andreyev. They would be told their mother and brother had deserted them and their father, Yuri Glazov, had died in the service of his country.

Reznikov burned the Glazov file and flushed the ashes down the toilet.

\* \* \*

Asserting her Party status, the widow Andreyev immediately enrolled eight-year-old Aleksei in a nine-year school—the highest level of general educational institutions. Five-year-old Kiril would be enrolled in three years as soon as he turned eight.

As each boy turned ten, Sofia enrolled him in the Young Pioneers—a mass youth organization designed to turn young children into staunch Communists from an early age. The main trappings were the red banner flag and a red neck-scarf. There were salutes, parades, rallies, flag-raising events, camping, bonfires, festivals, and jamborees. Membership was roughly from primary school through adolescence.

Sometime between the ages of fourteen and eighteen, each boy would be moved up into the Young Communist League. But it was the Young Pioneers experience that drove a wedge between Aleksei and Kiril.

Before moving in with his Aunt Sofia, Aleksei had doted on his father. Yuri Glazov had taught him to be regimented, obedient, distrustful, cagey, dishonest, cruel—a fearsome bully.

Kiril, three years younger, had never had much contact with his father when he was sober, which wasn't often. Nor did he care for his aunt. For one thing, she took him away from his gentle and loving Aunt Marissa. For another, Aunt Sofia had thick legs and walked like a man—sometimes even wearing long pants! Her hair was black and very short. He often found himself staring at her stubby fingernails whenever she gripped his arm to drag him off someplace.

While Aleksei prospered in the junior communist organizations, becoming feared rather than liked, Kiril rebelled as best he could by disobeying orders, breaking discipline, and refusing to participate in overtly patriotic conduct.

When Sofia had had enough of Kiril's disobedience, she decided to teach her young charge a lesson. Reminding him he was the son of an Enemy of the People, and that the state could do what it wished with him— from sending him to a Gulag camp to deporting him to some remote place in the Soviet Union, or even dumping him in some state-run orphanage—she took him to such an orphanage to underscore her point.

It was late November. The first thing Kiril saw was children without shoes, their bare feet frostbitten. Sofia described how starvation and malnutrition were the norm and child-inmates were left to forage through rubbish. She pointed out acute shortages of everything from shoes and clothing to blankets, and then took him to see four *lucky* children who shared a filthy lice-ridden mattress without blankets while the *unlucky* ones slept on the floor. Reliable heat was non-existent, as were washing facilities. Trips to the bathhouse were, at best, every other month. The absence of toilets forced the children to relieve themselves anywhere—yards, hallways, even where they slept—which, of course, led to disease. Typhus, dysentery, malaria, scurvy, and rickets were rampant. Corpses lay where they died until someone with a face-mask got around to removing them. The mortality rate in some orphanages—particularly in the Ukraine—was one-hundred percent, she told him. Beatings by older children and staff were common. So were sexual attacks.

Kiril refused to give his aunt the satisfaction of bursting into tears even as he bit his lip until it bled. Only after he was alone in his own room did he allow himself to cry. For weeks he cried himself to sleep every night.

But he got the message.

"There, but for the grace of State and Party, go I."

While Aleksei thrived—not academically, but in contact sports and extracurricular activities—Kiril learned as much as he could about as many subjects as possible. He had never forgotten his visit to the orphanage. He vowed he never would. Someday, somehow, he would liberate himself from the Soviet Union.

From 1936 to 1938, there were four major show trials in the Soviet Union as Josef Stalin rid himself of his enemies, real and imagined. Three of every five marshals were eliminated, along with 90 percent of the generals, 80 percent of the colonels, and every regimental commander—a total of some 30,000 military officers. The entire Politburo was purged, as was most of the Central Committee of the Communist Party, and countless intellectuals, bureaucrats, factory managers, and foreign communists who lived in the Soviet Union. Mass arrests, torture, imprisonment, execution without trial, and an absence of authentic judicial process was the rule, not the exception. The NKVD's own estimate was two-fold: roughly 700,000 men, women, and children shot in 1937-1938 alone and hundreds of thousands more shipped to the Gulag work camps.

The charges against these political prisoners ran the gamut from sabotage, spying, and counterrevolution, to conspiring with foreign powers. Most of the accused confessed under torture. As to those who steadfastly refused, they too were guilty because Stalin *said* they were.

Aleksei was eighteen years old when the trials began. He followed the proceedings with morbid interest, identifying with the prosecutors. He was convinced the charges were legitimate, the confessions and proof conclusive, the convictions and sentences just. In the Young Pioneers, the Young Communist League, and then as an observer of the Stalin show trials, Aleksei Andreyev was learning two important lessons. That fear was a powerful weapon. And that to induce fear one had to possess power. Wielding both would bring even strong men to their knees.

Kiril, who had just turned fifteen when the show trials began, instinctively recognized they were a sham. Stalin was murdering innocent people so he could consolidate his power and feed off the slogan popularized by Karl Marx in 1875: "From each according to his ability to each according to his needs."

From that time on, not a day passed when Kiril did not feel the weight of collectivism and statism pressing down on his soul.

# CHAPTER 3

L iving with Sofia Andreyev, a die-hard Communist since 1922, had by 1938 driven thoughts of Anna and Kolya, and even of his father, from Aleksei Andreyev's mind. Under his aunt's tutelage, and after a decade in communist youth groups, nineteen-year-old Aleksei had become a dedicated Communist. Ordinarily, as the son of an Enemy of the People, he would have had no chance to enter training for any of the Soviet intelligence or security services. But proud of what she had turned the boy into, his aunt got him admitted to training for the secret police— by then known as the NKVD. The organization had a huge jurisdiction. Performing mass extrajudicial executions. Operating the Gulag's forced labor camps. Deporting Russians and other nationalities to unpopulated regions of the U.S.S.R. Guarding Soviet borders. Conducting espionage. Assassinating political opponents. Influencing foreign governments. Enforcing Stalinist policies in other countries' Communist movements. Recruiting foreign spies. Interrogating arrestees. Coercing confessions. As befitting such an organization, NKVD training was physically arduous, mentally challenging, morally ambiguous, and often brutal. Aleksei loved every minute of it.

Having raised the two brothers during their most formative years, Sofia Andreyev knew that because Kiril so hated the State, he would have to be channeled into adult work that was largely divorced from politics. And because he'd always excelled in math and science and shown an interest in anatomy, his aunt had convinced him to try for medical school. Being admitted wasn't hard. Kiril had finished the nine-year school with honors. He possessed a rudimentary knowledge of English and German, and his Aunt Sofia was a formidable presence in the Novogorod Communist Party. What also worked to his advantage was how the State, in the 1920s, had made a special effort to increase the number of doctors—partly in anticipation of a coming war with Germany. New medical schools were opened. One year was cut from the course of study and Latin was eliminated as an entrance requirement. All of which shifted the emphasis away from written examinations and increased the number of social and political subjects in the curriculum. Ever since his frightening experience at the orphanage, Kiril had avoided political problems. By the time he entered medical school, his early childhood taint, neutralized by his aunt, was over a decade old. Ironically, having a brother in the NKVD didn't hurt either. But no matter how comfortable he was in the apolitical cocoon of medical school, Kiril continued to feel isolated and alone.

On September 1, 1939, forces were set in motion which would fundamentally impact the lives of both brothers. On that day Nazi Germany—and, sixteen days later, the Soviet Union—launched a pre-planned joint attack on Poland. The combined onslaught against an essentially defenseless sovereign country would be prelude to a war between the two aggressors at a time in the not entirely unforeseen future. Indeed, Stalin knew Hitler would attack the Soviet Union. He just didn't know when. In anticipation of this falling out between partners, the NKVD rushed Aleksei through his final training and into the field. As for the medical school Kiril was enrolled in, it accelerated his final course, dispensed with exams, and graduated him months ahead of time.

On November 30, 1939, the Soviet Union invaded Finland. A miscalculation, as it turned out. While the Red Army outnumbered the Finns two-and-a-half to one, the Soviet troops were ill-equipped for the freezing, snowbound, winter weather. And thanks to Stalin's 1936-1938 purges of the Red Army's officer corps, there were no competent commanders. Despite fierce Finnish resistance and substantial support from the Allies, nature proved determinative. Not until the spring of 1940, after the snow had melted, were more able commanders available to lead a new Red Army offensive. The Finns finally capitulated, relinquished territory that the Soviets coveted, and Dr. Kiril Andreyev got to spend a few months mostly treating frostbite cases.

In mid-1940, the Soviets took over Latvia, Lithuania, and Estonia. Aleksei was posted there to suppress anti-Soviet sentiments. But the tide turned on June 22, 1941 when the formidable Nazi war machine attacked the Soviet Union in Operation Barbarossa. Aleksei, by then a lieutenant in the NKVD, was recalled to Moscow to hunt Nazi agents.

Kiril, already in Finland, spoke some English. He was sent to the Eastern Front—to Murmansk—where Soviet doctors were needed, and where the Germans were already experiencing huge casualties. Murmansk, not far from Russia's borders with Norway and Finland, was the largest city north of the Arctic Circle. Being a port city—a crucial link to the Western World—it was expected to play a large role in the Soviet Union's receipt of American and other allied Lend Lease. By September 1941, three months after the German invasion of the Soviet Union, Lend Lease war materiel began to flow by Arctic convoys into Murmansk—tanks, artillery, ammunition, airplanes, trucks, and jeeps. As grateful as Stalin was for American and allied assistance, and as much as he understood how necessary it was for Americans to be stationed in Murmansk—how else to manage the countless tons of materiel flooding the port?—his paranoia dictated there be as few Americans as possible.

Even so, there were enough Americans for Kiril to hone not only his English, but a lot of American slang as well. Over time, he realized his NKVD watchers had lost minute-by-minute interest in him. Having settled into a routine, they were satisfied he was somewhere on the base; after all, there was nowhere for him to go. Taking full advantage of this sliver of independence, Kiril made it a practice whenever he was treating his American patients for relatively minor ailments—frostbite, alcohol poisoning, pneumonia, broken limbs, and accidental gunshots—to learn everything the GIs were willing to share with him about their country. Its culture and geography. Its economic system and how the free market actually worked. Fascinating accounts of individual rights. And most important, America's *Declaration of Independence* and *Constitution*. Kiril took a kind of defiant pleasure in this last, knowing that it would be treasonous for him to possess a *copy* of either document!

One day, as he set the broken arm of an American GI with a legal background, Kiril and the GI were so deeply engaged in discussion that he barely noticed how new patients were lining up just outside the clinic door. Until he realized that the first man in line wore the uniform of a Soviet Air Force officer who was pressing a bloody rag against a gash just under his hairline. Quickly finishing up with the American GI, he gestured for the officer to step forward.

"Your English is excellent," the officer said.

Kiril's jaw tightened.

*How much did you overhear?*

"My name is Stepan Brodsky," the Soviet Air Force officer said with a smile, then added *sotto voce*, "You have nothing to fear from me, doctor."

Kiril studied the man. They were about the same height, though the Russian officer was a bit more muscular. His blond hair was closely cropped, his eyes hazel. But what impressed Kiril was Stepan Brodsky's ability to turn his inquiring eyes into blank unreadable discs depending on whom he was talking to.

What made them fast friends over time was the discovery that they both lived and breathed the same dream—defecting from the Soviet Union to the United States of America.

When Stepan was reassigned to Moscow, he and Kiril vowed to keep in touch.

The war went on. As materiel continued to flow from Arctic convoys into Murmansk American servicemen remained, giving Kiril the chance to become more and more fluent in American English and the opportunity to learn more and more about his devoutly-wished-for destination: the United States of America.

\* \* \*

When the war ended in 1945 and the Murmansk pipeline was shut down, Kiril was ordered back to Moscow. He looked up his brother Aleksei, now a captain in the NKVD, hoping to enlist his assistance in finding their Aunt Marissa. Aleksei offered to help, but either the war or the NKVD had buried all traces of her. As for his inquiries about Stepan Brodsky, Kiril learned his friend had been drafted by the NKVD to be a translator in the Soviet zone of Berlin. Although Brodsky had been admonished not to fraternize with anyone outside the NKVD, the two were soon in contact.

Kiril began looking for work as a physician. Although his medical education had not been of the best quality and not nearly long enough, his practical experience in Finland and Murmansk had turned him into a more than capable generalist. But with so many war veterans returning home, there was a surfeit of doctors. For the next few years Kiril took whatever medical work he could find. Drawing blood at laboratories. Filling in at emergency rooms. Assisting physicians at public health clinics. Taking x-rays at special Communist Party hospitals.

One day, about six years after he'd left Murmansk, Kiril was working as a nurse in a private Kremlin hospital reserved for top officials. During an operation, an anesthesiologist—a high-ranking Politburo member—collapsed from what later proved to be a heart attack. While attendants prepared to operate, the chief surgeon instantly turned to Kiril and asked if he knew anything about the IV anesthesia drip in the patient's arm.

"I do," Kiril replied.

The surgeon—muttering that if the patient died, all of them would no doubt suffer the same fate—handed Kiril the instructions. Kiril kept the anesthesia flowing, the surgeon removed an about-to-rupture appendix, and there were smiles and handshakes all around. The appreciative and renowned surgeon, Dr. Mikhail Yanin, took Kiril under his wing, taught him how to operate a heart-lung machine—its purpose to bypass the heart during open-heart surgery—and used Kiril in so many operations that he became one of Moscow's leading heart-lung physicians. As such, he was invited to join Yanin's heart surgery team.

# CHAPTER 4

New Year's Day, 1960—a national holiday in the Soviet Union that traditionally begins with a late dinner on New Year's Eve. Smoked fish, sliced sausage, steaming borscht, black bread—and non-stop vodka toasts that undoubtedly had caused last night's twelve-car pileup on an ice-covered highway leading to the hospital. Dr. Kiril Andreyev sighed inwardly. "What time is it?" he asked a technician.

"Twenty past eight, doctor."

Kiril didn't bother to mask his frustration. His eyes, a deeper brown than his hair, were somber. The habitual set of his mouth was firm, masking tight control. And endurance. Occasionally, one corner of his mouth slipped down, suggesting a touch of melancholy.

He sat on a low stool, monitoring the control panel of a boxlike machine on wheels. After examining the pump-heads on top, he followed the downward flow of colorless liquid through clear plastic tubing. The flow was unimpeded.

The nurses had prepped the patient. An anesthesiologist

paced back and forth, and Kiril was on the thin edge of following him.

The operating room doors finally swung open. A man with curly gray hair confined under a green surgical cap strode in. "I have just learned of a catastrophe," Dr. Mikhail Yanin growled. "For the surgical department of this hospital that bears my name. For Soviet medicine!" Yanin announced with characteristic melodrama. "Our trip to Canada was cancelled last night. No funding, they say."

Dr. Yanin glanced at Kiril, aware that his protégé was gripping the sides of his chair even as he managed to keep his face expressionless. Kiril was even better at subterfuge than *he* was, Yanin realized with a touch of pride.

He knew what Kiril had to be feeling right now: a sense of loss and longing as piercing as his own. A Canadian medical-device company had developed a new heart-lung machine that was faster, more reliable, and much less expensive than anything on the market. In an effort to spur sales, CanMedEquip had invited hundreds of cardiac specialists from the developed nations for a weekend of dining, entertainment, and *live* demonstrations of their superior new machine.

And like Yanin, Kiril was no doubt thinking back to September 1945 and the notorious defection to Toronto, Canada of Soviet Embassy cipher clerk, Igor Gouzenko . . .

"The State giveth and the State taketh away," Yanin said gently with a sympathetic glance in Kiril's direction.

"Any chance they'll change their minds?" one of the techs asked.

"Why should they?" Yanin snapped. "They're in charge. The government has money for space stations but not for me to immerse myself in the latest surgical technology, courtesy of my Canadian colleagues. In spite of faulty equipment and seemingly endless shortages, I am expected to accomplish miracles. Worst of all, I am being robbed of a rare opportunity to observe Dr. Kurt Brenner, a world-class heart surgeon, at work!"

The doors swung open again, this time admitting two stone-faced men in dark suits.

Yanin stared at them, momentarily speechless. "How dare you enter my operating room unannounced? Get out. Get out at once!"

One of the men impaled Yanin with a laser-like glance and looked around the operating theater. "Dr. Kiril Andreyev?"

Kiril rose to his feet. "At your service," he said flatly.

"Come," said the man with a curt nod of his head.

"Please," Yanin intervened in a subdued voice. He knew, now, who the men were. "We have a grueling schedule this morning. I need Dr. Andreyev to—"

"Get someone else."

"You don't understand." Yanin's voice was deferential. "Dr. Andreyev anticipates every move I make. He can hook up a heart-lung machine with his eyes closed. Dozens of things can go wrong in cardiac surgery. My plastic tubing is not of the best quality," he said. "If it springs a leak during an operation, it would need immediate repair. Should the blood in the oxygenator drop below a certain level, air could be pumped into the patient's blood stream. If the heart won't start once the operation is over, we have only five minutes to get the patient back on the machine— five minutes or the patient will die."

No answer this time. Stone-face motioned for Kiril to leave.

"I'm sorry, Dr. Yanin," Kiril said . . . and deliberately took his time following the two men out.

A black limousine waited at the curb. Kiril slid in the back seat with the two goons. As he slipped his hands into the pockets of the hospital gown he'd had no time to remove, the limousine shot forward. He didn't need to ask where he was going, or why. Glancing out the window, he saw a familiar banner. Gigantic, it swayed gently in the breeze.

## GLORY TO THE COMMUNIST PARTY
**THE GUIDING FORCE OF THE NEW SOCIETY!**

He eyed a passing parade of faces, early risers on their way to work. People quick to grumble, he mused—but at what? The scarcity of oranges in December? The fact that caviar was available only to foreigners and government officials? He saw women in babushkas lined up for their tedious daily shopping queues. But did they ever direct their anger at the apparatchiks who had a stranglehold on the economy? Unlikely.

They had grown used to the system, he thought. They took for granted that they were slaves. And though his heart went out to these poor creatures whose lives had been reduced to day-by-day survival, he forced himself to look away. It was almost as if the mere sight of them might attach itself to his body like some infectious disease.

There was only one way to avoid that kind of living death, he knew. Never stop dreaming of freedom. From the time he was old enough to think, to reason, he never had.

# CHAPTER 5

The limousine pulled up in front of an imposing structure. With its row upon row of windows and glossy black marble facade, the building had a guileless look—a showplace on tourist itineraries said to house government offices. This was true. The spacious windowed offices were occupied by high-ranking members of the secret police. The windowless core of the building, not visible from the street, contained one of Moscow's most infamous prisons.

Kiril entered a small anteroom. As usual, the wooden benches that hugged the walls were filled with an odd assortment of people. Young, old, middle-aged. Shabby suits and shapeless dresses. Tensed shoulders and averted eyes. The one thing they had in common was fear.

"Go right in please, Dr. Andreyev!" the secretary said officiously.

Kiril nodded his thanks, not wanting to give her the satisfaction of knowing he was nervous. As he walked toward a burnished oak door, it occurred to him that if his brother's office had a sign, it would have said: DEFECTIONS AND CONFESSIONS.

He walked in. As usual, his brother's desk was in friendly disorder. Papers, books, assorted pipes, a half-eaten sandwich—and files, files, files.

Aleksei Andreyev wore a loose, ill-fitting jacket. Bits of tobacco nestled in the wrinkles of his shirtfront. His eyes behind pale-rimmed glasses were light blue with a tendency to blink rapidly. He raised his head, acknowledging Kiril's presence, and returned to an open file.

As he settled into a chair, Kiril thought of his friend Stepan. If Air Force Captain Stepan Brodsky had had an official job description, Kiril thought with a hidden smile, it would have been FOREIGN VIP SECURITY.

He wondered if Stepan knew the trip to Canada had been canceled.

"Well?" Aleksei said when he finally looked up. "What do you have for me?"

"As you can imagine," Kiril said, "Dr. Yanin is upset about the trip to Canada being canceled. But does his anger and annoyance mean he was planning to defect when he got to Toronto?" Kiril asked rhetorically. "Absolutely not."

"What makes you so sure?" Aleksei responded irritably.

"For one thing, Dr. Yanin is genuinely distressed about being denied the opportunity to meet Dr. Kurt Brenner, the famous American heart surgeon. Frankly, Aleksei, I wouldn't mind meeting Brenner myself."

"Frankly," Aleksei said drily, "we wouldn't mind getting our hands on him either."

"Whatever I can do to help," Kiril said with a straight face just as Stepan walked in and greeted him with a warm smile.

"I take it you won't be needing my unit to handle Canada in the near future," Stepan told Aleksei. "What I suggest—"

*Not to worry, Stepan. Canada isn't our only ticket out of here. I'll keep trying, and so will you. God knows we've been at it long enough.*

Kiril remained in his chair, waiting for Aleksei to dismiss him like an office boy. He didn't have long to wait.

"Kiril?" a preoccupied Aleksei said, gesturing toward the door.

"See you later, Stepan," Kiril said cheerfully, getting to his feet. "You too, Aleksei."

*If you only knew about me and Stepan—and yes, about Dr. Yanin, you smug bastard. Did you really think I'd betray my mentor?*

# CHAPTER 6

A leksei didn't waste any time.

As soon as Kiril left, he told Brodsky to clear everything from his schedule. "Your top priority is VIP security for a two-day Four

Power summit. April 30th to May 1st in Potsdam."

"Potsdam, East Germany? How much time do I have?"

"Relax," Aleksei said. "You have a few months to work out the details."

"Why Potsdam?"

"Time for a mini-history lesson, I see." Aleksei lit his pipe and pushed back in his chair. "Glienicker," he said thoughtfully. "It went through many architectural phases—wooden, brick stanchions with a movable wooden center to accommodate steamer traffic, and eventually a suspension bridge. What makes it unique is that half the bridge is in East Germany, half in West Berlin."

*The bridge that straddles East Germany and West Berlin!*

Brodsky willed himself to stay calm. If only he were as adept as Kiril at hiding his emotions.

"What makes it historic," Aleksei continued, "is the

Potsdam Conference in the summer of 1945. It was the first meeting between General Secretary Joseph Stalin and the late Franklin Delano Roosevelt's successor, Harry Truman. The General Secretary had charmed an ailing Roosevelt. Truman, as it turned out, was not so malleable." Aleksei paused to take a bottle of vodka and a glass from a desk drawer. Russian style, he emptied the glass in one gulp.

"But I'm getting ahead of myself. During the closing days of the Great Patriotic War, the Nazis began blowing up all bridges leading into Berlin. Glienicker suffered a slightly different fate—a random artillery shell. By the end of April '45, a makeshift wooden bridge parallel to Glienicker's damaged steel had been built in order to restore the important road link between Potsdam and Berlin. Between '47 and '49 the bridge was rebuilt and reopened as Bruecke der Einheit. Bridge of Unity."

"The word unity seems an odd choice to describe our relations with the West Germans," Brodsky said drily.

"Indeed. According to some accounts, as repairs were underway in Ceceilienhof Palace on the eve of the 1945 conference, Glienicker Bridge was referred to as Bruecke der Freiheit—Bridge of Freedom—to commemorate work done by American GIs and Russian soldiers."

*Wait until Kiril hears that*, Brodsky thought.

Aleksei's pipe had gone out.

Anxious to hear more about the upcoming Potsdam conference, Stepan lit a cigarette and offered one to Andreyev, leaving pack and lighter on the desk. "What's so important about this conference," he pressed.

"Chairman Khrushchev and President Eisenhower will meet to discuss Berlin and a nuclear treaty," Aleksei said, his voice—slightly thick from the vodka—assuming a conspiratorial tone. "At least that's what the Americans, the British, and the French think the agenda is."

Frowning, Aleksei put out his cigarette—a sure sign, Brodsky thought, that the conversation was about to come to an abrupt end. He couldn't resist slipping in one more question. "At least give me a hint, Colonel," he said casually.

"The Chairman has something else in mind," Aleksei said in a tone reserved for subordinates. "Let's just say the Americans don't own the skies."

\* \* \*

KGB Colonel Aleksei Andreyev had good reason to make such a cryptic remark. His thoughts wandered back to 1957 when President Dwight D. Eisenhower had obtained the Pakistan government's permission to park America's super-secret spy plan—a fixed wing high altitude U2—at Peshawar Airport, from which the plane would launch photo intelligence sorties over the Soviet Union.

Now, in early April 1960, the CIA's U2 had just flown over four top-secret Soviet military installations: a strategic bomber airfield, a surface-to-air missile test site, a missile range, and a nuclear test site.

Aleksei's superior, General Vladimir Nemerov, was livid. Even though the American spy plane had flown hundreds of miles over the Motherland for seven hours, neither Russian MIG-19s nor their SU-9s had been able to intercept it. The CIA operation was an intelligence coup of the first order!

Another flight had been scheduled in a few weeks, several days before the start of the Eisenhower-Khrushchev summit in Potsdam. Civilian CIA pilot Francis Gary Powers was to fly his U2 high over the Soviet Union, photographing Soviet Intercontinental ballistic missile sites.

Aleksei smiled. This time, Soviet intelligence had been forewarned by its agents in Italy. Air Defense Forces would be on red alert.

Waiting.

# CHAPTER 7

A pale sun peeked through dirty puffs of gray, a mid-April promise of spring. Kiril shivered in his unlined raincoat at a sudden blast of wind. Entering the café, he ordered breakfast and let his eggs grow cold as he waited for Stepan Brodsky.

"Coffee?" he asked as soon as Stepan walked in.

"Nothing, thanks."

Kiril left a few rubles on the table to cover the bill. They walked out and headed for a construction site roughly three blocks away. With the reverberating sound of jackhammers making it impossible for listening devices to pick up their conversation, Stepan reiterated his earlier conversation with Aleksei about Americans not owning the skies.

"But *where* I'm going—Potsdam, East Germany—offers a golden opportunity for me to defect," Stepan said, gripping Kiril's arm. "I'll be so damn close to West Berlin!"

"Then you must seize the opportunity," Kiril said fervently. "I'll help you any way I can."

*Don't worry about me, Stepan. I'll find another way out.*

As if reading his thoughts, Stepan said, "A friend of mine—an American diplomat—will be at the summit. If I can make a deal for myself, I'll find a way to include you. I have a strong suspicion that the bargaining chip for *both* of us is your brother's remark about Americans not owning the skies. Something's going on that ties in with the Four-Power summit."

"But you can't ask Aleksei without arousing his suspicions." Kiril mused. "We better talk tactics, Stepan."

Which they did, for another half hour. They agreed that Kiril's goal was to shed some light on Aleksei's cryptic remarks—the sooner the better. They disagreed about using the cancelled Canadian trip as the lever to get him talking.

"You know how paranoid Aleksei is," Kiril said. "If I ask him to reinstate the Canadian symposium, he'll conclude that my intention is to defect. After all, it really *was* my intention three months ago."

"Ironic, isn't it? But what choice do we have?" Stepan countered.

Kiril shrugged. "None."

An hour later, Kiril entered his brother's office, having decided on what he thought of as a direct, unapologetic approach.

"You wanted to see me?" Aleksei asked in his usual abrupt fashion.

"Is there any way that funding for the Canada trip can be found?" Kiril said, equally abrupt.

Kiril's opening salvo predictably triggered suspicion in Aleksei's glance. Ignoring it, Kiril pulled up a chair without asking—and on closer scrutiny realized his brother's eyes were a bit red-rimmed.

*Hitting the vodka again, Aleksei? Now there's a piece of good luck!*

"Why Canada?" Aleksei snapped.

"I'm a doctor," Kiril said tartly. "Dammit, Aleksei,

we have a lot to gain from the new heart-lung machine technology being developed there."

"It's not up to me," Aleksei said, sounding somewhat mollified. "And even if it were, I have more important matters to think about."

Fishing around in a side drawer of his desk, he took out a pint bottle of vodka and a couple of small glasses. "Join me?"

"Why not?" Kiril replied.

*Especially if I can manage to nudge you from mild inebriation into borderline drunk.*

They raised glasses and drank.

"How's this for an idea," Kiril said, pushing his glass forward for a refill. "Even if you can't bring the Canadian trip back to life, at least leave poor Dr. Yanin alone." He grinned. "If your men keep interrupting our surgical team's operations, we won't be able to function with even the outdated equipment we already have!"

Aleksei cracked a smile. "Never realized you had a sense of humor, Little Brother."

"Never realized you drank so early in the day."

Aleksei shrugged. "I have big problems."

He was drinking from the bottle now.

"Pressure from the top," he mumbled, slurring his words.

"That bad?" Kiril said, feeding brotherly concern into his tone.

No answer. Kiril braced himself and plunged in. "When you were talking to Stepan yesterday about his new assignment, you mentioned something about the Americans not owning the skies."

"Your pal told you about the Potsdam summit, did he?"

"Only in passing."

"So he's being discreet? He'd better be. That goes for you too," Aleksei said, wagging a forefinger for emphasis. "There's an old saying—a cliché now, but true enough during the Great Patriotic War. "Loose lips sink ships.""

Understand? Air Force Captain Brodsky is making our VIP arrangements is all. Know what the CIA's been up to? Photo-intelligence flights over the Soviet Union. For a long time, our MIG-19s and SU9s couldn't touch them."

"*That* high up?" Kiril said, genuinely fascinated.

"Tens of thousands of feet."

"But photographing what?"

"Whatever those bastards want," Aleksei muttered. "Everything from grazing cows to surface-to-air missile test sites," he said darkly, his normally pale face flushed with anger and alcoholic overload.

*Loose lips is right! If you were sober, Aleksei, you'd appreciate the irony of this conversation.*

"How long has this travesty been going on?" Kiril asked in a tone of righteous indignation.

"Long, long time. Our MIG-19s and SU9s couldn't touch them."

"So what are we doing about it?"

"Plenty. But not to worry, it's almost over. The CIA scheduled another flight a few days before the Eisenhower-Khrushchev summit. And *this* time," Aleksei said in an exaggerated whisper, "we'll be ready."

"For what?" Kiril said, puzzled.

"Think about it," Aleksei said with the patience of a professor whose most promising student needs prodding from time to time. "We start the summit in a friendly spirit, eager to cooperate with the Americans and their British and French allies. Suddenly our missiles shoot down this spy plane—a perfect excuse for Chairman Khrushchev to explode and walk out with his delegation. The United States of America won't be so united after that," Aleksei said smugly. "Not only will the Soviet Union's friends around the world condemn the war-mongering United States for threatening world peace, but many American citizens will follow their lead."

"I don't understand. What's in it for the Soviet Union?"

"Leverage, Kiril. For now, how Berlin is to be subdivided. Later, nuclear treaty negotiations will be on the agenda."

No more questions. Don't press your luck.

Aloud, Kiril said, "I can see why you have more important things to think about than resurrecting the Canadian symposium."

"Can you really?"

As Kiril held Aleksei's glance, he was stunned at his brother's abrupt transition from an amiable borderline drunk to a stone-cold sober intelligence officer—so sober that, without warning, Aleksei snapped forward in his chair.

"Breathe a word of this, Little Brother," Aleksei said with knife-edge sharpness, "and you are a dead man."

# CHAPTER 8

Aleksei Andreyev was surely the most devious person Kiril had ever known. To deal with him was to encounter wheels within wheels, never knowing what was artifice or distraction, propaganda or disinformation. What Aleksei had just revealed despite his apparent drunkenness . . . was it an act? Why tell Kiril a state secret of the highest order? Did Aleksei have an ulterior motive? Was he using Kiril in some way? Would Aleksei have him followed to see if he ran to his friend Stepan with such explosive intelligence? Was Khrushchev's Machiavellian plan even true?

So many possibilities, Kiril thought. How could he arrive at any definitive conclusions? He needed to be alone. To think.

After a lunch of black coffee and pirogi stuffed with cabbage, Kiril took a bus to the hospital. Luckily, there were no operations scheduled for the day. He had Dr. Yanin's surgical section to himself.

He sat in his cubicle-sized office and processed the morning's events, the questions he had just raised. He realized how important it was to preserve what he had just learned from Aleksei. But how?

His first impulse was to write an account of the entire episode in longhand. He vetoed the idea almost immediately. Such a report would be lengthy, cumbersome. Worse, if it fell into the wrong hands, it could turn into a death warrant.

Better to take advantage of his retentive memory and fall back on a number of key words to jog it, he decided.

He pulled out some note paper and wrote "April" on the chance that someone might read the note paper in English. Then "20" for the date—deliberately misleading; Kiril had been at Aleksei's office five days earlier. He followed up with seven key words: Andreyev, U2, summit, walkout, leverage, Berlin, nuclear. It was meager fare, but enough to feed his memory, which in turn would permit him to recite almost verbatim his conversation with Aleksei.

As he stared at the notepaper he'd just used, he realized it was cheap Soviet stock. What if it were destroyed in handling? If, say, the ink ran? His eyes wandered absently around the room and came to rest on the microfilm version of a patient's chest x-ray clipped to some medical report.

He leaped out of his chair. As small as his handwritten list of words was, he could render it much smaller with the microfilm machine that he'd used countless times. He went to work reproducing the list onto two tiny negatives, each roughly the size of half a fingernail.

*One microfilm for me. The other for you, Stepan.*

Next, a crucial last step. Where to hide *his* copy?

He sat back and lit a cigarette. He would need a place that was both secure and readily accessible. He was idly fingering his Zippo lighter when he cracked a smile.

Step one, he thought, and went about removing the lighter's working parts—windscreen, flint-holder, flint, wheel, wick—leaving him with a metal shell from which he removed the alcohol-soaked cotton. Taking a wad of unused cotton, Kiril wrapped it around the microfilm, inserted the cotton back into the shell, and replaced the working parts.

Step two. He walked down two flights of stairs and into a hospital storage area filled with old furniture. Piled high were desks, chairs, bookcases, all with an overlay of dust and the overpowering odor of mildew. Climbing carefully over wobbly wood and metal, Kiril wrapped his cigarette lighter in a rag and placed it in the back of a drawer whose desk looked like it had been there since the time of the Czar.

# CHAPTER 9

Fearful of being followed by KGB agents working for Aleksei, Kiril waited a few days before contacting Stepan. Their meeting place was a bath house's blue-and-gold-tiled steam room at dawn as soon as the facility opened.

"The microfilm could be our passport out of the Soviet Union," Stepan whispered. "When I think of the risk you've taken . . . "

"What you're about to do is a lot riskier," Kiril said soberly.

"When I get to Potsdam, I'll tell my American diplomat friend the whole story."

Kiril frowned. "But will it be in time to save the U2?"

"Maybe. Maybe not. But even if the information comes too late, Khrushchev's orchestrated charade will be exposed. The Communists will lose their leverage regarding Berlin, and, later on, the nuclear negotiations."

"Let's hope so. Can we run through the rest?"

"Here's how it works," Stepan said. "Once my friend helps me defect from Potsdam, he gets the CIA to exfiltrate *you* from the Soviet Union—probably from Leningrad to

Finland. Like I said, that's how it should work. And it *will* work, Kiril."

Kiril couldn't tell if Stepan's flushed face was from the steam or from sheer excitement. "Better get dressed," Kiril told him. "Then meet me at the lap pool."

Kiril was wearing a terrycloth robe by the time Stepan got there. They sat on a bench. There were no patrons at this ungodly hour. Kiril had counted on that. He opened a paper bag and pulled out two cheese sandwiches. He kept one and handed the other to Stepan. "Careful how you open yours, Stepan" he warned. "Mine really *is* a sandwich. Yours has—"

"Microfilm, wrapped in a tiny piece of cellophane," Stepan whispered, as if he couldn't quite believe his eyes.

"It's time for you to leave," Kiril said reluctantly. "I'll kill another half hour in the lap pool."

"Right."

They started to shake hands and ended up in a bear hug.

"Be safe, my friend," Kiril said, and forced himself to look away.

The minute Stepan left, Kiril was filled with foreboding. Sliding into the lap pool, he traveled the length of it with a ferocious overhand stroke. He kept up the pace for half an hour.

But utter exhaustion did not erase his premonition of disaster, nor the nagging questions that followed in its wake.

Disaster for whom?

For you, Stepan?

For me?

For both of us?

# CHAPTER 10

At precisely 7:00 P.M. on April 30, 1960, Paul Houston entered the noisy pre-conference reception in Potsdam, East Germany.

Not surprisingly, Moscow red had been transported *ad nauseam* to East Germany's grand Cecilienhof Palace, he thought drily. Red walls. Red gilt-trimmed chairs like the ones in the main conference room upstairs. Red tablecloths on buffet tables.

Clusters of solicitous East German waiters were circulating with drinks. A handful of civilian and military officers—American, British, and French—mingled with three Soviet officers.

Two of the three Soviets were dark and squat like sawed-off tree trunks. The third was a rotund blond with round metal-rimmed glasses. All three men were resplendent in uniforms that looked as if they'd come from the costume department of a Gilbert and Sullivan operetta.

". . . May Day toast to *another* memorable Potsdam conference!" the blond Russian enthused in English. "Gentlemen, the past few months have not been in vain.

Negotiations over wider American, British, and French access to Berlin have become snarled, yes? Never mind. By this time tomorrow, our leaders will have untangled the snarls. Harmony prevailed at Cecilienhof Palace sixteen years ago. It shall prevail again! As a good hunting dog grabs hold of his quarry, our great leaders shall grab hold of our doubts, our disagreements . . ."

Finally, glasses were raised, putting a welcome end to the Russian's melodramatic monologue.

Houston had little patience for the usual Soviet Orwellian refrain. The original Potsdam conference in 1945 had eased world tensions.

*Sure it had.*

It had established the principles for a lasting peace.

*Right.*

How anyone could respond to the notion that the first Potsdam conference had *accomplished* anything but politically motivated turmoil was beyond him. Not in the face of postwar Germany as it was carved into four occupation zones: American, British, French, and Soviet. Certainly not in postwar Berlin, which currently sat in the middle of East Germany, and was subjected to the same Four-Power division.

What *had* been accomplished, thanks to wily *Uncle Joe* Stalin, as FDR had affectionately called him, was West Berlin's untenable position after being locked in—surrounded by the Communists.

Needing a break from the bombast, Houston went outside and walked briskly down a long paved driveway bordered by close-cut grass and hemmed in by sculpted bushes.

Halfway down the driveway, he turned around and took in the architectural excesses of "Schloss Cecilienhof." Erected between 1914 and 1917 for Germany's Crown Prince Wilhelm and his wife Cecilie, it had the look of a metastasized English Tutor country house: red-tiled roofs, 6 courtyards, 55 carved brick chimney tops, and more.

More of everything.

Because Houston knew the palace's history, the same thought came to mind whenever he saw Cecilienhof: *What a waste!*

Construction was to have been completed in 1915. Delayed due to the outbreak of World War I the year before, it was not until August 1917 that the Crown Prince and his bride were able to move in. A year later, the prince and his father were forced into exile. Cecilie had stayed on but was forced to flee from the approaching Red Army in February 1945.

Five months later, Cecilienhof Palace was once again refurbished—this time for the Potsdam Conference that had taken place fifteen years ago, between July 17 and August 2, 1945.

Houston pictured the men who had met at the round table in the conference hall. Winston Churchill, and later Clement Attlee, Joseph Stalin, and Harry Truman. He recalled the world-shaping events that had been agreed upon here . . . Churchill's and Truman's July 26, 1945 *Potsdam Declaration*, which insisted on Japan's unconditional surrender. Later, their partially successful attempt to bring the Soviet Union into the war in Asia.

The cast of characters had certainly changed this time around, he reflected. Former General of the Army Dwight D. Eisenhower. Nikita Khrushchev, the *"Butcher of Ukraine."* Harold Macmillan, the Conservative Party son of an American mother. Charles de Gaulle, leader of the World War Free French.

In spite of everything else on his mind, Houston had to admit he was looking forward to the conference.

\* \* \*

Houston and Brodsky had slipped through the raucous

partiers by different routes. A quarter-moon had just begun to cast its dark gray light on the ornate grounds of the palace. Dense foliage and hedge-like bushes would provide excellent cover for the two men.

Outside, Houston hurried down a couple of steep steps. Trees were turning into silhouettes. A tall form stood in the shadow of a hedge.

"Stepan?" he called out softly.

A hand gripped his. "Hello, Houston."

It was the old joke between them. Brodsky liked greeting him by his last name—the name of an American city he hoped one day soon to see for himself.

When Paul Houston offered Stepan a cigarette, Brodsky automatically went for his cigarette lighter. It didn't work. Houston held out a match, wondering why Brodsky had cracked a smile as he slipped his cigarette lighter back into his pocket.

As soon as they were well away from the palace and securely surrounded by trees, Brodsky turned to Houston. "You know how long I've wanted to defect, Paul. But always, your CIA came up with excuses for not helping. I won't go into the litany. For one thing, it's too painful."

"For me too," Houston confessed.

"I know. I'm going to tell you a story. What your CIA and your State Department choose to do with it is up to them. But I'll tell you now—'upfront,' as you Americans like to say. In return for what I have, I want my freedom and I want it now."

Houston looked at him intently. He had never heard Stepan sound so uncompromising.

Brodsky spelled out the whole story, and then held up his lighter. "Here's the deal, Paul. I keep the microfilm in my lighter until you tell me your people will go for it—my freedom in exchange for high-level intelligence. And not just mine. Someone else's."

"Someone who's still in the Soviet Union?" Houston

said skeptically.

"My closest friend. We go back a long time. He risked his life to get the microfilm—and not just to help me. He's wanted to defect as long as I have. Every day he remains in the Soviet Union, his life is in grave danger. So tell your people it's me now, my friend as soon as possible—from Moscow to wherever your CIA can exfiltrate him. Maybe from Leningrad to Finland?"

Houston looked uncomfortable. "Getting you out is hard enough, Stepan. But someone else who's still in Moscow? That's a tall order."

"Try to imagine what it's like to be an exile in your own country," Stepan said softly. "My friend and I have felt that way all our lives. I cannot—I *will* not—abandon him."

"Something just occurred to me," Houston said. "If the Soviets shoot down the U2, giving Khrushchev a good excuse to walk out tomorrow morning—how can your film prove the Russians intended to blow up the summit even *before* it began?"

Stepan smiled. "Don't take this personally, but my friend was one step ahead of you. The microfilm contains a date stamp."

A look of fierce determination crossed Houston's face. "I'll try tonight by secure line. What worries me is that I'm dealing with bureaucrats. They have a certain mindset."

"Meaning?"

Houston shook his head in disgust. "They're shortsighted. Pragmatic. They have a tendency to play it safe in this era of so-called good will with the Soviets. 'Moscow is edgy,' they keep telling me. 'We've seen too many defections to the West lately'."

Brodsky paled.

"First things first," Houston said, gripping Stepan's arm. "Keep the lighter while I work on getting you out of here. Then we'll see about your friend."

# CHAPTER 11

The next morning—May Day in Potsdam, East Germany—the summit began early.

Dwight Eisenhower, Nikita Khrushchev, Harold Macmillan, and Charles de Gaulle sat at a large square conference table, their military and civilian staffs seated behind them. Microphones had been placed in front of each participant. On a green felt tabletop were arrayed the usual pitchers of water, glasses, pads, pencils, and the like. Each of the four men had large ring binders nearby. Translators were out of sight.

The agenda and considerable preparatory work with the foreign ministers of the other countries had been completed well in advance by the American Department of State. Essentially there were two issues literally on the table. Foremost was the fate of Berlin. Was it to remain divided, militarized? The second issue involved a much-discussed nuclear arms treaty that was to be the subject of a subsequent summit.

As the four world leaders shuffled papers and the audio technicians tested sound levels and recording equipment, high in Soviet airspace pilot Frances Gary Powers' supersonic U2 had been detected. A Soviet air defense general ordered the attack. His fighters were ordered to engage in suicidal maneuvers by ramming the American U-2 if there was no other way to bring it down.

Initial interceptions failed. Powers was up too high for the fighters, his U2 out of range.

Until it was hit by a surface-to-air missile.

Powers bailed out of the crippled aircraft even though, to avoid being taken alive, he'd been supplied with a poison-tipped needle hidden by CIA spooks in an American silver dollar. Contrary to strict orders, Powers didn't use it.

At about 5:00 P.M. during the summit's afternoon session, an aide approached Khrushchev and whispered in his ear. As he listened attentively, his face reddened. Suddenly he erupted from his chair and began shouting in Russian. The translators could barely keep up. To everyone not in on the act—and not all of the Soviets were—Khrushchev's bombast seemed legitimate.

It virtually wrote the script for what Soviet Ambassador Dmitri Zorin would reiterate later that day in New York City.

The Soviets had Francis Gary Powers. And to the chagrin of the American intelligence establishment, they had not only Powers but also considerable wreckage from the super-secret U2 aircraft.

"Since our partnership in the Great Patriotic War with the countries represented here, too often Western hostility has blunted my country's good intentions!" Khrushchev bellowed. "I have just been informed by Moscow that the imperialist United States has violated Soviet airspace and spied on our socialist nation. The purpose of this summit was to resolve important problems concerning Berlin and nuclear annihilation. Yet behind our back, the United States has been flying over the Union of Soviet Socialist Republics. Why? To take photographs of our defenses against imperialist subversion and aggression."

President Eisenhower's face was impassive. CIA at Langley had received a coded flash cable in the middle of the night from Paul Houston, warning that the Soviets would try for the U2, and that if they succeeded, would use it as an excuse to walk out of the summit.

Having readied himself for that possibility, Khrushchev's bluster had no effect on Eisenhower, who had readied himself for that possibility.

Charles de Gaulle smirked, although it was not clear why or at whom.

Harold Macmillan tried to suppress a smile. Those who noticed figured that MI-5 or MI-6 had put him in the picture.

Khrushchev continued his rant. "We have your man, 'Proudest'!"

Eisenhower suppressed a smile over Khrushchev's mispronunciation of *Powers*.

Khrushchev raised a plump fist. "In the name of the Soviet Union, I demand an apology from the President of the United States." He glared at Eisenhower. "I demand assurances that nothing like this will ever happen again."

Looking Khrushchev squarely in the eye, Eisenhower said, "You won't get an apology from me."

Khrushchev and the rest of his delegation stormed out.

Chaos. Three of the Four-Power delegates were ushered out by their security personnel. Staffers packed. Reporters rushed for telephones. Limousines pulled up in front of Cecilienhof Palace.

Houston went into the bar for a stiff drink.

Stepan Brodsky joined him. "That was quite a show," he said.

"Wasn't it, though?" Houston said soberly, staring into his drink. "I got through last night to the CIA. Thanks to your information, President Eisenhower had advance notice."

"I'm glad, Paul. Any news about me and my friend?"

When Paul Houston looked up, Brodsky shuddered

inwardly. Houston didn't have to answer his question—not with that ravaged face, those bloodshot eyes. "Last night I had a long-shot chance that my government wouldn't turn me down," Houston said tonelessly. "But after what happened here today— I'm so sorry, Stepan, and so damn helpless."

Brodsky squeezed his shoulder. "You better get going, Paul. The limousines have already pulled up in front of the Palace. I'm expected outside too."

They abandoned their bar stools and headed for the exit.

When Houston was a few steps ahead, Brodsky called after him. "I want you to know something, Paul. Working with you these last few months has been like having a small glimpse of all the things I've missed in my life. Thank you for that."

Houston paused to answer . . . and walked on. He could not trust his voice.

He was waiting outside when he next caught sight of Stepan, who had stopped to speak with Ernst Roeder, an East German photographer friend of his.

# CHAPTER 12

At roughly 6:00 P.M., with Nikita Khrushchev's pseudo-tantrum still ringing in his ears, Air Force Captain Stepan Brodsky swallowed his fear as the two Mercedes-Benz limousines sped through the woods on a road bathed in moonlight. Ahead was Glienicker Bridge, spanning the Havel River that separated Communist East Germany and free West Berlin.

The moon had disappeared behind a cloud by the time the limousines, following one another like disconnected pieces of a caterpillar, reached an obstacle course of concrete barriers. After roughly 200 feet of zigzag maneuvering, the lead limo containing Paul Houston and Ernst Roeder entered a cobblestone square at the mouth of the bridge. The second limo, with an East German driver and Stepan Brodsky in the back seat, followed.

Both Mercedes stopped between two guard houses. One flew East Germany's flag, the other the Soviet Union's hammer and sickle.

From his rear seat, Houston stared at the suspension bridge that loomed just beyond the cobblestone square,

Glienicker's dull steel webbing looking shiny, almost festive, in the wash of floodlights.

Brodsky, seated behind his driver in the second car, looked to his left.

A red-and-white-striped border pole barred the way across the bridge. Three uniformed men stood nearby. A Soviet soldier. An East German Vopo. And an East German officer with white-blond hair . . .

*Colonel Emil von Eyssen, chief of security at the Four-Power summit that had just ended in chaos.*

With studied casualness and the air of a man who wanted a last-minute word with someone in the first limousine, Brodsky exited his vehicle and approached the open window.

"Hello . . . my friend. A cautionary word," Brodsky said. "The guards are looking *edgy* tonight. Too many defections to the West lately."

No fear in his voice. Brodsky knew, as he returned to his car, that Paul Houston would see it in his eyes.

Houston's throat constricted, instantly sizing up the situation. He was dimly aware that Ernst Roeder was rolling down his window.

"I cannot resist taking advantage of the light from these obscene floodlights to get a shot of the verböten side of the bridge," Roeder grumbled. "Since I prefer not to photograph through glass—"

"You know the regulations," Houston answered automatically. "No photographs of bridges. No open windows on your side when the East German Volkpolisei check you—"

*The Vopo . . . Damned if it wasn't the anti-American bastard who hassled him every time he crossed Glienicker Bridge—so much so that he'd inquired about the man's name. Two syllables. Began with a "B." Berger, Brenner, Bruno—Bruno, that was it!*

"No photographs, Ernst," he whispered. Then: "Switch

seats with me. Quickly!"

Still staring at the bridge, Houston calculated that it was roughly a hundred feet from the cobblestone square where they were parked to where the bridge itself began. He zeroed in on the bridge's midpoint—and a large yellow sign facing him that spelled out the Communists' claim on Stepan Brodsky's life: *DEUTSCHE DEMOKRATISCHE REPUBLIK.*

Below the sign, like living exclamation points, stood two more East German guards.

The Vopo bent to his task, expecting Roeder's East German ID card to be pressed against the window. He gaped. *Not* a West German. An American diplomat—and on the wrong side of the car, window rolled down, passport in his hand!

In the split second before Bruno's surprise and annoyance shifted to anger, Houston took a deep drag on his cigarette and blew a cloud of smoke in the Vopo's outthrust face.

Cursing, the Vopo snatched the passport out of Houston's hand.

"Give it here, you sonofabitch," Houston said. "Only the Soviets get to touch my passport."

"Big shot American." The Vopo clutched the passport to his chest.

"My passport," Houston snapped. "Or do you intend to search this car? You have no authority. You wouldn't dare," he taunted.

"*I will search,*" Bruno snarled, underscoring each word as his hand moved toward his revolver.

"Out!" Houston ordered Roeder. And to his bewildered driver in the front seat, "Get out! Leave your door open with the motor running."

*Do it, Stepan. It's now or never!*

Stepan Brodsky, imposing in his Soviet Air Force officer's uniform, strode over to the confrontation, a scowl on his face, an unmistakable what's-going-on-here question in his eyes.

The Vopo hesitated, and then backed away, his eyes still locked on Brodsky's uniform.

Houston's heart was a heavy drumbeat in his chest as he watched Brodsky's gamble play out during the next few seconds. Slide under the wheel of Houston's limousine. Floor the accelerator.

Brodsky's back slammed against the seat cushion. The Mercedes shot past a startled Soviet guard, smashing its way through the border pole. The vehicle's speedometer soared.

Indifferent to the shriek of sirens assaulting his eardrums, Houston watched Colonel Emil von Eyssen race to the mouth of the bridge, megaphone in hand, as Brodsky gunned the powerful motor of the Mercedes.

When von Eyssen aimed the megaphone at some machine gun emplacements in the watchtowers, it seemed to Houston that he stopped breathing. He concentrated only on the trajectory of tracer bullets. They had reached out for the fleeing limousine but, so far, had harmlessly struck pavement and burst into sparks.

Every fiber of Houston's being propelled the Mercedes forward across the bridge, willing it to go faster.

Bullets whipped over the top of the car. An East German guard at Glienicker's midpoint collapsed into a soft pile.

"Get down!" von Eyssen screamed to no one and everyone, needing clear fields of fire.

Then: *"Feuern!" Fire!* roared von Eyssen's megaphone-amplified voice.

*"Die Reifen! The tires!"*

Von Eyssen's voice carried over the ear-splitting sirens, the clatter of machine guns.

But the shooters in the watchtowers knew their job. Even as von Eyssen screamed the orders, a rear right tire blew apart, spewing rubber all over the blacktop. The Mercedes veered sharply to the left, rammed into that side of the bridge, bounced off, and swaying crazily, careened toward the opposite side, its left flank even more exposed to the line of fire.

*Mere feet from the bridge's midpoint, from West Berlin. You're so damn close, Stepan.*

Houston choked as a bright green tracer round connected with the Mercedes' gas tank just as the car smashed into Glienicker Bridge's unforgiving steel.

Gas-fueled flames engulfed the Mercedes and enveloped the steel bridge supports. The smell of burning rubber was overpowering.

Debris fell on the inert form of Stepan Brodsky. He had been thrown clear.

*"Feuer einstellen!" Cease fire!*

In the din of wailing sirens and the confusion of shouted orders, two men raced for the burning wreck, their footsteps swallowed by the engine of an East German patrol boat hovering beneath Glienicker Bridge.

Paul Houston got there just before Ernst Roeder.

Brodsky was crawling through spilled gasoline and his own blood.

His body was twisted like a piece of charred steel. One outstretched hand slowly reached for a small object that had spilled from his pocket. It was lying between him and the edge of the bridge a few inches away.

Brodsky slid forward on his chest, touched metal.

Before Houston could retrieve Brodsky's cigarette lighter, a black boot nudged it barely out of Stepan's reach.

"You sadistic sonofabitch!" Seizing a broken piece of the car's bumper, Houston swung—just missing von Eyssen's head.

Clicking his heels in mock deference, a smiling von Eyssen joined the men now swarming over the bridge.

Houston knelt down. He started to reach for Brodsky's lighter when he felt a hand on his shoulder.

"Watch my back," Ernst Roeder muttered as he slipped a smooth silver object from his jacket pocket—a

Minox miniature camera no more than a few inches long. Concealing it in one oversized hand, he took three surreptitious photographs in rapid succession before returning the camera to his pocket.

Then, "Good lord, he's still alive," Roeder whispered.

Houston made a grab for the lighter. But not in time.

With what seemed like a last burst of energy, Brodsky pushed his cigarette lighter over the edge of the bridge.

Then his hand lay still.

# CHAPTER 13

At the same time Stepan Brodsky lay dying on Glienicker Bridge, in Manhattan black-booted men in loose white tunics and red sashes performed deep knee bends and gravity-defying leaps as they formed a large loose circle. Inside the circle, young barelegged women whirled, red-and-black peasant skirts whipping above their knees. The exuberant cries of the dancers threatened to drown out the cheerful strains of an accordion. Suddenly the men and women broke into a heel-stamping finale, then bowed and waved at the crowd in traditional Russian fashion.

About twenty-five fashionably-dressed people stood in a walled-in garden half the size of a basketball court. Tall-stemmed sunflowers and stately shade trees ran along the walls all the way to the East River. They stood looking up at Grace Manning, their blonde blue-eyed hostess, as if waiting for permission to applaud the dancers.

Grace stood in front of a brass and teak bar, a fetching picture in a red-and-black peasant blouse and matching skirt identical to the women dancers. "Ladies and gentlemen," she said, tapping a thin brass knife against a red goblet; pausing until she had complete silence. "Thanks are in order to the ambassador of the Soviet U.N. Mission for this combination May Day celebration and sneak preview of tomorrow night's gala opening at Lincoln Center. But before we treat ourselves to some tantalizing Russian delicacies, every recipe courtesy of the Soviet U. N. Mission"—she gestured toward a sumptuous buffet table—"I should like to propose toast."

On cue, butlers appeared with trays of brimming glasses.

"It's vodka. Don't say I didn't warn you," a smiling Grace Manning cautioned her guests. "The champagne comes later. I propose a double toast," she said, raising her glass. "First, to the talented dancers from Ukraine who have brightened what surely would have been a dull Sunday afternoon in New York. Second, to the gentleman who arranged this exciting glimpse into his country's cultural heritage, United Nations Ambassador Anton Zorin!"

The trim-looking Zorin downed his vodka Russian-style—in a single gulp. His glass was quickly refilled by a hovering butler. Most of the guests, but not all, sipped their vodka somewhat tentatively.

"Now it is *my* turn for a double toast," the ambassador said in fluent English. "To our distinguished host, Russell Manning." He raised his glass high. "And to Russell's pride and joy, Medicine International, an organization that lives up to its slogan—World Peace through World Health—and by so doing contributes significantly to the relaxation of world tensions!" he enthused.

A beaming Russell Manning ran a hand through waves of silver hair. "One cannot indulge in toast-making," he said, "without acknowledging America's most prominent heart surgeon and noted humanitarian, Dr. Kurt Brenner. Dr. Brenner will represent the United States at Medicine International's forthcoming Artificial Heart Symposium in West Berlin."

Kurt Brenner acknowledged the applause with a nod

and a half-smile. The silver-blue of the East River and the brighter blue of a cloudless sky were perfect backdrops for his tall, stately figure in an impeccably tailored off-white linen suit. Brenner's eyes were velvet-brown, his face deeply tanned. His hair, in stunning contrast, was white.

He waited for his glass to be refilled. Waited, as Grace Manning had, until he had everyone's full attention. "It looks like double toasts are in fashion," he said with a faint smile, and wondered if the people who returned his smile were responding to his sense of humor or to the praise Russell had heaped on him. Both maybe. "To my Russian, French, and British colleagues in absentia, who will be joining me in West Berlin," Brenner said in his rich baritone. "And to the success of Medicine International's Artificial Heart Symposium, which I look forward to with great anticipation." He smiled broadly—this time for a photographer from the Soviet News Agency.

The guests lost no time in switching from vodka to champagne, and even less for descending upon the sumptuous buffet table.

"Isn't this exciting!" exclaimed a breathless brunette version of their hostess. "Grace practically took an oath that the food's authentic. Chicken Tabaka with garlic sauce. Fish in aspic. Pickled cabbage. Oh, and crabmeat. I hear it's impossible to beg, borrow, or steal crabmeat in Moscow these days."

The dancers looked longingly at the buffet table, uncertain as to whether they were allowed to approach it. Clustered in a small group off to one side, they showed no sign of the grace and vigor that had characterized their performance.

No one seemed to notice them. A couple of men in dark baggy suits stood among them. No one noticed them either.

"—cannot grasp why Americans don't demand a standard of medical care at least as high as that found in the Soviet Union," Ambassador Zorin was lecturing Brenner.

"You're certainly way ahead of us there," Brenner said diplomatically. "I've always admired your policy of making the health of your people a government responsibility."

"Quite so," Zorin said. "Once a citizen is enrolled in his or her neighborhood clinic, every medical need is met. Medical care for our children—"

"Now *there's* a subject close to Kurt's heart," Grace Manning chimed in, taking familiar hold of Brenner's arm.

"But of course. We in the USSR have heard a great deal about your cardiac clinic for underprivileged children," Zorin said—and paused as a butler approached him regarding a telephone call in the library.

Interesting, Brenner thought. Zorin didn't look the least bit surprised about that incoming call . . .

* * *

"Don't look so disappointed," Grace Manning quipped as Zorin left the room. "Surely you weren't intending to squeeze a donation out of the Soviet Union?"

"Don't be a bitch." Brenner's lips curved into a characteristic half-smile—part amusement, part contempt.

"Why shouldn't I?" she retorted. "You're such a busy man these days. Lectures. Charity work. Important people to see. I'm beginning to think you only came to my party because Russell wanted to show you off to the Ambassador. Russell tells me you're absolutely desperate for money these days."

Brenner shrugged. "A combination of the recession and some injudicious investments. I've neglected you lately because I've been in Washington a lot. Government grants are becoming as scarce as hen's teeth."

"Poor dear," Grace said, mollified. "Too bad most of Russell's handouts end up in underdeveloped countries instead of heart institutes on the upper Eastside of

Manhattan. With all your money problems, how on earth do you find time for surgery?"

"I have a competent and highly trained staff," he said in a bored voice. "Can we talk about something else?"

"Let's talk about your perfectly enchanting wife," Grace said peevishly. "Since she doesn't know we're having an affair, I'm wondering if the woman is just plain rude."

Kurt Brenner was wondering who else had noticed Adrienne's absence. What was he supposed to tell people? That his wife refused to socialize with Ambassador Zorin? That lately she avoided socializing with her own husband? It was sheer luck their latest rift hadn't hit the gossip columns.

"Not rude," he countered. "Just wrapped up in that job of hers."

"Adrienne Brenner, journalist. Charming occupation for a woman with *her* social background," Grace said with disdain. "You look like you could use another glass of champagne, dear heart," she teased and reached out to a passing butler. Her hand accidentally caught the man at a bad angle, sending his tray of glasses to the floor with a shattering crash.

"Clumsy fool!" Brenner exclaimed.

"Is this an example of the famous Dr. Kurt Brenner temper?" Grace said, taken aback. "It was *my* fault, not the butler's."

"What if a piece of glass had sliced into my hands?" Brenner snapped.

Before she could respond, a grim-faced Ambassador Zorin returned to the garden, and waving to the men in the black suits, spoke to them.

Grace Manning, ever the alert hostess, deserted Brenner and made a bee-line for the Ambassador.

Zorin turned to her. "I am sorry to spoil your lovely party," he said, "but I must leave at once. We all must." He gestured at the dancers being herded back into the house by the men in black.

"How perfectly horrid of you, Mr. Ambassador," Grace pouted. "But at least Russell and I can look forward to seeing you at the Artificial Heart Symposium next year when—"

"I'm afraid you won't see anyone from the Soviet Union at your symposium," Zorin said, his thoughts elsewhere— and instantly regretted not having lowered his voice. A circle of expectant faces stared at him.

A reporter joined the group. "Would you care to make a statement, Mr. Ambassador?" he asked, mildly curious.

Zorin adjusted his glasses while he collected his thoughts. He had been waiting to be notified about the orchestrated collapse of the Four-Power summit. Now that it was a *fait accompli* and Khrushchev had walked out, there was no reason not to be frank.

"The barbs of Western hostility have pierced my country's good intentions," Zorin said gravely. "I have just been informed by Moscow that your country has invaded Soviet airspace. It has been spying on our nation for some time now. The Soviet delegation, led by Chairman Nikita Khrushchev, has walked out of the Potsdam summit. While we were enjoying Russian folk dancing in New York and drinking toasts to the relaxation of world tensions," Zorin continued, "an American spy plane was overflying our country to photograph sensitive installations."

Murmurs rolled through the guests.

"Unfortunately, the repercussions of this international crime touch us all," Zorin said, warming to his subject. "It spells the end of Soviet participation in cultural exchanges, in competitive sports events, in—"

"My Artificial Heart Symposium?" Russell Manning asked, aghast. "Surely your government won't withdraw its participation because of some minor political incident?"

"We already have," Zorin said flatly.

Brenner gripped Manning's arm. "I hope you're not

thinking of pulling the plug on the symposium, Russell," he said lowering his voice. "There are other participants. Think of the money you poured into the new medical center there. Think of the dedication ceremony, the publicity."

"I'm not sure, I'm just not sure. We're supposed to be in the middle of an East-West thaw, for god's sake! I hate politics," he whined, thrusting out his lower lip.

"Mr. Ambassador," Brenner said as Zorin turned to leave. "While I consider myself a patriotic American, I must confess that I'm offended by my government's behavior. Spying in this day and age? Despicable!"

The reporter, no longer bored, was scribbling away.

Zorin turned toward Brenner, the suggestion of a smile on his lips.

"It has taken years for people of good faith from our two countries to establish a bridge of friendship," Brenner said with feigned sincerity. "I only hope that bridge is strong enough to withstand such ill-advised and provocative conduct."

"Speaking of bridges, Mr. Ambassador," the reporter pressed, "isn't the one across the Havel River in Potsdam called Glienicker? And didn't American GIs and Soviet troops, with assistance from Ukrainian laborers, work together after the war to repair it?"

Brenner turned pale.

"True," Zorin told the reporter. "All the more reason for my country to be enraged at the needless collapse of our peace negotiations. As the Havel River now separates our delegations in Potsdam, so too it separates our two countries."

Zorin, followed by his entourage, left the Manning townhouse through an elaborate front entrance.

Hands jammed into his pockets so no one could see them shaking, Brenner headed in the opposite direction. Reaching the brass-and-teak bar in the garden, he grabbed the nearest bottle, not sure whether it was gin or vodka.

Not caring that whatever it was burned his throat on the way down.

*Glienicker Bridge. Ukrainians!*

A coincidence? Brenner wondered. Maybe. Maybe not.

He had always prided himself on his rational approach to life, his utter disdain for superstition.

Not anymore.

# CHAPTER 14

It was a typically stifling early May in Moscow. The woman with the bovine face pressed her cheeks with a handkerchief, feeling a rush of guilt over the vodka she'd indulged in during the May Day holiday two days ago.

The telephone on her desk jangled shrilly. ". . . Yes, sir, he's here. I'll send him in." She hung up and turned to Kiril. "They're ready for you, Dr. Andreyev," she said cheerfully. "Second door to your right."

The room Kiril entered had no windows. Two men sat behind a battered desk. One wore a yellow jacket that had seen better days. He looked barely old enough to shave.

Kiril's eyes flicked to the other man. Balding. Mid-to-late fifties. Florid face with a wary, almost deferential, expression.

"Please take a seat, Doctor," the older man said, indicating an empty chair opposite them.

The minute Kiril sat down, a brilliant flash exploded, pinning him to his chair in a white glare. He could no longer see either man.

"Aren't you being a touch melodramatic?" he said

caustically. "I was asked to come here and, as you know, I came voluntarily. I'm going to shut my eyes, gentlemen. Then you can decide whether you want to strong-arm me or have a civil discussion without that light in my face."

Silence. A long time when you're counting the seconds . . .

*A small victory,* Kiril thought as the lights went off.

"We have questions about an Air Force officer named Stepan Brodsky," smooth-face said testily. "Would you call yourselves friends?"

"Why would I deny it?"

"When did you first become acquainted with him?" The older man's soft-spoken tone remained deferential.

*What's going on? Why haven't I heard from Stepan since the summit broke up? Is he in trouble? Did he make it to the West?*

"We met about fifteen years ago," Kiril said. "I was a medical officer in Murmansk, and he was liaison to the American Lend Lease troops."

"How did you and your pal spend time together after the war?" smooth-face asked.

Kiril shrugged. "How do friends spend their time?"

His thoughts turned to the countless hours they had spent learning German. Of how Kiril had shared his expertise in American slang. His knowledge of the American *Constitution,* limited government, individual rights.

"Why did Brodsky join the Soviet Air Force?" the older man asked.

"He never told me."

*But he had. To steal a plane someday so he could defect.*

"I don't know who you think you're fooling," smooth-face snapped.

"Don't feel rushed, Doctor," the older man told him. "Just try to be more specific about how you and Stepan Brodsky spent your time."

The pressure that had been building dissipated like air

being let out of a tire. Kiril related a half-dozen activities, all of them innocuous. Sports. Cinema. Occasional double-dating. A rare hiking trip.

*Even as he remembered how he and Stepan had studied plan after plan in an ongoing effort to get out of prison, as they thought of it. Stepan haunted diplomatic gatherings where his credentials might land him invitations to other countries. Kiril, for the same reason, explored medical exchange programs. Both of them pored over maps of East Berlin and East Germany to prepare themselves should the opportunity ever arise to defect from either place.*

Smooth-face picked up the questioning. "I presume you and Brodsky are acquainted with the same people? You have the same friends?"

"I have very few friends—"

"Why is that?"

"Because of the demands of my work. As for Captain Brodsky's friends, I assume he has some but I've no idea who they are. We do know several people jointly, of course."

Smooth-face folded his arms. "How long have you known Brodsky was a traitor?"

Kiril shot to his feet. "What the hell are you talking about? Captain Brodsky a traitor?"

*Something did go wrong in Potsdam! Was Stepan tortured? Do they have the lighter? The microfilm?*

"I'm leaving," he announced, gathering his courage. Knowing damn well it was Aleksei who'd probably set up this interrogation in the first place. "If you care to pursue this outrageous slander," he said, "I suggest you take it up with my brother."

"Please resume your seat, Dr. Andreyev," said the older man, directing an icy glance at his impetuous young colleague. One never knew how Dr. Kiril Andreyev stood with KGB Colonel Aleksei Andreyev, he thought. The sensible thing was to tread carefully, not come on like a—a battering ram! "Did you, in fact, know that Stepan

Brodsky was planning to escape?"

In the small stretch of silence that followed, both interrogators leaned forward in their chairs. Dr. Andreyev—up to now imperturbable—looked stunned.

*"I didn't know it,"* Kiril said slowly, his mind an agony of questions.

*Where was Stepan? Had he abandoned his plan? Do they know about me?*

Smooth-face wasn't about to be distracted. "We have proof that you met with Captain Brodsky shortly before he went to Potsdam. Do you really expect us to believe he revealed *nothing* about his escape attempt?"

"Nothing, I told you. What's going on? Is Stepan all right?"

"Not exactly."

"What the hell is that supposed to mean?"

"Captain Brodsky was shot dead trying to escape across Glienicker Bridge," the older man said calmly. "We have no more questions, Dr. Andreyev. Thank you for your cooperation. You will remain here please."

The two men left the room.

Kiril sat down, his legs too weak to hold him upright. He felt numb. The numbness rose slowly, inexorably, up the length of his body until his shoulders slumped as if from the sheer weight of it.

*Why should I fight it any longer, Stepan? I am as dead as you are.*

But even now, Stepan reached out to him.

Kiril pictured a favorite haunt he and Stepan had christened the "Western Bar." They had enjoyed nursing a couple of beers as they watched shaggy-haired kids in faded jeans and miniskirts lose themselves in a defiant attempt at gaiety. Then when they were ready to leave, they would raise a glass in a solemn toast that had become a ritual.

*Say it*, he told himself. Say it *now* before it's too late!

"To the United States of America," he whispered in the solemn tone of a vow, and a farewell.

He was still weeping as he clung to the image of the Western Bar when a figure in a soiled military tunic yanked him up by one arm and said, "You come with me."

# CHAPTER 15

Aleksei Andreyev had unruly hair—more yellow than blond—eyes as pale blue as a robin's egg, and an unsettling expression. Unsettling because it simultaneously suggested placidity and a readiness to pounce.

"Kiril!" he said heartily by way of greeting as his brother was hauled into his office. "You look distressed."

"Distressed?" Kiril said wearily, making no effort to hide his utter devastation. "Your thugs tell me my closest friend is a traitor. That Stepan tried to defect so they shot him to death. How the hell do you expect me to feel? What do you want with me, Aleksei?"

"I might ask you the same question. Sit down." Aleksei indicated one of the chairs opposite his spacious desk. "Why did you come to my office a few weeks ago?"

"Don't be coy. You know why." Kiril dropped into the chair. He could barely stand. "I wanted your help getting permission for Dr. Yanin's operating team to participate in that Canadian medical meeting."

"Of course you did. So you could go to Canada with them, Kiril? And then what?" he said patiently. "Defect like your friend just tried to do?"

"Think what you like," Kiril said indifferently.

"Has it occurred to you that, precisely because of your undistinguished career all these years, you haven't been cleared to make such trips? After all your childhood pretensions—that burning desire to be a doctor—I thought you'd amount to much more. I know about the harsh years when work was scarce. What you did manage to get were—how shall I put it?—menial jobs. Putting up intravenous drips for other doctors. Handing them instruments. Operating their machines like a mechanic."

Aleksei's eyes probed Kiril's face for a reaction. Not finding it, he leaned back in his chair. "Then along came your big break," he continued, the annoyance in his voice clashing with his placid expression. "You become a 'glorified mechanic' for the eminent Dr. Mikhail Yanin."

Eminent enough to be invited and re-invited to the West, Kiril thought. Aloud he said, "It didn't take long for *this* 'glorified mechanic' to make himself indispensable to the best surgeon in Moscow."

"True. Still, I managed to overcome our tarnished family history. Forgive me for being immodest but even if Aunt Sofia hadn't taken me under her wing, nothing would have barred my way," Aleksei said smugly. "If there's anything the woman ingrained in me, it was how to be resourceful. I learned how to ferret out one's enemies. How to distinguish between a man's strengths and his weaknesses. I seem to recall your early interest in medical research. Did you know that's how I started?"

"In research?" Kiril said, incredulous.

"Of a special kind. Ever heard of the Index, Little Brother?"

Kiril had heard of it, all right. A staggering collection of biographical information, infinite in scope and indiscriminate in content. Anyone of even remote interest to the KGB was targeted.

"Aunt Sofia grasped right from the start that the Index was a perfect fit for my special talents. Over the years, I've made myself useful to a great many influential people," Aleksei said with a faint smile of reminiscence.

"You mean that over the years you've become a blackmailer *par excellence*," Kiril said with disgust.

"One tramples or one is trampled on," Aleksei said philosophically. "But our aunt was not so sanguine about *your* future, was she, Little Brother? Oh, you were studious enough. Uncomplaining. Obedient. Top grades. Still, you'd built a kind of wall around yourself that shut people out, especially as you got older. 'Kiril even shuts *me* out, the ungrateful brat!' Sofia told me once. What's so funny?"

"Our Aunt Sofia was more astute than I gave her credit for."

"I could have helped you professionally had you come to me," Aleksei mused. "Why didn't you?"

"That's like asking a priest why he never made a pact with the devil."

"You *are* your mother's son," Aleksei said with a mock sigh. "Your antisocial attitude is precisely why I've kept an eye on you all these years. I could have had you arrested, you know. Or confined in one of our mental institutions, like Vladimir Bukovsky and men of his ilk. But I didn't. Maybe blood really is thicker than water," Aleksei said magnanimously. "Or, maybe I'm a generous person when it comes to relatively harmless transgressions. Like your learning German."

It took Kiril a split second to realize how naïve he'd been. Of course Aleksei would have put out feelers for something like his language capabilities . . . and for god knows what else.

"I learned German to read medical journals," he said matter-of-factly. "I also hoped that someday I'd have an opportunity to talk to our German comrades in the East."

"And learning English?"

"Same reason."

"You flirted with the Gulag," Aleksei said bluntly.

"Thanks for the warning."

"Take it seriously, Kiril. This is not the time to make trouble. It's bad enough that we had to pull out of Medicine International's Artificial Heart Symposium in West Berlin," he said sourly.

"You sound disappointed," Kiril said slowly, even as his mind raced while he tried to figure out why.

"Let's just say I was looking forward to a friendly chat with the eminent Dr. Kurt Brenner at close range and on friendly ground—a missed opportunity."

"What business could the KGB possibly have with a world-class heart surgeon like Dr. Brenner?" Kiril scoffed.

"So Brenner is a hero of yours, is he?"

Aleksei turned toward a massive figure who stood just inside his office door. "Bring me the Dr. Kurt Brenner file, Luka."

"Sergeant Luka Rogov," Aleksei said as the uniformed Mongolian returned with a bulky file tied with rough cord.

"We've already met," Kiril said drily. "Your Mr. Rogov dragged me in here, remember?"

"I have to make a call," Aleksei said, ignoring Kiril's sarcasm. "A private matter I must attend to. But before I permit you to leave, I cannot resist seeing your reaction to what's in this file." Smiling, he handed the file to Kiril.

Something in that smile, even more than his brother's words, made Kiril open the Brenner file with trepidation.

It was an odd mix. Copies of military service documents. Diplomas. Grainy newspaper articles. Airline tickets and hotel statements—

And a transcript of Dr. Kurt Brenner's remarks at the home of Medicine International's Director, Russell Manning, during a May Day party in Manhattan a few days earlier.

Kiril found what he was looking for all too quickly.

*"I must confess that I'm offended by my government's behavior. Spying in this day and age? Despicable!"*

Then: *"It has taken years for people of good faith from our two countries to establish a bridge of friendship. I only hope that bridge is strong enough to withstand such ill-advised and provocative conduct."*

Kiril made himself read it again. He read it twice more, as if the repetition forced him to believe what he was reading.

*How could Dr. Kurt Brenner disparage America—a country that, more than any other, was the very personification of freedom?*

He shook off a sense of sacrilege so pungent it filled his mouth with bile. A prominent American heart surgeon, a man whose profession was saving lives, being deferential to the ambassador of a slave state!

Kiril was slipping the papers back into the file when he noticed a thick batch stapled together—roughly twenty pages of a medical report about the next generation of heart-lung machines. Grateful for the distraction, he dug in and was soon mesmerized by the new technology available in the West. He was roughly halfway through when he came upon a 5-by-7-inch photograph—a mistake, he figured. Why else would a photograph have been stapled into the middle of a report?

The first thing that registered was the name typed at the bottom of the photograph: DR. KURT BRENNER.

Then he was staring at the man. Brenner's hair was white, in stark contrast to the deep tan of his skin. His eyes were dark brown, his cheekbones high. His mouth curved with amusement—and something else, something Kiril couldn't quite put a name to. Something he didn't like. Still, apart from certain dissimilar features and the man's fashionable attire and self-assured sophistication, the resemblance was startling.

Kiril was a consummate realist. Brenner was no mirror

image . . . and yet did he dare hope?

The office was cold. Even so, drops of perspiration appeared on his neck and slipped down to his shoulder blades. Had Aleksei seen the photograph? Doubtful. His brother would have had no interest in such a technical paper. Even if Aleksei had glanced at it accidentally, surely he'd have called it to Kiril's attention. He slipped the photo into his pocket and tuned in to Aleksei's voice through the slightly open office door.

"—no time for your petty problems," Aleksei was saying, his tone a mix of impatience and anger. "The repairs will have to wait. After all, Glienicker Bridge has been collapsing ever since the war. My orders from General Nemerov are to keep all unauthorized personnel off the bridge until the investigation is complete. Your orders are to set up the necessary dredging equipment before I get there . . . *Three weeks*? . . . Godammit! Let me know as soon as you get the equipment back from Lake Constance. It's important we dredge up Brodsky's lighter. The General's been pushing me hard. *Why?* A would-be defector named Stepan Brodsky, who just *happened* to be a Soviet Air Force Captain, and who just *happened* to work for me. Who just *happened* to organize my part of the security for the Four-Power summit and just *happened* to almost pull off that defection on Glienicker Bridge. Oh, and Brodsky's last act on earth just *happened* to prevent me from obtaining his cigarette lighter. What do you suppose was in that goddamn lighter, Emil—cotton?!"

Kiril was stunned.

*Stepan's cigarette lighter was still missing? If they were dredging, he must have pushed it into the Havel River!*

As he waited Aleksei out, Kiril worked calmly, stoically, on planting the germ of an idea that, despite Aleksei's paranoia, just might prove irresistible.

# CHAPTER 16

Aleksei reentered the room to find Kiril sitting, trance-like, the Brenner file open on his lap.

"I see from your expression that you found Dr. Brenner's lack of sympathy for his own country disturbing," he said cheerfully. "Your hero—"

"Has feet of clay," Kiril snapped. "He's no patriot. As for the word *despicable*, it's an apt description of the bastard."

Aleksei laughed. "I agree, but for different reasons."

"You never did answer my question, Aleksei. What business could the KGB possibly have with Kurt Brenner?"

Aleksei began filling a pipe, his fingers milky white against the dark wood of the stem. "What would you say were the chances of someone with Dr. Kurt Brenner's impressive credentials defecting to the Soviet Union?"

"Whatever else you are, Aleksei, you're no fool. Would-be defectors head for the West, not the East. There's also the problem of medical facilities. Ours can't begin to compare with what the West has to offer. You mention Brenner's impressive medical credentials. What would be in it for him?"

Aleksei lit up and watched the lazy upward drift of the smoke. "Suppose it were a question, not of what Brenner had to gain by defecting, but of what he stood to lose?"

"I thought your specialty was extorting confessions," Kiril said drily, "not seducing westerners to Mother Russia."

"How shortsighted of you. Think of me as an expert at collecting the fascinating bits and pieces that form the mosaic of a man's past. Anyone who could reverse the usual direction of defections and persuade a prominent figure like Dr. Kurt Brenner to 'relocate' from West to East would be held in great esteem in certain circles."

"No doubt.     And     by 'persuade,'     I     take     it     you mean blackmail?"

"What else? Not that I'm so naïve as to think I could pull off a coup like that," he said sourly.

"What if you could?" Kiril said slowly.

"Could what?"

"To hell with Medicine International's symposium in West Berlin next year! What if the Soviet Union were to hold its own medical conference in *East* Berlin—say a one- or two-day affair? What if you scheduled it for a few days *before* Medicine International's symposium in West Berlin? Brenner would still have an opportunity to work with Dr. Yanin and our heart specialists in East Germany. Knowing how it must have rankled him when the Soviet Union abruptly withdrew from the West Berlin symposium, Brenner would almost certainly accept."

*Clever of you, Little Brother. First you push me to send you to Canada, supposedly in the name of science but in fact so you could defect. Now you want me to send you to East Berlin—right where your pal Brodsky almost pulled it off. On the other hand . . .*

"Brenner *would* be unlikely to refuse, wouldn't he?" Aleksei said thoughtfully. "Especially if we were to invite some prominent heart surgeons from the People's Democracies. The West Berlin symposium doesn't happen for what—another sixteen months? I'd have plenty of time to make plans."

"And plenty of time to implement them," Kiril observed.

Aleksei's pipe had gone out. Switching to cigarettes, he offered one to Kiril and held out a match. "Why the sudden desire to cooperate with the KGB, Little Brother?" he said, pushing back his chair.

"I'll cooperate even more if you'll let me. In case you're busy just before the conference, I'll entertain Brenner."

"Don't you think Dr. Yanin would be a more suitable substitute host?"

"He would if he spoke English."

"But you don't know Berlin. You don't know East Germany."

"You're wrong," Kiril countered, not having to feign bitterness. "Thanks to Stepan, I know a great deal about both. From time to time, he would describe East Berlin in great detail. Shall I anticipate your next 'problem'? That I lack the credentials for the job? I'm your brother. I'm also a longstanding member of Dr. Mikhail Yanin's surgical team—much of it, I admit, behind a heart-lung machine. Before that, I was a doctor with nearly twenty years of experience. I'd say that qualifies me to describe the life of a Soviet heart surgeon. In glowing terms, of course."

"You amaze me, Little Brother. Why do something so out of character?" Aleksei said softly, leaning forward to stare at Kiril.

Kiril, his face impassive, felt like an insect being examined under a magnifying glass. "If Brenner *does* defect, which, frankly, I doubt, I could say that observing the undeniably brilliant Dr. Kurt Brenner at work would enliven things at the Yanin surgical center. I could say that whatever else he is, Brenner is a heart surgeon without peer. That he'd need his own surgical team here in Moscow. I'm egotistical enough to think I could persuade him to train me as chief assistant surgeon. I'm tired of watching from the sidelines," he said, feeding weariness into his tone. "Given half a chance, I could be as good as Yanin, maybe better."

"So childhood ambition dies hard," Aleksei said. I have to admit that the thought of *you* as my co-optee in this enterprise is intriguing."

"Co-optee, as in cooperate? I find *that* amusing," Kiril countered.

More than amusing. If Kiril could help me pull Brenner in, isn't it a risk worth taking?

"I'll do it," Aleksei said without ceremony. "But on one condition, Kiril."

He waved Luka Rogov back inside.

The Mongolian's head was shaved, his face flat. His eyes were deep-set and slanted, his skin neither brown nor yellow, but some of each. The coarse black hairs of his full mustache framed his mouth.

"Tell my brother about *your* credentials, Luka."

"In 1945 I help liberate Berlin. I was six years in Red Army," Rogov said, his eyes gleaming with the memory.

"I discovered Luka Rogov during the war, lost track of him, then found him years later on a Moscow street. He comes from a small town near the Mongolian border. His name has been modernized, but not his soul. Can you guess why the Lukas of this world are invaluable in security matters? They know how to obey orders. I don't think I need to add that Luka enjoys his work."

Aleksei studied Kiril's indifferent expression. "Let me clarify my position," he said. "When you were a child, you used to fear me. I see that this is no longer the case, even though you have much more reason to fear me now. If I permit you to visit East Berlin next year—let alone play host to Kurt Brenner—Luka will be your constant companion. If you make any move to follow in the footsteps of your late friend Brodsky, Luka will take 'extreme measures.' There's a story that circulates among my colleagues about the sister of a general, picked up in Moscow for black market speculation. The police who contacted the general expected him to dismiss the charges. I still have in my possession a copy of his order. 'Speculation during wartime is treason. Shoot her.' Any questions?"

"Just one." Kiril tossed the Brenner file folder onto Aleksei's desk. "What makes you think Brenner will accept the invitation? Dr. Yanin tells me Brenner has consistently declined invitations from communist countries—apparently because of his wife's anti-communist bent."

"Not this time, he won't. Not after his recent May Day reaction in New York to the Potsdam incident. Not after his eagerness to defend our country at the expense of his own. And certainly not after his disappointment over our withdrawal from September's Medicine International symposium in West Berlin."

"I see."

"Then too," Aleksei mused, "I suppose Brenner could claim he was eager to visit his birthplace."

"I don't understand."

"He was born in what is now East Berlin."

"You're not serious!"

"Oh, but I am. Not that it matters one way or the other. Herr Dr. Kurt Brenner will accept our invitation for only one reason. Fear."

"Mind telling me what you're blackmailing him about?"

"I do, actually." Aleksei smiled thinly. "We intelligence types play by the need-to-know rules."

# CHAPTER 17

In the days after he left Aleksei's office, Kiril noticed that Galya's attitude seemed to have changed. She acted more guarded. Paid close attention to everything he said—especially about the East Berlin medical conference he was working on for the following year.

Once he surmised that Aleksei had recruited Galya to spy on him, Kiril spoke guardedly and with circumspection. Still, her presence in his life made it difficult for him to prepare for his attempted defection. He had never been to East Berlin and knew little about the city generally, even less about its geography. Without calling attention to himself, he'd had to study East and West Berlin's geographical relationship to each other, and theirs to East and West Germany. He pored over street maps of Potsdam and West Berlin. Learned all he could about Glienicker Bridge and the Havel River that flowed beneath it. Made a mental note to find out about the East German launches that patrolled under the bridge. None of this was easy to do in a police state, let alone while under ongoing surveillance by a woman with whom he had a professional, as well as a personal, relationship. By snatching some time here and there, visiting libraries with plausible excuses, talking to the few friends he could trust, walking casually through museums, Kiril had to admit he was making progress, albeit much too slowly.

* * *

Aleksei Andreyev had no such constraints. Immediately after his intriguing chat with Kiril, he turned his researchers loose in Moscow and tasked the New York and Washington KGB stations with turning the life of the eminent Dr. Kurt Brenner inside out. He already knew Brenner had been born in what was now East Berlin, and he was privy to Brenner's war record. But he wanted to know more about the years in between. Much more. More, perhaps, than Kurt Brenner knew about himself.

In the next several months, the intelligence flowed in a steady stream. Because of the lack of pre-Revolution records, the civil war following the Bolsheviks' seizure of power, and then two world wars, Aleksei's researchers could ascertain only that Brenner's mother had been born in Czarist Russia sometime around 1901. After that, all traces of her had disappeared in Russia and in the Soviet Union until the 1920s, when she surfaced in Berlin, married a German citizen, and had a son.

Aleksei had learned earlier that in 1922, Brenner was born in what later would become East Germany. He even knew the name of the borough: Pankow. Aleskei surmised that in 1931, the Brenners, in the wake of the Nazi rise to power and apprehensive of the threat facing assorted groups—Jews, Communists, Democratic Socialists—had emigrated to the United States.

Brenner's mother and father were physicians. Their son, Aleksei learned, had been a prodigy as early as age ten. School work was never a problem. Kurt Brenner consistently mastered scientific games designed for his age group. His parents had subscribed to magazines on his behalf, *Popular Science* among them. When he was twelve, Brenner started to hang around his parents' medical office, asking questions. Harvard College accepted him in 1936 when he was only fifteen—a pre-med major, a biology minor. Three years later, he had his B.S., and in February 1942 his Ph.D in microbiology. There was no doubt that Kurt Brenner was a wunderkind.

But there was a dark side, Aleksei noted with considerable interest. Prodigy or not, Brenner never seemed to be surrounded by a circle of real friends. He was aloof and driven. Even more intriguing, few of his peers trusted him. He had a reputation for breaking his word. For being late to some affair or not showing up at all. For infuriating a pal whose girlfriend was supposed to be off limits. Relationships with girls were invariably short-lived. When he was older, his love life followed the same pattern—casual affairs that ended badly.

Several months before his graduation from Harvard, Brenner had coolly assessed his situation. The Japanese had bombed Pearl Harbor and were racking up gains throughout Asia. The Germans had declared war on the United States and were rolling through Europe. Brenner would become a physician—a heart surgeon. That was carved in stone. But being twenty-one years old and soon to lose his graduate school deferment, he was about to be drafted—which meant he would have no control over what they'd do with him despite his fluent German and his stellar academic credentials. A classmate who had been drafted the year before, and who had a Ph.D in advanced civil engineering, was stuck in the infantry—not a pleasant prospect.

Typically, Brenner came up with a plan, a report of which had found its way into the KGB archives. He had convinced an Army recruiter into believing he had a job offer from a microbiology foundation that was doing classified research for the government—something vaguely having to do with chemical warfare, and that he was entitled to an "essential industry" deferment like, say, coal miners. *If* he took the job, that is. But what he really wanted, he'd told the recruiter, was to enlist and be trained as a medical corpsman. That way, he would get a jump on medical school.

Several weeks later, Kurt Brenner—prodigy, Bachelor of Science, Doctor of Microbiology—had become, in three years, Sergeant First Class Brenner. Called *Doc* by the soldiers he served with, Brenner was back in Germany, the land of his birth.

Aleksei scanned the report.

Brenner will rue the day he did that. It's what led to our hold on him.

He dug into the more recent threads of Kurt Brenner's life. After medical school at Harvard and a residency at a famous Texas heart institute, Dr. Kurt Brenner was awarded several prestigious surgery fellowships. He joined the cardiology faculty at New York's Columbia Presbyterian Hospital, where he soon began to shine as an outstanding heart surgeon. He borrowed money to start the Manhattan Pediatric Heart Institute. He was the recipient of many medical and philanthropic awards.

Aleksei reached for a file labeled "miscellaneous."

Parents unreservedly proud of their son.

Marriage in 1955 to Adrienne Kalda, journalist and outspoken anti-communist. No children.

Excessive drinker, but not alcoholic.

Profligate with money.

At least two extra-marital affairs in the past five years, one with Grace Manning, wife of Medicine International's Russell Manning.

Aleksei smiled, reminded that Medicine International's

Artificial Heart Symposium, scheduled for September, was proceeding apace but there were a host of problems.

According to his sources, by the time Russell Manning returned to New York in late winter after an extended vacation, Kurt Brenner had sent M.I. a list of conditions before he'd accept their formal invitation. As the undisputed star of the show in the forefront of international artificial heart research, Brenner was demanding a lot of perks. Private chef. Large suite on the hotel's top floor. His own heart-lung machine operator from New York. An American assistant surgeon and anesthesiologist—both of them board-certified. His own translators. Even his favorite operating room nurse.

*Which may explain why Brenner is having trouble convincing his wife to accompany him.*

There was more. The West Germans were being skittish about sharing the billing with French surgeons. The French wanted Brenner to operate on a Frenchman. Financing from either the German government or the Soviet Union could not be guaranteed. The hosts might have insufficient hotel space. And on and on.

Aleksei savored the moment.

*Looks like it's time to invite the illustrious Dr. Kurt Brenner to the other half of Berlin.*

* * *

Brenner was stunned.

The letter had arrived via a special courier from Washington, D.C. He held the single sheet of paper as though it had been dusted with anthrax.

Rising from his soft camel-colored leather office chair, Brenner crossed the room and closed the door. He returned to his chair and reread the letter from the German Democratic Republic, Washington, D.C.

*My dear Dr. Brenner:*

*The Ambassador of the German Democratic Republic was delighted to note recently in The New York Times that you have accepted an invitation from the highly regarded Medicine International organization to participate in its Artificial Heart Symposium several months from now.*

*His Excellency was disappointed to read that while the Symposium will explore recent developments and examine the technological advances that are just beyond the horizon in the fast-moving field of artificial hearts, there will be no hands-on demonstration.*

*It is in that connection that I write.*

*By the oddest coincidence, about a week before the Medicine International symposium in West Berlin, the Humboldt University Medical Center in East Berlin is sponsoring a conference on a related topic: "Does the future of cardiology belong to artificial hearts, or to human transplants?"*

*His Excellency, the Ambassador, cordially and with utmost sincerity, has asked me to invite you to deliver the keynote address and perhaps honor the faculty and invited guests by performing a simple open heart procedure— possibly something like a mitral valve replacement.*

*When the Ambassador mentioned his idea to the Chancellor of Humboldt University, the Chancellor enthusiastically embraced my issuing this invitation, and suggested that it include Mrs. Brenner, the noted journalist.*

*Again coincidentally, Chancellor Dmitri Malik recalls having met you during World War II and looks forward to seeing you once again. The Ambassador told me that he understood from Chancellor Malik how extremely disappointed he would be if you were unable to attend. Apparently he believes there is much to recapture about what he referred to as "the old days."*

*The favor of a prompt and affirmative response would be greatly appreciated.*

*With sincerity and the utmost respect, I remain your faithful servant,*

> *Dr. Gerhardt Hans Walter Spiegel,*
> *Special Assistant to the Ambassador*
> *German Democratic Republic*

"Jesus Christ," Brenner said softly to himself. "Jesus Christ."

He focused on the seventh paragraph, realizing that the rest was window dressing. Dmitri Malik wanted him in East Berlin. If Brenner didn't accept the invitation, Malik was threatening to expose the Glienicker Bridge incident.

And they wanted Adrienne.

# CHAPTER 18

Kurt Brenner experienced the old stir of excitement as Adrienne pushed through the revolving door and walked toward him in that easy rapid stride of hers. Sleek copper-colored hair. Green eyes with a catlike upward slant. Lovely.

Her tall, lithe figure attracted admiring glances. As usual, she was oblivious.

The cut and color of her pants suit—severely tailored black—stressed her slenderness, making her look vulnerable. He knew better.

"Late as always, but always worth waiting for," he said, smiling.

"Sorry. My meeting took longer than I expected." She slipped her shoulder bag to the floor and slid into the booth.

He reached for her hand. "When are you coming back to me? The apartment is like a mausoleum without you."

"That depends."

"I know," he said. "But even though we agreed to settle things in Paris after the West Berlin conference, I have to talk to you now."

"I'm not going to West Berlin. It's just another back-slapping, good-ol'-boy excuse for physicians to massage their egos. I have too much to do here trying to get my hands around an Iron Curtain article I'm working on. Besides, I can't get a visa out of the East Germans. I have a friend from the State Department working on it, but so far there's been no movement."

"You know," he said irritably, "I realize your anti-communist views are a matter of principle. But what I *don't* grasp is why you seem to take it personally."

He steeled himself, expecting her to lash out. She surprised him by reaching for his martini and draining the glass.

"Order for me, will you? Whatever you're having. Be right back."

Adrienne opened a teak door with a discreet brass plaque: LADIES. She leaned her forehead against cool black marble. Kurt's criticism had the ring of truth. Why *do* I take these things personally?

She ran the faucet and splashed cold water on her face. She was absently running a comb through her hair when the answer jumped out at her, as if liberated by her subconscious . . .

*Because it feels self-evident that free people should care about those who aren't. Because it shouldn't take any imagination to picture a wife on one side of a closed border, her husband stuck on the other. Because a stranger's body riddled with bullets could just as easily be your lover, your best friend, every mother's son or daughter.*

In fairness, Adrienne thought, could she blame Kurt for not grasping what she herself had just realized?

Which led to a more complex question: Was she really prepared to end her marriage, she asked herself as vivid memories flashed to the surface.

Six years ago, Adrienne Kalda had shared the balcony of an amphitheater with a bevy of young medical students fairly bubbling over with excitement. Excited herself by her recent promotion from drudge researcher to staff reporter, Adrienne was nervous at the prospect of her first assignment—an interview with the famous Dr. Kurt Brenner.

But peering down as Dr. Brenner entered the operating theater, she lost track of time as excitement turned into something else . . .

It was as if she were watching from a great distance what seemed like a dance performance with the most beautiful choreography she had ever seen. Every gesture was purposeful but unhurried. Relaxed but with no wasted motion. She was mesmerized by the sight of an exposed human heart. Of machines hissing. Strong light blazing. The faint odor of anesthesia. She saw nurses and assisting surgeons effortlessly maneuvered about the operating table by a master director. The elusive angle of an incision being probed by two equally deft hands. A perfectly positioned needle sewing up the patient's chest cavity.

Her post-operative interview was pathetic: tentative questions awkwardly put.

Why couldn't she keep the awe out of her voice?

Tamping it down by sheer will power, she asked about the famous Brenner temper. Were the rumors true about elbowing aside flustered assistants in the midst of an operation? About flinging an instrument at some nurse whose timing was a few seconds off?

Laughing good-naturedly, Dr. Brenner had owned up to such "outrageous" behavior—but only from time to time, he added. This so disarmed her that she forgot her next question.

To cover her embarrassment, Brenner said with a smile that took her breath away, "I have an idea. Since you've just been promoted, and since I recently opened a heart surgery clinic for underprivileged children, we both have something to celebrate. Why not do it together?

Champagne, dinner, dancing—"

"Tonight?" she said stupidly. "You must be exhausted."

"Quite the opposite. I'm exhilarated."

Their courtship, like their first date, had been exhilaratingly brief.

Their marriage had made headlines. The famous heart surgeon and the neophyte journalist.

One of the things Adrienne appreciated most about her husband was how supportive he was of her fledging career. Another thing she cherished was his confidence in her ability to rise without milking his contacts. Nor did Kurt begrudge her the frequent and sometimes long separations when she traveled in relentless pursuit of a good story—especially when a trip ended with a brief holiday for both of them in some exotic locale.

Hers was a charmed life, one she never took for granted.

Until a few years later when she realized that the man she'd married had drastically changed.

It was all the more unsettling because the change had nothing to do with her—at least not directly. Kurt had metamorphosed into Dr. Kurt Brenner, world-famous heart surgeon, with a dazzling smile, the pseudo-confident style of a playboy, and an increasingly unpredictable temper in the operating theater. Or so it was rumored.

She refused to believe it. From time to time she returned to the amphitheater. Sitting in the same balcony, she would watch Kurt work his magic, eager to recapture what had made her fall in love with him.

Afterward, she would be relieved that he hadn't lost his skills.

But she could no longer deny what *else* she had witnessed: nurses and even assistant surgeons fighting for his attention . . . and Dr. Kurt Brenner, peerless heart surgeon, enjoying the competition.

They had argued about it. Reconciled. Talked things out. There were times when she thought she was getting through. Times when she succumbed to the famous Brenner charm. Times, like now, when she called her own stubbornness into question.

She sighed, tired to the point of indifference, and headed for the dining room. Before she could even sit down, Kurt preempted the conversation.

"There's been a new development about the West Berlin trip, Adrienne. That's why I asked you to lunch."

"Kurt, how many times do I have to—"

"What if I told you the *East* Germans will give you a visa? If you're so eager to write some sort of exposé, I would think you'd jump at the chance to have a first-hand look from behind the Iron Curtain."

"Why would they give me a visa?" she asked, incredulous.

Brenner filled her in about Humboldt University Medical Center's conference on artificial hearts versus human transplants and how he would give the keynote address and perform a simple open-heart procedure.

"What do you *really* get out of it, Kurt?"

"I get to show off my lovely wife in both East *and* West Berlin," he said.

*And I keep Major Dmitri Malik happy until I find out what the hell his game is.*

# CHAPTER 19

Adrienne entered the oak-paneled taproom of the Manhattan Press Club and spotted him immediately, ensconced in the soft-leather comfort of a dimly lit booth.

"Hello, Paul. Happy Labor Day."

"And to you, Adrienne."

"Thanks for seeing me on a holiday weekend. It's my only free time, these days. You doing okay?"

"Reasonably well under the circumstances."

Well, you look wonderful. I wish women aged as well as men."

"So you like a touch of gray in a man's hair, do you?"

"I do when it's real," she said. "Kidding aside, how are you bearing up?"

"Let's just say it wouldn't surprise me if my hair turned color in the last fourteen months."

Adrienne frowned. "That rough?"

Houston shrugged.

"I take it the Soviets have succeeded in getting you fired from the State Department."

"Not quite. After a year-long investigation of what

happened on that bridge, I've been asked to retire. Quietly."

"I'm really sorry, Paul."

"Don't be. I was planning to quit my day job as soon as I got back from Potsdam last year. Now I'm not so sure. I think I'd much rather be sacked."

"*Why*, for heaven's sake?"

"My colleagues—those at the State Department, at least—are trying to convince the East Germans that the so-called *border incident* shooting had no official sanction. That it was nothing more than an unauthorized cowboy stunt staged by me alone. Being fired will make me feel better."

"We've known each other a long time, Paul. For a diplomat, you've been involved in some pretty convoluted . . . 'operations' but I've never asked you if they're limited to the State Department. I'm not going to start now."

"Good woman. We'll drink to it."

Adrienne smiled and sat back.

"I'm going to East Berlin with Kurt in several weeks, and about a week later, the Medicine International symposium in West Berlin," Adrienne announced when their drinks arrived. "Something to do with artificial hearts and human transplants."

"You, of all people, are willing to go behind the Iron Curtain? What am I missing?"

"Isn't it obvious? As the wife of the Symposium's honored guest, I'll have access to things that are ordinarily off-limits."

"And you'll write about what? As if I didn't know," he said with a faint smile.

"Human rights—or more precisely, the lack of them. Frankly, given my reputation as a journalist, I'm surprised the East Germans are letting me ride on Kurt's coattails."

"Maybe because your last few articles have honed in on the Soviet Union, so you're viewed as anti-communist, period—and yes, I've seen that kind of skewed reasoning firsthand. These people don't see the wider connection."

"Which is?"

"That your consistent theme is anti-totalitarian."

She grinned. "It's so refreshing, not having to explain myself. By the way, do you happen to have a photograph of Stepan Brodsky?"

"I can do better than that. I'll arrange for you to meet a man named Ernst Roeder. He's a well-connected East German photographer. Roeder takes two kinds of photographs. The ones destined for the Communist newspaper, *Neues Deutschland*—New Germany—the others for a very different outlet—a small, mostly underground magazine called *Das Wort*."

"*The Word*," she mused. "A friend of mine mentioned it once. Very grim stuff."

"Some of it. Remember the famous shot of a wizened old woman in East Berlin begging for food in front of Communist boss Walter Ulbricht's office?"

"I'll say! How could anyone forget?"

"That was Ernst Roeder's work—anonymous, of course. Even so, with those kinds of photographs, Ernst is taking a big risk."

"But if his photographs are anonymous . . ."

"Doesn't matter. There's an artistic phenomenon known as a *signature*, and I don't mean a written one. Experts can spot a genuine Van Gogh—even an unsigned painting— by its style, subject, composition, color, brush strokes, *etcetera*. The same with photographs by Ansel Adams. Alfred Hitchcock's films have a signature even without a director's credit. Roeder's photographs have a signature, too—one that's distinctive in both *Neues Deutschland* and *Das Wort*. The only thing that keeps Roeder and photographers like him behind the Iron Curtain is the chance to fight the regime in the best way they know how."

Impressed, and touched, Adrienne asked, "How do I contact him?"

"You don't. I'll see that he contacts you."

"And he's reliable?"

"There's something you should know about Ernst Roeder," Houston said evenly. "He was on Glienicker Bridge in May of last year when Stepan Brodsky was killed. He and Brodsky were friends. The idea was that Ernst would shoot some film as Stepan tried to make it across. If he succeeded, the pictures would show a defiant rebellious defection from communism. If not . . . well, something else. Ernst managed to take a few photographs of Stepan as he lay dying."

"He's allowed to take *those* kinds of photographs?!"

"Certainly not. Ernst Roeder has two things going for him," Houston said with a wry smile. "He's a large man— more like soccer coach than a celebrated photographer. But Roeder is cagey. He uses a conventional Leica or Speed Graphic for authorized photographs. For more surreptitious shots, his oversized hands can easily conceal a miniature camera. A Minox, for example."

"Very enterprising, carrying two cameras," Adrienne said thoughtfully.

"And dangerous. Don't try it. Too many tourists have ended up in a communist prison—or worse—for something as innocent as a sunset that happened to have a piece of some bridge in the background."

"*Bridges* are off limits?"

"Bridges and a lot of other things in East Germany."

"How well-connected is Ernst Roeder?"

"Very. His brother-in-law is a colonel in East German intelligence."

"Now *there's* a double-edged sword," Adrienne observed.

"Indeed." Houston glanced at his watch. "Let's get down to business. What do you want to know?"

She dipped into her shoulder-bag and pulled out a notepad.

For the next hour and a half over lunch, Paul Houston gave Adrienne Brenner a detailed intelligence briefing about the Communist regime in East Germany.

# CHAPTER 20

The sign on the table said: SPECIAL SECTION FOR PERMISSIONS TO VISIT ABROAD, and under it, CENTRAL COMMITTEE, U.S.S.R. Alongside was a pile of filled-out forms, each one containing cautiously written answers to carefully drafted questions. Two men bent over one of the forms.

"I don't like it," muttered one of the men as he followed the line of questions with a sharpened pencil and stopped at the question labeled "Family Status." The man had a pointy chin in perfect symmetry with the tip of his pencil.

His rotund colleague didn't bother to look down. "The application seems to be in perfect order," he said, examining his stubby fingers.

"Have you forgotten what happened to Simonov last month?" the first man shot back, not in the least reassured. "A severe reprimand for giving an exit permit to a man with a short tail. This applicant has no tail at all!"

"He has no need of one. You know who his brother is."

"I still don't like it. Whenever something goes wrong, we're always asked the same question. How many hostages were you counting on?"

"What a lot of fuss over nothing, Lev. He's only going to East Berlin."

"Just the same, I want to ask him a few questions."

"Fine by me."

When his name was called, Kiril noticed that the people standing closest to him inched away, a few casting him a resentful glance—as if he should have known better than to join the group and possibly cast suspicion on them all. As if his six-foot one-inch frame were a personal threat.

He approached the table with the calm expression of a man who has nothing to fear . . . as if the two men really *were* innocuous bureaucrats instead of plainclothes officers in the KGB.

"Your residence registration certificate," said the thinner of the two.

Kiril handed over the certificate.

"Your internal passport. Your military card," he snapped.

"Both those documents were turned over to the proper authorities three months ago."

His interrogator began leafing through some papers attached to the back of Kiril's questionnaire.

"How many forms have you completed in the last three months? How many personal appearances have you made? How many photographs did you submit?"

"Many forms. Dozens of appearances. Photographs?" Kiril closed his eyes. "About twenty," he said, opening them.

"Why, in your more recent photographs, are you wearing dark sunglasses?" the pencil-pusher asked.

"I explained that in my answer to Question Eleven. Several days ago I developed a minor infection. My eye is still very sensitive to light." He removed his glasses so that both men could see for themselves.

Dismissing Kiril with a contemptuous wave of one hand, pointy-face ordered the entire group to approach the table.

"Do you all understand the loyalty pledges and the secrecy agreement you have signed?"

There was a general murmuring and a nodding of heads.

"Very well. You will not receive *these*"—one hand came down hard on a pile of green leather booklets—"until you have read and memorized *these*." The KGB officer's other hand touched a pile of red booklets with gold lettering. "Only then will you be ready to take the loyalty and secrecy oath."

Kiril reached for a red booklet. "RULES OF BEHAVIOR FOR SOVIET CITIZENS ABROAD" it said on the cover, and under that in smaller letters: *For internal distribution only.* As he thumbed through the booklet, he couldn't help thinking the rules were written in a style suitable for children. Do not drink. Do not visit places of doubtful entertainment. Do not talk with foreigners outside the presence of a reliable witness. Do not use the normal mail facilities of the host country. Do not fail to report suspicious behavior on the part of associates and traveling companions. Above all, do not forget that every Soviet citizen is a potential target of provocation by mercenary anti-Communist elements, all of them eager to recruit the unwary into their ranks.

Twenty minutes later, Kiril left the building. The sound of iron doors slamming shut behind him gave him an almost giddy sense of finality.

The feel of the green leather booklet in his pocket gave him a sense of lightheadedness. He walked through a courtyard and into the street as if his feet never touched the pavement.

*Free*, he thought wonderingly.

Free, at least, to leave the building, he thought with a jolt of fear. It isn't the West, but it's a giant step in that direction. At least I'm free to leave the Soviet Union!

He passed ponderous granite structures with six-story-high portraits hanging over ornate facades—comic-strip versions of his country's "illustrious heroes," past and present. He saw string after string of red flags waving hypnotically in the breeze. But high above the sprawling flatness of Moscow, a few tall buildings rose in self-conscious defiance. Kiril felt a moment's kinship with them.

There was no queue at his trolley stop, but as usual, people packed themselves into each car with the zealousness of combat soldiers embarking on a mission. As soon as the trolley car doors closed behind him, he was struck by the contrasting stillness inside.

He stared out the window. Row after row of prefabricated apartment houses rolled past—pale yellow cinderblocks, each a shabby functional echo of its neighbor. Half an hour later, he worked his way to the front of the car, exited at the next stop, and headed for one of the cinderblocks—his home for the last ten years.

As he climbed the stairs in the drab hallway, he was assaulted by a pervasive dinginess. The thought of never again having to walk up these stairs and down this hallway gave him an odd sense of detachment. He passed through the communal kitchen and unlocked the door to his room. It was simply furnished for simple needs. A narrow bed. A few shelves and wall hooks for clothes. A small scarred table and a couple of chairs. Apart from some medical books piled at one end of the table that provided the only spot of color, there was nothing to suggest the character or personality of its occupant. It was a suitable room for a transient-in-spirit, he thought, closing the door. He switched on an overhead light. A plastic suitcase lay open on the bed next to his raincoat. Some bottles and an eye dropper were on the table. A towel with brown stains hung over the back of a chair.

A clock on one of the shelves reminded him that Galya was due any time now.

Removing his dark glasses, he examined his left eye in a mirror. The redness was almost gone. He had passed inspection this morning. But he might not be so lucky if he didn't remember to keep after it once every hour, when possible, until people stopped asking questions.

After packing only what he'd need, he opened a small bottle, and stuck the eyedropper in. With the odor of lemon pulling at his nostrils, he put a few drops of lemon juice in his left eye and held his breath against the sting.

He felt his scalp gingerly—still raw from the chemicals and repeated rinsing. But a mirror check drew a tight smile. His hair was just a touch darker than his natural color brown. Galya was the only one who might notice—unlikely in the dim light of a lamp. He turned off the overhead.

On his way home he had stopped off at the hospital and retrieved his cigarette lighter. Dropping it into his jacket pocket, he sat down to wait.

At the familiar tap-tap on the door, he called out, "It's unlocked."

Galya came in. "I won't stay long," she said, eyeing his small open suitcase. "You must have so much to do. Not much to pack, is there?" she observed with a tinge of bitterness. "I know there's more to life than stylish clothes and beautiful jewelry," she said bleakly, "but even so . . ."

He tuned out, not wanting to be a complicit enabler when it came to Galya's obsessive need for pretty things. Not when she should be lashing out at the apparatchiks who blocked, not just a fun trip to Canada, but freedom to do whatever she wanted with her life.

"—hurts the most when I go to the cinema," she was saying. "At first I'm captivated by the glamorous heroine— her clothes, her jewelry, even her high-heeled shoes! The next thing I notice is how *casual* she is about her wardrobe. And then I glance at the only semi-decent item I own—a black dress that's four years old and stylish as a muddy overshoe . . ."

"Never mind," he said gently, touching her cheek. Knowing how vulnerable she was because she had never fully grasped that the luxuries she wanted were symbolic of a much wider principle . . . her right to be free. "Don't give up, Galya," he told her. "One day you'll have some of the things you want."

Kiril sounds so solemn . . .

She leaned forward to kiss him. "Call me soon as you get back?"

"You know I will," he said, hating the lie on his tongue.

"Know what I think?" she teased. "I think you've contracted a bad case of first-trip-out-of-the-country-itis. I'm told it has a very sobering effect on its victims."

"An apt diagnosis, Nurse Barkova. Shall we drink to it?"

"Can't. I'm late for an appointment."

She gave him a quick hug and was out the door.

\* \* \*

Galya hurried inside the Metro station and headed for a row of wooden telephone booths along one wall, stopping outside a vacant one to dip into her full change-purse for a two-kopeck coin. Ignoring the envious glance of the woman behind her, Galya snapped the purse shut. This was one shortage, at least, that no longer affected her. Not for the last two years, anyway.

She shut herself in the narrow booth and waited for her call to be put through, conscious of two competing rhythms—the tapping of her fingertips against the telephone base and the ticking of her wristwatch.

She touched the tiny face of the watch, the elegant gold band. Beautiful. She shouldn't have worn it. If Kiril had noticed . . . But he hadn't. By the time he got back from his trip, she'd have a good story to explain it.

"Yes?" The voice on the other end of the line was typically impatient.

"It's Galina Barkova."

"Ah, yes. What have you to report?"

"Nothing really."

"Comrade Barkova." The voice was patronizing now. "I don't expect you to uncover some dire plot to overthrow the Kremlin. Your assignment is to observe much subtler things. An unguarded remark here. An antisocial view there. An overall state of mind. Incidentally, how *is* Kiril's state of mind these days? Are his spirits unnaturally low since the death of Stepan Brodsky? Has his behavior altered significantly in any way?"

"Not really."

"What about his upcoming sojourn to East Berlin in a few days? Is he looking forward to it?"

"I think so, yes. He didn't really say. He just . . ."

"He just *what*?" Alexei snapped, going into alert.

She felt trapped by the tight embrace of the phone booth. By the ticking of the watch as it counted off the seconds.

"When I got up to leave, Kiril seemed so—I don't know, solemn."

*As if he never expected to see me again.*

"Oh, that." Aleksei chuckled. "You are an attractive young woman, Galina Barkova—my most charming agent by far. To be parted from you for even half a week could upset any red-blooded man. Shall we see that Kiril is not upset for long?"

"I don't understand."

"How would you like to go to East Berlin with our Dr. Andreyev?"

"But I have no papers, no money, no exit permit," Galya stammered. "I don't even have proper clothes."

"Details, my dear. I'll see to them."

"What shall I tell Kiril?"

"I'll take care of it. Maybe I'll set something up so Kiril can assist Dr. Brenner in some medical capacity. That way he'd need a nurse he's used to working with—namely, you."

She bit her lip. "What will I *really* have to do, Colonel?"

she said cautiously.

"No more than what you've been doing for the past two years. Keep an eye on him. Others will be watching as well, but there are things a woman can sense more easily than a man. And I promise you, Galina, do a conscientious job, and you'll be amply rewarded. I've been thinking about a private flat. It could prove useful to me if you had a place of your own."

She closed her eyes, thinking of her roommates . . . someone's eyes always looking, someone's ears always listening. She said shakily, "You're *sure* nothing bad will happen to Kiril?"

"It's touching, your concern for his welfare. But don't lose sight of the fact that his welfare is *precisely* what you'll be protecting. Remember what I told you at the start of our little joint venture? Some men have to be protected from other men. But men like my brother must be protected from themselves."

# CHAPTER 21

Plush white carpeting swallowed footsteps. Billowing silk drapes fluttered noiselessly in the air-conditioned space. Chairs of glove-soft leather encircled the room. The soothing notes of piano music distracted the room's occupants from the repetitive sounds—part whine, part growl—of taxiing jets somewhere beyond the drapery.

"This is so much nicer than the regular waiting areas!" enthused Dr. Max Brenner.

"It's Pan Am's first-class VIP lounge," Kurt Brenner told his father, amused.

"For very important persons like my son," Max countered with unabashed pride.

"Just following in your footsteps."

"Ah, but you sped past my footsteps long ago."

Max Brenner looked around. "All these people—they're here to see you off?"

"Most of them. Matter of fact, I ought to be circulating."

"Go right ahead, it's your party. And Kurt, don't be upset about your mother. You should know by now that her refusal to attend your two symposiums isn't personal.

She won't set foot in Germany—period."

"At least you had the good grace to see me off," Brenner snapped, his good humor evaporating. "When are you joining her in Zurich?"

Max glanced at his watch. "I have a connection from New York to Switzerland in about three hours. Plenty of time to get ready for a wedding," he said brightly. "The granddaughter of some very old and dear friends. I'd wish you luck in your symposiums, East *and* West, son, except that I'd be doing you a disservice. It wasn't 'Lady Luck' that brought you to the pinnacle of your profession. You earned it with hard work and perseverance."

"How can I be impatient with my greatest fan?" Brenner said, cracking a smile. "Thanks, Dad."

"Hungry?" Adrienne asked her father-in-law as Kurt went off to mingle with his guests. "Since you have a few hours to kill, the rubber-chicken meal you're likely to be served on Swiss Air won't be able to compete with Pan Am Deluxe. How about a plate of hors d'oeuvres and a glass of wine? What's your pleasure, a glass of Chardonnay?"

"Just what the doctor ordered. But shouldn't you be circulating too?"

"Probably. The truth is, I'd much rather be with you."

He squeezed her arm. "I hope my son realizes just how lucky he is."

Adrienne managed a smile.

*If you knew the truth, Max dear, it would break your heart.*

After Max left, Adrienne lost track of time as Kurt mixed with the crowd, spending brief calculating minutes as he moved easily from person to person. From one small gathering to another.

When it was time to leave, Brenner helped Adrienne into her cape, took her arm, and led her out. "As much as I enjoy this sort of elaborate sendoff," he confessed, *sotto voce*, "I'm eager to board and get the hell out of here."

Adrienne was so fatigued that, with the aid of a sleeping

pill and a comfortable seat pushed as far back as it would go, she fell asleep.

Brenner, in no mood for small talk, let alone arguments, was relieved. He had a lot to think about, starting with the only reason he was going to East Berlin.

He'd been summoned like a schoolboy, he thought with a flush of anger. He rang for the stewardess. When she appeared at his elbow, he ordered a gin and tonic. "Make it a double, will you?" he said.

Staring moodily as the liquid in his glass swayed torpidly with the plane's vibrations, he was reminded of the lethargic waters of the Elbe River as it wound its way past the camp where he'd spent the last days of the war ministering to the sick, the wounded. And the dead.

\* \* \*

"Medic! Medic!"

By March 1945, three years after he had enlisted in the United States Army to avoid being drafted, twenty-three-year-old Kurt Brenner, with a B.S (pre-med), an M.A. (biology), and a Ph.D (microbiology), had become Staff Sergeant First Class Kurt Brenner—*"Doc"* to the American soldiers he had served with in Germany since the invasion of Europe nearly a year earlier.

Brenner raced across an open field, dropping to his knees beside the mangled body of a soldier who had stepped on a land mine. He held one eyelid open. The pupil stared back, unseeing. Removing the young man's dog tags from around his neck, Brenner walked away, swamped by emotion.

*Months and months of blood and guts—literally. How much more can I take? The brass keeps saying the war will be over anytime now, but it's already April, and we're still not in Berlin! We're still taking casualties!*

He was thinking about the latest intelligence—die-hard Nazis concentrated in and around Berlin—when the usual cry for help sounded.

"Medic! Medic!"

Shaking off his reverie, Brenner took off running toward yet another mangled GI.

By early April, when American forces were roughly 120 miles from Berlin, Staff Sergeant Kurt Brenner was still grousing. Once Berlin was taken, he figured, the war would be over and he'd be on his way home. Time for the next step in the career he'd carefully planned before the war, he thought with a flood of relief.

But all American units heading for Berlin were stopped in their tracks. Held back by General Eisenhower's orders from his Commander-in-Chief to allow the Soviets to take Berlin, Brenner and tens of thousands of others waited. Toward the end of April, the waiting appeared to be over. On the 22nd, the Soviets were in the north and east suburbs of Berlin. The next day, they had surrounded the city. A week later, the Red Army had taken most of the city, although fierce fighting continued at the Brandenburg Gate and the Reichstag. On April 30, 1945, Hitler committed suicide. In Europe, World War II was officially over.

But not for Doc Brenner. Although the Yalta Conference had provided for the Americans, British, and French to have occupation rights in Berlin, the Communists did not allow them to enter until roughly July 4, 1945.

\* \* \*

On their drive from the blood-soaked beaches of France to the former Nazi capital, American soldiers were exposed to scenes that conjured images of hell. The bloated bodies of GIs who'd stormed French beaches. The sightless, the limbless, the lame and the halt. Nor was the detritus of war limited to combatants. Dead civilians—men, women, children—were strewn about like rag dolls. GIs tripped over carcasses of dogs and horses. Churches had lost their roofs. Homes were flattened, as if the Devil's fist had smashed them into rubble. But the camps were an unmatched chamber of horror. Prisoners more dead than alive. Rigor mortis giving corpses the look of stacked firewood. Mountains of human bones. Piles of personal items, from eyeglasses to hair.

To these blistering images, burned into their consciousness, the advance parties of the American military added the fate of Berlin. During the war, American and British pilots had dropped 75,000 tons—1,500,000 pounds—of bombs on the city. Before the war there were a million-and-a-half dwellings in Berlin; by the end, 300,000. Of Berlin's huge fleet of buses, only thirty-seven were serviceable, and less than one tenth of the city's subway cars were of any use. As for Berlin's many canals, virtually every bridge that spanned them had been destroyed by the Nazis. Worse, raw sewage was turning canal water into cesspools covered with scum that became favorite haunts for billions of flies and mosquitoes.

Shallow graves dotted city streets, parks, and public squares. Dead bodies lay unburied under the rubble. Edible food, if any could be found, was at a huge premium. Venereal disease was rampant. Thousands of women, raped by Soviet troops, had been abandoned by their families and cast out to fend for themselves.

Into this surreal city in early July 1945 came Kurt Brenner's outfit. Setting up camp in the woods on the outskirts of the American zone across the Havel River from Soviet-controlled East Germany, the men were tasked with providing security for American staff personnel who were starting to move into the American zone. It took a long time before Brenner's battalion began to achieve some degree of normalcy.

\* \* \*

"Yo, Doc! The CO wants you on the double!"

Brenner sighed but took off running. He passed bedraggled German civilians headed toward the American zone as they tried to put distance between themselves and the Russian troops occupying the East. He'd seen endless streams of the poor bastards in the last few weeks as they plodded along, their miserable possessions wrapped in dirty sheets. The lucky ones were pulling wagons, household items piled high.

"Hop on the truck, Doc," the CO said with a cursory wave toward a canvas-roofed vehicle the GIs called "a deuce-and-a-half" because it could carry a 2½-ton load. A couple dozen soldiers were in the process of climbing into the rear. First Lieutenant Joseph Cherner stretched out his hand to pull Brenner aboard.

"Where to, Joe?"

"Recon close to Potsdam this side of the river," Cherner said. "Regimental commander's orders."

"What's the CO want with *me*?" Brenner groused.

"Best guess? The CO figures we could meet up with some Wehrmacht die-hards. We'd need a medic."

"Hope not. I'm asleep on my feet," Brenner said with a yawn. "After these guys get off the truck I'm crapping out. Wake me if I'm needed."

"Roger."

When Brenner opened his eyes, it was dark.

"Joe?"

"It's okay." Cherner was standing just outside the truck. "There's nothing going on. The CO just got orders to pull back."

"So where is he?"

"Down the road a piece."

"Cherner, you speak Russian, right?" First Sergeant Al Rosen bellowed. "Move your ass, soldier!" he said without waiting for a reply. "You too, Doc. And don't forget your stuff."

The two of them double-timed it up the dark road, straining to make sense of the silhouettes clustered about a small truck with its headlights switched off. "International Red Cross" was stenciled on both doors.

The flames of a small bonfire illuminated the scene. "Cherner? Brenner? Over here," the CO called out. Next to the fire stood a man in a shabby civilian overcoat with curly red-blond hair. "Mr. Johannsen here is with the Red Cross. Take a look at these kids, Brenner," the CO ordered. "See what you can do for them."

"*Kids,* sir?"

"Yeah, kids." The CO turned on his flashlight and moved its powerful beam about five yards further down the road. The light paused when it fell on a pair of tiny bare feet, and then moved up to the huddled form's nearly skeletal body.

Then another child. Another . . .

There were ten of them. The oldest looked to be about twelve. She was holding tightly to the hand of the youngest, who couldn't have been more than three. The rest seemed to be between four and ten years old. Brenner bent down for a closer look, and then gingerly examined them one by one. Girls with stringy matted hair. Boys whose heads had been shaved. Their tattered clothes and swollen stomachs, their enormous eyes staring out of bruised emaciated faces, gave them the look not of children, Brenner thought uneasily, but of aging dwarfs.

The CO, a stubby man with sharp probing eyes, angrily stuffed his hands into the pockets of his field jacket. "Talk to the older child, Cherner. She seems to be in charge of the others. Tell her we're here to help them."

"Мы здесь помочь вам," Cherner translated.

The child stared. Then, "Нет не разговаривать русский," she replied. "I not speak Russian."

Cherner took a closer look at her. The same Nordic coloring as his own—blond hair, blue eyes. Before his parents had emigrated to America and their name, Chernovsky, had been shortened to Cherner, his mother said people wrongly assumed they were Norwegian . . .

Cherner cleared his throat. "Зробіть ви розмовляйте Українською?" "Do you speak Ukrainian?"

"Так." "Yes."

He turned to the CO. "They're Ukrainian, sir."

"Talk to them. Find out what this is all about."

Cherner spoke to the girl in quietly reassuring tones. After a few minutes, she answered him haltingly.

As soon as Brenner did what he could medically, Cherner steered the kids to First Sergeant Rosen, where GIs began feeding them Army rations. Spam, sausages, biscuits—and the most popular item—chocolate bars. It was obvious the children had never tasted anything like chocolate in their lives. The First Sergeant was beaming. Some of the GIs were teary-eyed.

Cherner glanced at the stenciled words—International Red Cross—on the doors of the small truck. "How were you able to rescue the children?" he asked Johannsen.

"You know about the camps?" Johannsen asked.

Cherner and Brenner glanced at each other. Cherner nodded grimly.

"A concentration camp called Sachsenhausen is not far from here—about 22 miles north," Johannsen said. "Back in April, it was directly in the path of a fast-moving Russian armored column. The Nazi commandant, an SS Colonel, had standing orders from Himmler to 'evacuate' the camp before the Russians got there. I tried to persuade him to release the survivors—especially the children. He just smiled and began moving everyone out in two seemingly endless columns. Sick, starving, half-dead creatures. They were prodded along by bayonets. Those who couldn't keep up were shot and left where they fell . . ."

Johannsen shuddered at the memory.

The older girl, still holding the three-year-old, sidled over to Cherner.

"I ran my truck beside the line of march next to the commandant who was in the lead," Johannsen continued. "I implored him to free at least some of the children. That perhaps he had children of his own. When he smiled too, I figured he was about to move on without answering. Damned if he didn't look down from his horse and say, 'Mr. Johannsen of the International Red Cross, I can see that these ten children are together. Consider them a parting gift to your fine organization as a token of my good will.' The older girl, here, took me for an American," he continued. "I don't speak her language, but it was obvious from the start what she and the older kids were terrified of. 'Nyet Russkies. Nyet Russkies,' they repeated over and over."

Cherner turned to his CO. "They have good reason to be terrified, sir," he said in a voice choked with emotion. "The Russians consider it a sport to kill Ukrainians—at least the ones they don't use as laborers or cannon fodder."

"What did you find out from the girl?" the CO asked.

"Her name's Irina. Their parents are dead. She as much as said it's up to her, now, to protect the others. Little Mother," he said softly as the girl, eyes partly hidden by her matted hair, hugged the three-year-old to her chest. "What shall I tell her?"

"That we're Americans," the CO said tightly. "That we'll find a place to hide them where they'll be safe from the Nazis *and* the Russians."

"I have to go back," Johannsen told the CO. "There may be wounded survivors in those ditches," he said bleakly. Johannsen shook the CO's hand, nodded his thanks at the GIs, got into his small truck, and drove off.

"Go get the deuce-and-a half, Cherner," the CO ordered. "You and Brenner take the kids. The rest of us will walk.

There's a deserted farmhouse a few miles back, not far from the river. Wait for me there. And Cherner?"

"Sir?"

"Keep your lip buttoned. You, too, Brenner. The fewer people who know about this the better. It never happened."

\* \* \*

Under the protection of the CO, and with the connivance of other troops during the few weeks after the Americans moved into their occupation zone, the Ukrainian children were also moved several times. They were being cared for by one of the few remaining orders of Catholic nuns Hitler hadn't decimated. Most of the GIs who'd been helping the children initially had moved on, losing track of them.

Kurt Brenner hadn't thought of them at all, too preoccupied with how to speed up his pending discharge. He'd already been admitted to Harvard Medical School, but there was a problem. He wasn't due to be discharged for three more months—October 1945—and classes began in late August. Harvard had made it clear that if Brenner couldn't start with his class, he'd have to wait until the following academic year.

*Like hell I will.*

"Medic!" a voice shouted.

Brenner finished his sandwich, tossed a half-full can of beer into the muddy river, and watched as the swift current sent it spinning downstream. He hurried up the steep incline of the riverbank to Glienicker Bridge, where the American Corps of Engineers, aided by liberated Ukrainian workers, had floated an unstable pontoon bridge across the Havel River.

Permanent repair work was progressing well. At nearby Ceceilienhof Palace in Potsdam, GIs were replanting hedges. A line of slow-moving 21/2-ton Army trucks, loaded with building materials, headed for the Palace to repair walls, ceilings, and moldings. Brenner had been detailed to the general area as a medical corpsman—by then, mostly treating GIs with construction injuries.

He wrinkled his nose.

*I wish they'd repair the smell around here.*

It was going on three months since Berlin had fallen, but the stench of open sewers and the occasional dead body still permeated the air. It was an ongoing complaint with the GIs. The goddamn Krauts had emptied their cesspools into the Havel River.

"Medic! Where the hell *are* you?"

*Still here, unfortunately*, he brooded.

Brenner stepped over planks and stray pieces of iron, keeping carefully to the side of Glienicker that was propped above the water line by wooden pedestals parallel to the pontoons.

At the bridge, while he attended to a soldier's cuts and bruises, he fell into a conversation with a Russian officer he knew, but whose job was a mystery to him. He and Major Dmitri Malik had played chess a few times. While Brenner could beat the man with his eyes shut, he usually let Malik win against the day Brenner might want a favor. Then, too, there was the profitable black market business that the two of them were engaged in.

Launching into his usual complaint, Brenner mentioned that he was going to miss the start of medical school and lose an entire year. That guys who'd arrived in Europe—mostly infantrymen—were rotating home before he was.

They had been speaking English. So when the major suddenly looked around, lowered his voice, and switched to German, Brenner was startled.

"Tell me, Doc, what do you need to get orders moving you out sooner?"

"That's what frustrates the hell out of me, Major. It takes next to nothing. Just a clerk at division—probably a corporal—who inserts an earlier date on my transportation orders and sticks them in some box. Why do you ask?"

"I have friends everywhere," Malik said, dodging the question.

*Of course you do, Major.*

They ran into each other on the bridge a few days later. After the usual pleasantries, Malik said, "How would you like to leave Berlin in a week or so, Kurt?"

Brenner thought he hadn't heard right. After a moment he said, "You can pull it off *that* quickly?"

An eloquent shrug. "That depends on you," Malik replied.

"Anything, Major! Penicillin. More medical supplies. Petrol. Dope."

Malik looked bemused.

"If it's money," Brenner said, his mind racing, "I'll send you some as soon as I get back to New York—within reason, of course. A few thousand? Maybe five?"

"I have something else in mind," Malik said, his smile enigmatic. "You've always wondered what my position was but never had the nerve to ask. I'm NKVD—Soviet Intelligence. My work is with Operation Keelhaul."

# CHAPTER 22

It was dark as Brenner left Soviet headquarters in East Berlin and picked his way gingerly through brick-littered streets, stopping only to show his pass to a pair of Russian soldiers at Checkpoint Charlie before crossing from the Soviet zone back into the American.

It was all arranged. Tomorrow morning the Ukrainian kids would be picked up by Soviet authorities, including the Communist version of the Red Cross. Malik had assured Brenner that under Operation Keelhaul, the children would be well taken care of.

His young subordinate, Lieutenant Aleksei Andreyev, had reinforced Malik's assurances. "We have a great deal more to offer these children than placing them in foster care—or worse, stuck in some displaced-person camp," Andreyev told Brenner.

"Come now, Kurt," Malik interjected, picking up on Brenner's skepticism. "If at the Yalta Conference, the President of the United States—Franklin Delano Roosevelt, no less—and now his successor, Mr. Truman, promised to 'encourage' repatriation for some larger political end, who are you to question the judgment of two American presidents?"

An unanswerable argument, Brenner told himself. Besides, why would anyone want to harm a bunch of kids?

It hadn't been easy finding them—not at first. Eventually, Brenner had tracked down First Sergeant Al Rosen, who remembered him from when the Red Cross guy had rescued the children. A couple of drinks loosened Rosen's tongue. The children had been moved from place to place until they'd ended up with the nuns, he told Brenner. Arrangements were being made to have them moved to a DP camp in France.

After leaving Malik and his aide, Brenner walked aimlessly for hours, concentrating on the formidable obstacle course typical of post-war Berlin: broken pieces of pavement, mounds of rubble, collapsed buildings, gaping holes camouflaged by a thin layer of gray-black dust—

And came to an abrupt halt at the sound of angry voices. He realized he'd ended up practically at the main gate of the nunnery.

*The criminal automatically returning to the scene of the crime?*

It was where the Ukrainian children would spend their last night before being repatriated in the morning. So why was a Soviet truck parked in front right now? Brenner wondered.

*So much for "tomorrow's" arrangements.*

The Russians always kept one step ahead of you, he thought. It was worth remembering.

Ducking into the shadows, Brenner watched a group of Russian soldiers emerge through the nunnery gates led by—no surprise—Major Dmitri Malik. Ten whimpering children were hustled into the back of a truck. Brenner watched the truck pull away headed, no doubt, for Potsdam in East Germany.

An American jeep roared out of the shadows. Brenner

almost jumped out of his skin. Joe Cherner flung open the door on the opposite side of the jeep. "Good timing, Kurt," he said tightly. "I've been watching the nunnery off and on for weeks. Figured something like this might happen. Hop in. Let's see where the Russkies are off to. What are you doing here so late?"

"Same as you, Joe," Brenner said quickly. "I've been keeping an eye out from time to time. The Ivans are good at staying one step ahead of you," he added as an afterthought. It was true enough.

Keeping well behind the Soviet truck, Cherner followed until he was pretty sure where they were headed. "Glienicker Bridge," he muttered.

By the time they got there, a Russian truck had pulled up at the West Berlin end of Glienicker Bridge. Two American sergeants sat in a jeep facing West Berlin. Cherner skidded to a gut-wrenching stop right behind Ivan's truck.

"This bridge is officially closed to vehicular traffic until repairs are completed," one of the GIs announced.

"No problem, sergeant," Malik said politely. "We will walk." He signaled to his men, who proceeded to hustle the children out of the truck.

The column moved to the center of the bridge, Major Dmitri Malik in the lead, followed by other Russian soldiers who were hustling the children along. A grim-faced Lieutenant Aleksei Andreyev brought up the rear.

"Don't let them through!" Cherner yelled to the sergeant behind the wheel of the jeep.

"I can't stop them if they're walking, sir!"

"Then I will!" Cherner's voice was choking with rage.

Brenner shivered—and not from the cold night air. The bridge's emergency lighting was a blessing. In the dim light, he couldn't see the expressions on those small faces. But there was no way he could miss Irina. The girl was clutching the tiny three-year-old in her arms.

The sound of footsteps mingled with the slapping of

waves against Glienicker's damaged side. As Irina moved to the unobstructed section of the bridge, the children following behind her, she teetered slightly at the edge.

"Keep to the other side!" Malik warned—in English first, then Russian.

Brenner's breath caught in his throat. It suddenly occurred to him that the children couldn't understand either language!

It must have occurred to Joe Cherner too. He had leaped out of his jeep and was racing toward the middle of the bridge. Raising his sidearm, he fired into the air.

Malik and his soldiers turned into statues.

As if on cue, Irina paused. A ruptured support beam from one side of the bridge hung in the water like a broken limb, leaving a narrow breach. A few feet beyond, the pontoons bobbed in the water. The darkness made it hard to tell where the sky ended and the river began.

Suddenly Irina cried out and leapt into the breach. Three older boys followed instantly, three others hesitated but only momentarily. Two children—the youngest—froze. Russian soldiers scooped them up.

As Joe Cherner reached the scene, tears running down his face, the only thing his probing flashlight picked out was a shadowy patch being dragged downstream that might have been Irina's hair floating on the gray-black surface.

"Don't look down," Malik said philosophically, appearing suddenly at Brenner's shoulder. "By next week, you'll be saying goodbye to all this."

*Thanks a lot, Major. Let's hope Joe Cherner is so distracted that your remark didn't register.*

But it was Malik that Cherner pointed his weapon at. And not for long. The barrel of a rifle was pressed against the back of Cherner's neck.

"Show some sense, Lieutenant," Malik said coolly. "I have ten men here. Lousy odds, ten against one. My advice? Walk back to your jeep and move on. Forget this ever happened."

Cherner hesitated before holstering his .45. He turned on his heel and walked slowly toward his truck.

His friend Joe was smart enough to move on, Brenner thought, but forget? Never.

He wondered if the same was true of him.

# CHAPTER 23

Kiril stood on a stretch of unprotected tarmac at Schönefeld Airport, the major civilian airport of East Germany and the only one that served East Berlin. It was a cold, gray afternoon with no buildings or foliage to serve as a windbreaker. His fedora was soaked. His threadbare raincoat slapped against his trousers. Dark glasses obscured his eyes.

Beside him, Galya shivered uncontrollably even in a long coat lined with down, marveling at how Kiril could be so oblivious to the cold.

His mind was elsewhere. Would Dr. Kurt Brenner succumb to blackmail? he wondered. Damn Aleksei's secretiveness and his need-to-know rules! In Moscow, he had shown Kiril bits and pieces of the Brenner file, but not enough to get a clear picture of Dr. Kurt Brenner, famous heart surgeon—or Kurt Brenner, private citizen.

Then go over what you *do* know, he told himself wearily.

German father and mother. Both naturalized American citizens, both employed by their son's cardiac institute. Dr. Brenner's flamboyantly successful medical career. A long bachelorhood followed by marriage to a journalist. Brenner's widespread and apparently earned reputation as a humanitarian because of his nonprofit cardiac clinic for indigent children. Temperament: Brenner was known to cancel an entire day's surgical schedule and lock himself in his office on the rare occasion when a patient died on his operating table.

A man of contradictions, Kiril mused. A renowned surgeon who had declined every invitation to medical exchanges in Iron Curtain countries, yet heaped extravagant praise on Medicine International's Peace through Medicine activities in such places.

*Why had Brenner accepted the invitation to East Berlin with such alacrity?*

Kiril thought about some Western physicians who'd come to Moscow from time to time.

How everyone in Dr. Yanin's operating theater, from Yanin on down, had been excited at the mere prospect of learning about new ideas and technologies. The Americans, in particular, were open and generous about sharing their medical expertise—and friendly. But not judgemental. They saw—there was no way they could help seeing—the rigid control the Soviet government exercised over its citizens. No free exchange of ideas. No opportunity for hosts and guests to be alone. He recalled one American doctor who had given him a politically harmless detective novel in exchange for a volume of Russian poems but hadn't even noticed that both books had been examined by the KGB minders as if their pages contained a coded plot to overthrow the Kremlin.

Kiril's thoughts were interrupted by the arrival of two limousines. During their research, Kiril and Stepan had learned a lot about Western vehicles—cars and trucks manufactured in the Soviet Union after World War II by reverse engineering of a classic American automobile: the Packard Super-8. The Soviet "Packard," a ZIS-110 sedan, had a 6-liter, 8-cylinder engine under the hood, 140 horse power, and could reach a top speed of nearly ninety miles per hour—fast for those days. Stalin was rumored to have owned several Packards, so the story went, and he wanted the Soviets' first effort to manufacture a luxury automobile patterned after a stellar American car of the 1940s. Indeed, the ZIS-110 was so popular that Communist leaders from around the world—Mao, Tito, and Walter Ulbrecht of East Germany—favored them. So Kiril wasn't surprised to see two of them on the tarmac.

The lead limousine pulled up to where Kiril and Galya were standing, the second just behind it. The first vehicle's right rear door opened and a trim uniformed Vopo emerged, snapped open a black umbrella, and helped a short man wearing a top-hat to get out of the car. Top-hat carried a large piece of cardboard in the shape of a key.

*The mayor of East Berlin bearing a symbolic key to the city for Herr Doktor Professor Kurt Brenner?*

When Kiril had been stationed in Murmansk, he'd picked up a lot of American slang. The slang word he thought of now was "corny."

The second car disgorged a huge woman wearing clodhopper shoes, serge trousers, and a heavy wool overcoat. Her close-cropped gray hair was immediately soaked. As her car door was closing, Kiril glimpsed a man sitting in the rear seat.

"Here they come!" Galya exclaimed.

Kiril squinted toward the horizon and saw a tiny speck. As he watched it grow larger, the speck became a flying fish skimming over dark clouds. He felt a surge of optimism. Whatever else he might be, Brenner was an American. He would never succumb to a blackmail threat—not if the price were his way of life, his freedom.

The fish metamorphosed into a smooth silver body. Circling for a landing, the plane taxied to a halt in front of the small group.

The man and woman who emerged from the plane were Americans, all right. You could sense it in the lift of their heads. In the way they moved. Kiril focused on Kurt Brenner's walk—jaunty, with a brisk authoritative step. Unlike his own more deliberate way of moving. He burned the image into his brain. He would need to replicate Brenner's walk until it was second nature. Brenner was swinging a trim briefcase the way an American movie hero might cross a patio swinging a tennis racket. Another indelible image. He zeroed in on Brenner's hair. It was thicker than his, but not by much. He made a mental note to pick up some hair tonic.

The inventory stopped abruptly. He scrutinized Kurt Brenner's face, now only a few yards from his own.

*I have a good chance of making this work!*

He was so elated that he forgot the standing order he had given himself. Monitor people's reactions—especially Galya's.

He needn't have worried about Galya. She had barely noticed Brenner, too preoccupied with studying his wife. As he readied himself for making small talk, he glanced at Adrienne Brenner. She was tall, with an almost cat-like grace. She wore a forest-green cape, gold braid running across the shoulders and along the raised collar. Copper glints were all he could see of her hair, most of it captured under a wide-brimmed hat.

He couldn't quite grasp why something about this woman made him uneasy, nor why he slipped his arm around Galya's waist.

Adrienne Brenner took in the size of what had been billed as "the largest airport in East Germany." She thought about the research she'd crammed into the last few days. It hadn't prepared her for the moment when their plane was close enough for her to notice tethered goats. They were grazing on grass, on tarmac that was weathered and cracked . . . like rows of abandoned country roads going nowhere. She saw planes next to a hangar—only three? And men with submachine guns standing like uniformed statues at strategic points around the field. She'd been forewarned about that. Still, it unnerved her.

Frustrated that she couldn't put her small camera to work, she turned a polite face to the two officials who'd emerged from their limousines and managed to nod agreeably through ponderous introductions in German. As soon as the formalities were over, she extended her hand in silent greeting to the blonde woman who'd been staring at her—lovely, but oddly disconcerting. The man in raincoat and dark glasses was not so much disconcerting as . . . intense.

Amenities over and the key to the city presented, Kiril, per Aleksei's instructions, waited to see what the seating arrangements were to be.

The gray-haired woman took Dr. Brenner's elbow and guided him toward her limousine. With obsequious deference, she opened the ZIS's right rear door for Brenner, waited until he got in, and then joined the driver up front.

Not surprised at seeing who his seat-mate was, Brenner was nonetheless shocked at his appearance. Sixteen years had been good to Major Dmitri Malik. Straight black hair, streaked with gray now. A mocking quality in the not-quite-hidden recesses of a remembered smile. Eyes the same glacial pale gray.

"Hello, Doc," Malik said cheerfully with no trace of an accent. "The world has a habit of continuing to turn, don't you think? Vodka?" he asked, leaning forward to a built-in bar facing them.

"Thank you, no."

"A cigarette, then."

"Why not?" Brenner said.

He noticed that the window between them and the driver was closed.

Not that the two people up front couldn't be tuned into the conversation electronically . . .

Malik's manner, as he lit Brenner's cigarette, was deferential. "Your first trip to East Berlin, Dr. Brenner?"

Brenner almost choked on the smoke in his lungs.

*The sonofabitch is toying with me. Okay, you bastard, I'll play your game until I see what the score is.*

"I was here during the War," Brenner told him. "But that's a tale too long to relate in a short drive to my hotel," he said, getting in the last word.

# CHAPTER 24

So far, so good, Kiril thought as he sat on a jump seat in the Mayor's limousine, facing him and Adrienne Brenner. It was an opportunity to take the American woman's measure. Her window was down.

When they pulled up in front of a low brick building at the airport's exit, an East German civilian walked over and politely asked for her passport. "There will be no need for you to leave the car, Frau Brenner," he said in English. "I will be happy to attend to the formalities inside."

Adrienne handed over her passport. Opening her door, she said, "I'd like to have a quick look inside, if you don't mind." She got out without waiting to see if he did.

When the man hesitated, Kiril told him in German, "Not to worry. I'll see to it."

Inside was as commercial as a monastery, Adrienne thought. No gift shops. No displays of magazines and candy bars. No books or newspapers, of course. There was only one small dining area behind which a waitress with dark circles under her eyes and indifference in the shape of her mouth was serving soft drinks and sausages to a half-dozen customers.

"Our terminal is not impressive, I'm afraid," said a voice behind her.

"You speak English."

"I do," Kiril replied.

But with a thick Russian accent, she noted. "I gather you've seen airport terminals in the West?"

"Only in the cinema," he said with a faint smile. "Until yesterday, I was never out of the Soviet Union. Perhaps you have questions, Mrs. Brenner? If so, I'll be happy to answer them."

She was tempted to ask, Why are a couple of Russians— you and your girlfriend—our escorts instead of East German apparatchiks? And what's with the man in the soiled military uniform who never takes his eyes off you? As if I couldn't guess.

"—my job to see that your trip to East Berlin is a memorable one. We Russians have a motto," Kiril told her. "Показывать их в наших товаров. 'Show them the best of our goods.' I must apologize for this inauspicious beginning. If you like, I can give you a brief preview of some of the best the Deutsche Demokratische Republik has to offer before we proceed to your hotel."

"I'm game, Doctor . . . ?"

"Andreyev. Kiril Andreyev."

He waited for Luka Rogov to sit up front before giving the driver directions.

"The new civic center," Kiril announced as they drove by. "Forty blocks of office buildings, housing units, shopping arcades. Over there, an expensive new theater. Next to it, a concert hall."

Adrienne took in the huge circular plaza ringed with tall buildings. Spacious pedestrian walkways, but with few pedestrians. A wide boulevard with virtually no traffic. According to the most recent statistics, fewer than one East German in twelve owned a car.

"Your hotel." Kiril pointed to a high rise with an expansive sweep of his hand. "Over forty stories and three thousand modern rooms. I think you will enjoy your stay there. Our famous television tower." He indicated a thin tubular structure. "The second tallest edifice of its kind in all of Europe—almost twelve hundred feet high," he said with a tinge of pride. "The People's radio and television broadcasts come from there."

Adrienne nodded politely, not wanting to offend her guide. If American movies were his one source of familiarity with the West, you'd think the contrast would be more than enough to dampen his enthusiasm!

"Any questions?" he asked as the limousine moved on.

She thought for a moment. "Do the women in East Germany—in the Soviet Union, for that matter—have what Americans call equal rights?"

Kiril smiled his approval. "Women in the Deutsche Demokratische Republik have many rights, Mrs. Brenner. And I assure you, many Russian women have the same. In Moscow, it is a common sight to see women directing traffic, driving trolleys, climbing telephone poles, and working alongside men on construction sites. Depending on their fortitude, they dig ditches and haul heavy equipment. Some women are nurses, like my friend Galya." He paused. "But I think very few are physicians."

"You are an excellent guide, Dr. Andreyev," Adrienne said, pulling a notebook and pen out of her shoulder-bag.

*You are a treasure trove of information.*

"What am I looking at over there?" she asked, pointing.

"Neue Wache. Literally, New Guardhouse." It's a memorial to the victims of militarism and fascism."

She saw Greek columns and heel-clicking, goose-stepping East German soldiers.

"They change the guards every hour," he told her.

"Unter den Linden!" he announced with a touch of awe. "The Soviet Embassy. A museum, an opera house. Over there is Humboldt University. It has a newly renovated clinic where your husband's medical conference will take place." Kiril ordered the driver to stop, eager to see what Adrienne Brenner's reaction would be.

The famous Unter den Linden, Adrienne thought. A vast boulevard enlivened by four parallel rows of linden trees on each side. It was the most chillingly barren street she had ever seen. There were red flags on official black limousines parked along the street's center island. More red flags hung from the long, thin necks of lampposts. They bent obediently over the pavement and made her think of tall gaunt men, tagged and hunched in silent agony.

The boulevard reminded her of an abandoned parking lot but with one appalling exception. Where Unter den Linden began—or ended—she spotted some people. East Germans. They were milling about aimlessly. Despite a mass of shrubbery, nothing grew quite high enough to block the stone columns of Brandenburg Gate—and beyond the columns, the just-begun new Berlin Wall. "Can we stop the car for a moment?" she asked Andreyev.

Kiril nodded. "Halt."

Adrienne leaned out the window, wanting to see beyond the columns from the same perspective as an East German, hungry for a tantalizing glimpse of West Berlin, now beyond her grasp. She pulled out her notebook and did a quick sketch—poor substitute for a camera—but she didn't want it confiscated.

"Marx-Engles Platz," Dr. Andreyev said.

"Why does that sound familiar?" she wondered out loud.

"Probably because it was once part of the famous Lustgarten. Strange how history repeats itself. Hitler held huge rallies and military parades there. Now the East Germans do. Just last evening I witnessed a stunning torchlight parade of tanks and marching soldiers. Do you like parades, Mrs. Brenner?"

"Just the American kind. Kids marching with high

school bands and drum majorettes displaying their legs. No tanks. They can be hell on the roads," she said drily.

She had thought her bluntness would offend him. Incredibly, he seemed pleased. A real enigma, this Dr. Andreyev.

As the limo moved on, she couldn't help wondering why she sensed a grim purposefulness underneath his running commentary, like a discordant musical theme that contradicts the melody.

"We'd better wrap up this brief preview and head for the hotel before my husband thinks I've been kidnapped," she said reluctantly.

# CHAPTER 25

"Zum Wohle aller!" Kiril said. "For the good of all!"

A smiling Galya repeated the toast in her halting English, and then passed around glasses of champagne.

Kiril tipped his glass in a mock salute to an unsmiling Luka, who stood off to the side.

Adrienne Brenner took a single sip of champagne before setting her glass down. "I'm sure you're eager to check out the clinic, Kurt. Give me a few minutes to unpack a few things," she said, and walked into the adjoining bedroom.

Kiril eagerly looked around. He had never been inside a modern hotel suite before. His own room down the corridor—his and Rogov's—was one used by the hotel's travelling auditors. Just a couple of narrow beds with the barest essentials. The Brenner suite was spacious. And cheerful, he thought. A sitting room with a nubby couch and two matching chairs. A bedroom nearly as large, with an armoire of glossy oaken wood, flanked by dressers that took up the entire wall. An enormous four-poster bed—

An observation he quickly pushed out of his mind.

He sensed that the Brenners were not impressed—a

point in Kiril's favor. People accustomed to luxury would be reluctant to give it up. He added up the morning's other favorable points. On the first leg of his impromptu mini-tour, Adrienne Brenner had been both genuinely curious and remarkably open about her obvious distaste for most of what he'd called to her attention. She had not felt the need to be diplomatic about what she was seeing. Nor had she made any attempt to avoid politically awkward subjects. Even in his wildest imagination he had not been prepared for a woman who was so disarmingly direct. Her candor and independence intrigued him. He mentally transported her to Moscow and tried to imagine her standing before some bureaucrat, being told what to do, how to live, what to think. He could not imagine it.

If a police state were as real to her as it seemed, there was virtually no chance she would ever consent to live in one—certainly not in East Germany, let alone the Soviet Union. Would her husband defect without her? Unlikely.

His eyes drifted to Galya, still smiling, talking animatedly to Dr. Brenner. Flirting? He watched her cut through an elaborate cellophane-wrapped basket of fruit.

"Compliments of Colonel Aleksei Andreyev," Galya told Dr. Brenner.

Kurt Brenner felt as if he's been hit with an electric charge.

*First Dmitri Malik. Now his former subordinate. Does this Aleksei Andreyev think I've forgotten his name after all these years? Or is he counting on my remembering? A colonel, now, doubtless KGB, with the same last name as our "tour guide." What have I gotten myself into? What in god's name could they possibly want?*

As Dr. Brenner excused himself to join his wife in the bedroom, Kiril saw Galya scan the room's plush appointments. Her focus shifted almost imperceptibly to Adrienne Brenner's clothes. They were casually strewn across the four-poster.

*At first I'm captivated by the heroine's clothes, her jewelry, even her high-heeled shoes! Then I notice how she acts so casual about the things I long for.*

Poor dear Galya. It pained Kiril to see her listless posture. Her not-quite-lifeless eyes. The smile that never quite reached her eyes because she had not quite given up. How much longer before she did once she was condemned to spend the rest of her life in the Soviet Union?

As the five of them rode the elevator down—Galya and the Brenners in front, Kiril and Rogov in the rear—Kiril caught the faint scent of Adrienne Brenner's perfume. While they waited for their limousine, he felt in league with the wind—urging it on as it blew the folds of Adrienne Brenner's garment around her legs.

Wondering about the body underneath the cape.

# CHAPTER 26

"The Humboldt University medical clinic!"

Kiril's announcement had the clarion call of a trumpet.

Adrienne Brenner's expression brightened as she liberated pen and notebook from her shoulder-bag. Even Galya seemed to perk up, Kiril noticed.

Not Kurt Brenner though. As Kiril made perfunctory introductions to some of the hospital staff, he couldn't help noticing Brenner's tepid response—handshakes and glib phrases that seemed to slip automatically out of his mouth.

An alarm bell went off in Kiril's head.

*Brenner is just going through the motions.*

Did he dare cut through the man's preoccupation, even at the risk of being obvious? Luka Rogov spoke almost no English and understood even less. But Galya? he thought uneasily.

Kiril held off until the five of them were walking through the medical clinic's long, mostly empty, corridors. Whenever Brenner made some offhand remark about medicine that

Kiril could use as a transition, he would jump in with an artful description of nearly a half-century of Soviet medical progress—such as how Soviet medical schools graduated some thirty thousand physicians annually in three years! "I'm forced to admit, however," he said, "that because of such an attenuated program, our doctors would later have much to learn on the job." Kiril made a few more not-so-subtle attempts to extoll Soviet medicine, even as he undercut it.

Adrienne Brenner, as usual, wrote notes at a furious pace.

Brenner was still along for the ride.

As their party came to an area marked off-limits to visitors, Kiril ignored the sign with a wave and led them down a narrow hall, explaining that he was eager to show them some modern x-ray equipment he'd learned about only yesterday. They entered a room where a patient lay on a hospital bed, his massive chest covered with a number of black tubular objects, two of which were moving slightly. Brenner's eyebrow shot up—he knew immediately what he was seeing. Adrienne Brenner was staring at the patient as if memory could substitute for the cameras she'd been obliged to leave at the reception desk.

Apologizing profusely, Kiril said, "Wrong room. Sadly, leech therapy is a barbaric contrast with the modern x-ray equipment I meant to show you next door. I was told this patient is a Russian soldier wedded to the old ways. Anti-coagulation therapy is still common in some rural areas of my country, even though today's Soviet doctors can usually clear obstructed veins in a more scientific manner."

Their tour of the medical clinic over, Kiril made good use of the time it took to walk to their waiting limousine. He mentioned East German physicians being members of the elite. Not that East Germany's Ministry of Health was without its own problems. Did Dr. Brenner know that since 1958 many of these physicians had left the Deutsche

Demokratische Republik—luckily before the Communist Party had launched a campaign to improve the quality of political and ideological dogma in the medical profession? Did Dr. Brenner know that East German doctors—and Soviet ones as well—experienced an acute medical crisis? That hospitals and medical clinics had been forced to limit their services to emergencies? That, until recently, East German doctors had been forced to rely on inferior medicines produced in Communist bloc countries like the Soviet Union?

Dr. Brenner did not know. He did not seem to care, either.

\* \* \*

As soon as Brenner entered the limousine, he sat back and closed his eyes. He had never felt so out of control . . . and the questions kept coming.

*Where the hell was Malik? He was, after all, Chancellor of the entire University. Why invite him here in the first place? Despite that charade on their way in from the airport, I couldn't pry anything specific out of the bastard. And why the empty excuse for not joining me in my hotel suite for a drink?*

Brenner tried to break out of his reverie, but it was as if he was doing a balancing act between two different time zones!

Which, in a way, he was.

Back in the limousine, Kiril left the back seat to Galya and the Brenners, again taking the jump seat.

As the car pulled away from the clinic, Galya leaned back against the limousine's worn velvet upholstery. The faded Oriental rug under her feet had been beautiful once—a real luxury. She had been bored to distraction during the tour of the medical clinic, only half listening as Kiril went on and on. "I am tired," she said to no one in particular. "I would so much like to return to the hotel and make ready for dinner."

"Good idea," Brenner chimed in. "I could use a drink. I have a feeling jet lag is just around the corner."

"I know of a shortcut back to our hotel," Kiril said, and gave the driver directions before resuming his seat.

"A shortcut?" Adrienne Brenner said skeptically. "How is that possible? You arrived only yesterday."

*Clever lady.*

"I'm good with maps," he said, which was true enough.

As their limousine left the Unter den Linden area, the change was swift and dramatic. Starkly modern apartment houses gave way to seedy Stalin-like housing projects and buildings so caked with grime it was difficult to guess at their original color. Empty lots were dusted with crumbling plaster, suggesting the bombed-out ruins of World War II. Half-collapsed structures with sections of sagging walls gave evidence of being occupied. Their limousine attracted furtive, resentful stares.

Kurt Brenner emerged from his fugue long enough to mumble something about the somber architecture.

"A great nation's progress is not always self-evident, Dr. Brenner," Kiril said evenly. "East Germany has the highest standard of living of any Soviet-bloc country."

Adrienne Brenner stared at him.

*Damning with slight praise again, Dr. Andreyev?*

When she commented on the long line of shoppers waiting patiently at a street vendor's vegetable cart, Kiril said tonelessly, "Waiting in line for basic necessities is a way of life—and not just here. We have queues in my country as well."

It suddenly struck him that he felt at home here—almost as if he had never left Moscow. Different streets, yes. Totally different cities. Moscow was pale yellow—washed out. East Berlin was tarnished and gray, with a kind of grittiness in the air, as if the whole place could use a good scrubbing. But the ominous familiarity was in the silence. In the absence of bright lights.

It was the way people hurried, as if their biggest concern was to get off the streets and out of sight. It was what they wore—the same ill-fitting clothes he had looked on all his life. It was their demeanor—part lethargy, part despair.

He had to stop himself from looking at Adrienne Brenner as hungrily as Galya had looked at her clothes.

Except that he had no need to look at her anymore. Unconscious pride—it was in the set of her mouth, the lift of her head. Unstated confidence—it was in the way she moved.

Adrienne Brenner was living proof that somewhere beyond the limits of his existence was another world. Another universe. He felt the empty ache of longing, followed by a searing impatience that blurred his vision. His whole adult life had been a testament to patience. He had taught himself to suppress his anger. To scoff at his bitterness. To go slowly. To bide his time. It was this that had brought him to the edge of freedom. That had kept him alive.

*Don't abandon your oldest ally, your best weapon! Don't fall victim to the sights and sounds of East Germany. Of the Soviet Union. Keep it intact—your vision of those poor pathetic creatures lined up for their vegetables. Of the patience stamped on their faces.*

But even as he listened to his mind, he knew that his emotions were in revolt. After two decades of waiting in line for his freedom, his patience had burned itself out.

# CHAPTER 27

On their way back to the hotel, Kurt Brenner turned to his wife and reminded her about a pre-dinner cocktail party being held in their honor on the 38th floor. "We should both make an appearance," he told her.

"I guess," Adrienne Brenner said without enthusiasm. "But we'd better make it an early dinner. We have that field trip tomorrow, remember?"

"Field trip?" he responded with a touch of annoyance.

She shrugged. "Your host, Chancellor Malik, apparently thinks you could use a day off before the medical proceedings begin on Monday. We're going for an outing to the ancient town of Waren on Lake Mueritzsee."

As the four of them rode up in the hotel elevator, Galya said a silent prayer, pasted a smile on her face, and well before the elevator got to her floor said, "Dr. Brenner, in your rooms this champagne that I taste, I like very much. There is nearly a whole bottle left. Do you mind I have a little before I make ready for early dinner tonight?"

"Not at all." He handed her his key. "You're welcome to the whole bottle. Just be sure to leave the key on the bed and the door unlocked when you leave."

Ignoring the question in Kiril's eyes, Galya rushed to the Brenner suite as soon as the elevator let her off.

Her hand shook with anticipation—so much so that she had trouble unlocking the door.

\* \* \*

Adrienne had been uncomfortably aware of her cape all day long to the point where she'd taken to carrying it. But still people stared, even in the *"better"* part of town. She felt their eyes on her suit. Her jewelry. Her leather shoulder-bag. Sensing that it wasn't envy, she put the question to Dr. Andreyev on the way to the cocktail party.

"It's two things," he explained. "Fear, and a touch of resentment. Western clothes stand out because of their rich fabrics and stylish lines. And there's no mistaking the fit—so perfect it couldn't possibly be some hand-me-down from an aunt or an older sister."

"I can understand the resentment," she said, "but fear?"

"In East Germany, clothes like yours are the trademark of the privileged—Party people, their friends, their mistresses. It's no different in the Soviet Union."

Adrienne sighed. "I don't know about you, but I'm in no mood for cocktails and finger food. See you at dinner?"

He grinned. "You can't avoid me. We're at the same table."

Adrienne stepped into the elevator. When she got to the suite, the door slid open at her touch. Good. Galya had remembered to leave it unlocked.

She stepped inside—and stopped short in the foyer.

A black dress lay like an abandoned dust-rag on the bedroom floor. Her own clothes were spread out on the bed . . . all except a cream-colored gown. Galya was a vision of loveliness, the gown spilling in an unbroken line from its high virginal neckline to the floor. As she swept about the room, she was graceful elegance in motion—head held high, shoulders straight, arms slightly apart.

*It's as if Galya doesn't quite know whether to hold in the wonder of what she's feeling, or let it take wing.*

The beginnings of a smile pulled irresistibly at the comers of Galya's mouth. Her eyes had the luminous look of unshed tears. Gliding to a halt in front of a long mirror, she said to an imaginary figure, "Tell me, kind sir, is green gown which is best you like? *This* one, I think, is the most wonderful. The color is—how you say in America? This one is most sympathetic to *me*."

"It really is," Adrienne said softly, coming into the sitting room, stopping just short of the bedroom door.

Galya whirled around, fumbling frantically with the clasp at the back of her neck.

"Please don't be embarrassed," Adrienne said. "With your coloring and your blonde hair, the gown suits you perfectly. Would you allow me to give it to you?"

"You are too much generous," Galya said in a voice dipped in starch. "Are all American ladies so generous as you? But I have no need for such a generosity. Quite soon I am having money to buy beautiful gown same like this one."

Galya meant to close the bedroom door quietly.

She ended up slamming it. Her expression changed as rapidly as she changed her clothes—from embarrassment and envy to something darker.

# CHAPTER 28

At 8:00 the next morning, the Brenners, Galya, Kiril, and Luka Rogov met for breakfast in the hotel dining room.

"If this is supposed to be a day off, why did we have to get up so early?" Brenner complained.

"Not to worry," Kiril reassured him. "Chancellor Malik chose well for your outing. I've read up on Waren—a charming town on Lake Muritzsee." He took some notes from his pocket. "There are references to the town by an ancient geographer named Claudius as early as 150 A.D. In the centuries that followed, the town was devastated by fires and suffered greatly during the Thirty Years' War from 1618 to 1648. But in the eighteenth century, canal and railway building created economic growth, and in 1925 electricity came to Waren, followed four years later by a Roman Catholic church."

His tone changed. "In 1931 the Nazis were the largest party in the November elections. The following year they took over some political and administrative positions."

He saw that Adrienne Brenner, who'd been politely

attentive, was now paying close attention. Since her husband didn't seem the least bit interested, and Galya, eyes closed, had tuned out, Kiril focused only on Adrienne. "During the fascist era," he continued, "the Nazis followed a familiar pattern. Waren's Jews were persecuted, then expelled, and ultimately murdered. The Jewish population in the middle 1800s was roughly 150 men, women, and children. By mid-1938—even before deportations had begun in earnest—there were nine. By the end of that year, the Jewish cemetery had been desecrated and destroyed. In 1942, even the nine were gone."

Adrienne restrained a shudder. She could picture only too well what Dr. Andreyev was describing.

"I take it that Chancellor Malik would be offended if I begged off this jaunt to Lake Muritzsee," Kurt Brenner interjected.

"Apparently so," Kiril said. "But the lake is especially beautiful this time of year, the weather is warm enough for boating and swimming, and the ancient town buzzes with activity. Lake Muritz is the second-largest lake in the GDR—the only one that fits entirely within its own borders."

"Let's get on with it then," Brenner said, thinking that the sooner they left, the sooner they'd get back. "We'll meet out front at the limo after we collect our stuff."

"Let's meet in the lobby," Kiril suggested. "In about twenty minutes?"

Twenty minutes later, the Brenners stepped out of the elevator carrying large American beach bags. Galya had a Soviet version that Aleksei had provided, but smaller and less full. Kiril swung over his shoulder a mesh shopping bag he'd picked up at some flea market in Moscow. Luka Rogov wore his military uniform and carried nothing.

*Except a 7.62 Nagant revolver.*

"Follow me," Kiril said, and led them to one of the elevators.

"We can't get to the beach in an elevator," Brenner

said caustically.

"You'll see," Kiril grinned as he pushed the button for the top floor.

The elevator had more than adequate space for five adults, yet Dr. Brenner seemed agitated—but why? Kiril wondered. Brenner had begun to perspire the moment the doors closed.

"Where the hell are we going, Dr. Andreyev?"

"To the roof," he told Brenner. "We'll be flying to the lake in a helicopter," he announced with a touch of pride just as they reached the top floor.

The elevator doors opened. Chivalry aside, Kiril thought drily, Dr. Brenner was the first one out.

"Look," Brenner said with a show of calm as they climbed the stairs to the roof, "I can't do this. I'm still jet-lagged. There's no way I can sit for hours in a chopper."

"Not hours. Waren and Lake Muritzsee are roughly 60 miles from Berlin."

"Which means the limousine could have us there in what, an hour?"

"Actually, I suggested that. But Chancellor Malik was very keen that Herr Doctor Professor Brenner see the town and the entire panorama of Lake Muritzsee from the air."

Brenner got the message.

A Soviet helicopter was parked on the roof. The main body stood about ten feet high, its length roughly twelve feet. The bottom half of the body was painted orange, the top blue.

Adrienne stifled a laugh. The paint job made her think of a swollen sausage.

Above the body of the vehicle sat the flight deck, also orange. Orange paint ran from behind the front of the body toward the aircraft's rear and continued for another twenty feet where the three-blade tail rotor rested. The four-blade main rotor was attached to the roof of the flight deck, with four large front and side windows.

Brenner took one look at the helicopter's size and almost recoiled in fright. Approaching two men in flight suits who stood next to the aircraft, he walked up to the pilots and asked in German, "Is this your airplane?" The pilots looked at each other, confused. The one with the most gold braid on his shoulder—the captain?—cracked a smile.

"No. It is the property of the People of the German Democratic Republic."

*Terrific.*

Brenner suppressed the urge to ask if the *People's* property was safe.

As Kiril approached, the East German Air Force officer said, "Captain Rolf Gruner at your service, and you must be Dr. Kiril Andreyev."

"I am." They shook hands.

The captain introduced his co-pilot, a lieutenant.

"Our orders are to put ourselves and this aircraft at your disposal from now until sunset when, I was told, you have a dinner appointment with Chancellor Dmitri Malik," the captain said. "I'm responsible for flying this bird," he continued, "but as to anything else, I take my orders from you. May I ask who are the other members of your party?"

"Yes, of course. Honored guests of the DDR, Dr. and Mrs. Kurt Brenner. Galina Barkova, my assistant." Then, nodding at Luka, Kiril added, "This man is with me."

Both pilots understood immediately.

While Gruner did a last-minute walk-around check of the aircraft, Kiril, noticing Brenner's discomfort, turned to his wife. "If your husband thinks East German helicopters are inferior or in some way unsafe compared to American ones," he said, "I'd be happy to reassure him."

"It's not that," Adrienne said, smiling. "Kurt is claustrophobic. This helicopter *is* pretty narrow. Haven't you noticed how my husband practically breaks into a cold sweat whenever we step into an elevator? And the elevators here are spacious compared to the ones in Paris. They're not only tight, but maddeningly slow."

"Why don't I ask the co-pilot to show us around, explain how the helicopter works?" Kiril suggested. "That way I can translate our plush accommodations into English for you and Galya."

"Thanks. I'd like that," Adrienne said.

Kiril returned with the co-pilot in tow.

"This is a model MI-4 helicopter, manufactured in the Soviet Union since 1953. NATO's name for it is *Hound*," said the co-pilot. "When used by the military, it can carry a dozen or more soldiers and much equipment. This version, an MI-4-*L*, means the interior was remodeled to carry—how do you say?—VIPs. And *that* means it takes up to six adults, comfortably seated in the lower body of the aircraft. As you can see, three large windows on each side of the aircraft provide every passenger with an unobstructed view. The cabin, entered through a door on the left side of the aircraft is heated and sound-proofed. There is a toilet in the rear."

The co-pilot warmed to his subject.

"Depending on altitude and load, we can cruise at 140 miles per hour. Today our flying time should be just less than an hour to the lake, then however long Dr. Andreyev needs us to fly around looking at the sights. The weather promises to be cooperative. The engine is 1,675 horsepower—more than adequate. And now," he announced with a trace of formality, "we must board."

Captain Gruner was already on the flight deck. His co-pilot escorted the party to the open door on the left side of the aircraft. "Ladies?" he said, motioning first to "honored guest" Adrienne Brenner.

Looking inside, Adrienne saw a row of three airline-type seats facing the rear of the aircraft, their backs against a wall beyond which was probably the engine and, above it, the flight deck. In front of the seats was an aisle as wide as the plane itself and about five feet deep. Facing the three seats were another two, with an empty space the size of one of the chairs. The East Germans had removed one of the usual six seats since there were to be only five passengers.

*Very impressive.*

Adrienne climbed up a short ladder and took the farthest seat in the row of three. Galya followed Adrienne in and sat next to her. Brenner took the seat opposite his wife in the row of two. When Kiril took the seat next to Galya, she flashed him a look of excitement. Luka Rogov heaved himself into the remaining seat opposite Kiril.

Leaning into the cabin, the co-pilot called out, "Dr. Andreyev, should you want to talk to the flight deck, use that wall phone on your left. You will hear us through the speaker above your head."

As the co-pilot slammed the door, Kurt Brenner broke out in a cold sweat.

* * *

The helicopter ascended from the hotel roof as if pulled by a huge magnet, its five passengers silent as they waited for the aircraft's blades to lift it into the air. After a few minutes of vertical flight, the co-pilot's voice came through the speaker. "We have reached the altitude for horizontal flight over Waren and Lake Muritz. You will be able to see much on the ground. Please enjoy the view."

Silently cursing the absence of seatbelts, Brenner gripped the armrests on both sides of his seat.

Luka Rogov leaned toward Kiril and asked in Russian, "How long we up?"

Despite the cabin being sound-proofed, Kiril had difficulty hearing him and asked Rogov to repeat his question. Kiril looked at his watch. "About an hour."

As the helicopter flew north, Adrienne and Kiril took advantage of the large windows in the VIP aircraft to watch the landscape unfolding below . . . cultivated farmland and flat country with few high hills . . . lush green meadows studded with trees and dotted with small lakes.

The voice that came through the speaker this time was the pilot's. "Ladies and gentlemen, in a few minutes we will resume vertical flight, slow our descent considerably, hover for a moment, and ease onto the ground."

When Gruner climbed down from the flight deck, he announced that they were now in the Muritz National Park, only a few miles from town. "You will be picked up momentarily by a gentleman named Herr Dieter Gelb," he told them.

Gelb was probably *Stasi*—Ministry of State Security, Kiril thought.

As if on cue, a ZIS-110 appeared.

The lanky man in civilian clothes and pointy leather boots who stepped out had a thin-lipped mouth and the feral look of a shark. He shook Kiril's hand, then said in English: "Doctor Andreyev, I am Herr Dieter Gelb." Delivering what sounded like a scripted statement, Gelb said he'd been asked by Chancellor Malik to escort them in Waren Town. He had taken the liberty of arranging an itinerary. "Unless you have objections?"

There were no objections.

"It is precisely 11:18 A.M. For the next three hours— until 2:15 P.M., that is—I will be your host," Gelb said with an appreciative glance at the two women. "Promptly at 2:30 P.M., you will enjoy lunch on the terrace at the Hotel zum Storchen, after which you will be taken to the town beach for ninety minutes. Chancellor Malik has provided swimming attire for those of you who may lack it. Except for Sergeant Rogov, of course, who will remain in uniform."

"Of course." Kiril didn't bother to fill Rogov in. It would

never have occurred to his "shadow" to exchange his military tunic for a bathing suit.

"At 4:15 P.M.," Herr Gelb continued, "I will collect you at the beach, return you here, and your helicopter pilots will have you back at your hotel between 5:00 P.M. and 5:15 P.M., when you may prepare for your dinner with the Chancellor."

Their first stop was at two churches built in the fourteenth century. What followed proved to be a fascinating sightseeing tour—but only to Kiril and Adrienne Brenner, apparently. As they walked through a fifteenth century old town hall, followed by an eighteenth century fire station and a nineteenth century new town hall, Kiril had to admit that Gelb was a fount of information. Kiril and Adrienne flanked him as they walked cobblestone streets, asking historical and cultural questions that their guide answered knowledgeably and with alacrity.

Allowed to take photographs for a change, Adrienne used what she thought of as her boxy, pain-in-the-butt camera.

Galya, looking bored, and Brenner, long-suffering, trudged behind them. Luka stoically brought up the rear.

They passed monuments to the victims of fascism. To World War II refugees. To Communist resistance fighters.

As promised, promptly at 2:30 P.M., Herr Gelb had the six of them seated on the terrace of the Hotel zum Storchen for a sumptuous lunch. Kiril ordered for Luka. The time passed quickly. Kurt Brenner had again withdrawn into himself. Galya ate up a storm, though she was no match for Luka Rogov. Adrienne Brenner took some notes.

Somehow the conversation turned to World War II. Kiril knew that several thousand Russian prisoners of war, as well as men and women from German-occupied countries, had been turned into forced laborers in a local armaments factory. He knew also that in October of 1945, the local Soviet military commander had become the town's mayor . . . and that their NKVD headquarters was known as the

House of Horrors because of its well-deserved reputation for harsh interrogation and fiendish torture.

He could not resist bringing these facts into the conversation—in rhetorical fashion, of course—which, by now, was second-nature to him.

*Is it not true, Herr Gelb, that . . .*

"Surely, doctor," Gelb said at one point, making an obvious effort to control the tone and volume of his voice, "you must know that the treatment of our *German* POWs by the U.S.S.R. was unconscionable, and yes, barbaric. You must know also that the NKVD was criticized for being overzealous as we worked to keep *your* Motherland free of capitalist and fascistic elements."

Adrienne, who had been taking copious notes, felt a rush of fear—and not for herself; for Dr. Andreyev.

"This is supposed to be a holiday sightseeing trip, gentlemen," she chided. "Herr Gelb, your knowledge of history and culture in this part of the world is what we Americans would call a real treat! Thank you so much for sharing your expertise with us."

Gelb smiled and clicked his heels.

For a moment, Kiril thought he was going to kiss her hand.

# CHAPTER 29

Herr Gelb drove them to the beach, organized changing rooms, and settled his charges with beach chairs and umbrellas. "I'll have you back in plenty of time to get you to your dinner appointment with Chancellor Malik," he assured them.

The blazing sun was low in a blue cloudless sky, the small beach filled with bathers. Lake Muritz was surprisingly blue, much like a bay adjacent to the sea, the water barely beginning to turn seasonally chilly. Children romped, parents chased after them. Men and women swam, some venturing beyond the buoys and white rope that demarked the allowable swimming area.

Adrienne walked toward the water and sank ankle-deep in warm white sand. Arching her back, she stretched luxuriously, looked around at her fellow sunbathers, and for the first time lost the tension that had ridden with her like an uninvited guest through the streets of East Berlin. Glancing at the placid blue lake, she was reminded of travel brochure clichés: picnic baskets, castles in the sand, carefree chatter—

Except that the chatter was practically non-existent, she realized. How could people compete with the blare emanating from loudspeakers that perched on long poles buried in the sand? She heard the strident notes of a military march as it oom-pahed its way into a clash of cymbals, followed by the razored cadence of carefully enunciated German.

"What are they saying?" she asked Galya, who happened to be nearby.

"I understand few words only. For me, the foreign language is hard."

Adrienne smiled. "Your English is a lot better than my German."

"How kind to give me compliment on my not very good English," Galya sniffed.

Adrienne restrained a sigh. For the umpteenth time, she wished she could retract her tactless offer about the gown. But if last night's apology hadn't cleared the air by now, nothing would.

As the two women moved away from the shoreline, their silence assaulted by the relentless staccato of the loudspeaker-voice, a strong breeze caught fringes of the beach umbrellas they passed, snapping them with the same staccato beat.

Adrienne almost laughed when she spotted the ever-vigilant Luka Rogov. He had plopped down under an umbrella adjacent to an empty chair, even though Dr. Andreyev was sitting right next to him.

*Comrade Ahab in a perspiration-stained Russian uniform, keeping a watchful eye on his Moby-Dick.*

Andreyev wore the inevitable sunglasses. Interesting how they'd given him an air of mystery—but how commonplace they seemed on a beach. No, it wasn't the glasses that were off-putting, she decided. It was his yachting cap. He wore it tipped jauntily to one side. It struck her as . . . unseemly and out of place on a man who had gone out of his way to pointedly show her the underbelly of the Deutsche Demokratische Republik.

The sudden blast of another marching song ended her reverie just as he half-turned in her direction. "Dr. Andreyev," she called out, "would you mind translating—"

"Dr. Andreyev is chest deep in Lake Muritzsee," Kurt told her, wearing a Cheshire-cat grin. "Will Dr. Brenner do?"

"I . . . it was the dark glasses."

"Darling! I didn't think you knew how to blush."

"I'm glad you're amused," she said tartly. "Since your German is impeccable, mind telling me what's coming out of those loudspeakers?"

"Lectures, announcements. That sort of thing."

"They're broadcasting *lectures* to people on a beach?"

"Amazing, isn't it?" he said. "They're also checking identity cards. See that uniformed guard over there?" He started to put his dark glasses back on. "Is it okay?" he teased. "Or are you apt to confuse me with our mysterious guide?"

"There is no mystery in dark glasses," Galya remarked with a faint smile. "Dr. Andreyev must keep away light from eye infection. But is *big* mystery why your wife is mistaking him for her husband. I tell difference if *my* husband," she purred, reaching up to adjust Brenner's yachting cap at a more rakish angle. Looking him over with a mock-frown, she said, "Maybe Mrs. Brenner not notice *this*." She touched a mole on Brenner's shoulder. "Or *this*." Her finger traced a thin line down his chest, white against deep tan. Dropping her hand, she laughed like a defiant child, then turned to face Adrienne Brenner's anger.

*Damn you!*

Adrienne almost said it aloud—to Kurt, not the Barkova woman. To his arched eyebrow—a not-so-subtle sign that he was flattered. To the same half-smile that he flashed at operating-room nurses and cocktail-party hostesses.

"Having fun?" she said acidly. Turning her back on

them both, she laid out a colorful beach towel, sank into it, and closed her eyes.

The sun was a lightweight blanket on her body. Surrendering to its warmth, she shut out the world—tried to anyway. Her article was practically writing itself. Entire paragraphs darted in and out of her head. The only thing she'd dared reduce to writing were some memory-jogging words that would be meaningless to anyone else. Photographs were more accurate than memory—and much more incriminating, she consoled herself. If only she could manage to take the ones she *really* wanted. Lugging a conspicuously large camera around for the few photos she was allowed to take was a nuisance. On the other hand, she had to admit it was a terrific distraction on the rare occasion when she could whip the tiny Minox out of her shoulder bag and snap away.

She let it all go finally and surrendered to the delicious warmth of her sun-blanket.

Until she felt the blanket slip away, as if some presumptuous cloud had crossed the almost cloudless sky. Turning lazily on her side, she reached with half-closed eyes for the terrycloth robe she'd dropped next to her towel.

Her arm stalled in mid-air as if someone had grabbed it.

Kiril Andreyev stood looking down at her. His shadow across her body had blotted out the sun.

She felt the weight of his glance. Her own tight breathing. The shock of seeing his body outside the prison of an ill-fitting suit.

Even her eyes betrayed her. She couldn't take them off his hands as they reached for a towel. The insolent line of his legs, braced against the hard-driving wind. She was aware of the curve of her hip. Of a bathing suit that rose obediently to her neck but left her shoulders and back exposed—

The shadow ruptured like broken glass. He had turned

to respond to something Kurt was saying.

She dropped back onto the towel and closed her eyes, feeling cold even though the sun was back.

* * *

When the helicopter was ready to board the passengers for the flight back, everyone resumed the seats they'd occupied before. Takeoff was uneventful.

As soon as the aircraft reached the altitude for horizontal flight, Kiril addressed the Brenners. "Before we took off, I instructed the captain to fly as low as possible as we approach East Berlin. I thought you might like to see East Germany's newest attempt at improving its security against 'capitalist encroachment' on its sovereignty."

Adrienne Brenner went into high alert, immediately grasping what Andreyev was getting at. Convinced that there was a subtext to everything he said and did, and given the worldwide headlines a month or so earlier about East Germany's newest attempt to "improve its security," he *had* to be talking about *The Wall*.

Before leaving New York, she had learned as much as she could about what was happening. Then on August 12, 1961, just a few weeks before she and Kurt set foot on East German soil, the Council of Ministers of the GDR had put out a patently self-serving and facially absurd statement.

"I know what you're talking about," she told Andreyev as she flipped to a page in her notebook. She paraphrased the Council of Ministers' statement. How, in order to put a stop to the "hostile" activity of West Germany's and West Berlin's "attempt to regain lost territory and militaristic forces," border controls of the kind generally found in every sovereign state would be set up at the border of the German Democratic Republic. Adrienne looked up from her notes. "What prompted the creation of those so-called border controls, Dr. Andreyev?"

"Mind changing seats with me for a few minutes?" Kiril asked Brenner. "It will make it easier for me to answer your wife's questions."

Brenner shrugged indifferently and took the seat next to Galya.

"Five years after the end of World War II—between 1950 and 1953—nearly one million citizens of the GDP's workers' paradise moved to West Germany. As the American saying goes, they voted with their feet. A quarter-million left within the first six months."

Adrienne scanned her notes. "A million people in three years," she said evenly. "How long did this go on?"

"A few more years. In 1957 the Communists imposed a passport law severely reducing the number of people leaving East Germany. Ironically, it was as if pressure applied to one end of a balloon forced the other end to bulge. By the end of 1958, the percentage of refugees using West Berlin as an escape hatch rose from sixty to ninety percent. And don't forget, the subway was still running between East and West Berlin."

"All defectors had to do was take a *subway*?"

He nodded, almost as if he couldn't trust his voice. But Adrienne saw in his expression what he was unable to hide: a terrible sense of longing.

"How many people escaped?" she asked.

"By the end of 1961? Three and a half million East Germans—20 percent of the population. And because most of them were young and well-educated—physicians, teachers, engineers, skilled workers—some party officials were calling it a 'brain drain.' It got so bad that by 1960, only 61 per cent of East Germany's population was of working age. It was obvious that the combined efforts of East Germany and the Soviet Union were needed to avert a crisis."

"Are you telling me this combined effort has

already begun?!"

"Several weeks ago. At midnight on August 12 to 13. East German Vopos and soldiers began to close the East to West Berlin border. Streets running parallel to the border were torn up. Barbed wire was strung. Four days later, the regime began to lay large concrete blocks. Guards were ordered to shoot anyone attempting to cross the border. According to Soviet intelligence, all of East Germany and East Berlin will in time be entirely sealed off from the West."

"How exactly?"

"With chain fences. Concrete walls. Minefields in a no-man's-land 'death zone' between what will later become *two* walls parallel to each other and snaking for miles. Vicious guard dogs will be caged and released to find and kill people trying to escape."

"People whose only crime is wanting to be free," she whispered.

"The entire East German population will be caged in," he told her. "Family members will be sealed off from one another."

Reaching for the wall telephone, he told Rolf Gruner in German to get as low as he could over what Kiril thought of as the early stages of The Wall's construction.

"I'll do my best," Gruner replied after a moment's hesitation. "But I can't enter West German airspace and I sure as hell don't relish getting shot down in the East."

"Thanks," Kiril said as Gruner swung as close as he dared to the East Berlin side of the wall. He translated for the others, making sure Kurt Brenner, as well as his wife, heard him loud and clear.

Adrienne had stopped taking notes. Pressing her face to the large window next to her seat, she followed the helicopter's trajectory—treetop level. Her face felt oddly still . . . like a wax dummy's. She zeroed in on the smooth gray of concrete. The grainy unevenness of cement. The still-intact wall of some forgotten home. An unbroken series of bricked-up doors and windows. She shivered as a bright gold speck signaled malevolently—the sun's reflection caught and held by razor-sharp glass shards all along the top. Like a sewing machine needle on a band of retreating fabric, her eyes drilled down the wall. She spotted a roller device—lengths of pipe atop the wall that forged a path through the broken glass so that anyone groping desperately for a handhold would slip. Between the pipes she saw metal poles with outspread arms, taut wires stretching from one pole to the next. Electrified? she wondered, closing her eyes as she stifled the urge to weep for its future victims.

Gruner banked sharply.

"Our pilot wants to avoid not just West Berlin," Kiril explained, "but what might be called 'aggressive notice' from East Berlin radar."

They were flying low enough for Adrienne to see a large park with a huge bronze statue on a white pedestal. She asked Kiril about it.

"The park? It's the East Berlin Soviet War Memorial in Treptower Park."

"A memorial to what?" Adrienne asked cautiously.

"More precisely, to *whom*. It's a military cemetery— an enormous mass grave commemorating 5,000 Soviet soldiers who died in the battle for Berlin."

Adrienne restrained a shudder. "What is it about mass burials and unmarked graves that seems so . . . so unsettling?" she wondered aloud.

"When a man dies, he should be permitted the dignity and solitude of a private resting place, not—" Kiril's mouth twisted. "—not lowered into some anonymous collection of humanity."

Luka Rogov understood virtually nothing of Kiril's explanation. But his face brightened at the mention of the word *"Treptower."* He'd heard about Treptower, all right. Tugging at Kiril's sleeve, he said in Russian, "Look down there."

"At what? I see the park, a bronze statue—and now the cemetery."

"No, not cemetery of Great Patriotic War. Look at what comes after."

"I see a field of some kind," Kiril said, puzzled.

"Is secret, this field." Rogov lowered his voice as if he were a fellow conspirator.

"Then why tell me?" Kiril asked warily.

"From kindness," Luka said with a sly, setting-a-trap smile. "Field is new but not empty. You like know what is in it?"

He pressed binoculars into Kiril's hands.

"I *don't* like," Kiril said, handing the binoculars back.

"Your friend Brodsky is in this field!" Luka announced triumphantly. "Your friend and other traitors, all together in one big hole, like garbage in garbage dump. Look!" Luka said insistently, brandishing the binoculars. "Still have time to say goodbye!"

Kiril's head snapped back as if he'd just caught the sting of a whip.

*Not Stepan. Not in such a place!*

Swinging around in the small aisle until he faced Rogov, Kiril lunged for his throat.

With a swift upward motion, Rogov broke Kiril's hold with one hand. With the other, he brought the butt of his Nagant revolver against the side of Kiril's head. Staggering backward, Kiril fell against Galya and Brenner before dropping to the floor. Luka resumed his seat and holstered his gun.

His head bleeding, his mind reeling, Kiril pulled himself up as the others sat frozen in their seats. Reaching for the wall phone, he shouted orders in German to the flight deck.

Galya gasped.

"Godammit," Brenner muttered, gripping the arm rests again.

Adrienne Brenner's hand was shaking as she pressed a handkerchief against Kiril's head wound.

# CHAPTER 30

As soon the helicopter's wheels touched the ground, Kiril thanked Rolf Gruner for setting down. "We'll be staying only a few minutes," he reassured the captain.

Opening the helicopter door, Kiril jumped down, Rogov right behind him. Galya and the Brenners followed.

Adrienne glanced back at the helicopter, its blades still rotating slowly, perched on the field like some wary bird poised for flight.

All five of them stood looking at a couple of uniformed soldiers headed in their direction, submachine guns in hand.

"Vopos," Kiril told them. "Let me handle this," he added with a warning glance at Brenner before walking toward the soldiers.

Brenner caught snatches of German, followed in short order by angry demands for an explanation. But Andreyev's authoritative voice—he said something about it being an inspection—made the Vopos uncertain about what to do next. One decided he would go to the phone at the guard shack three hundred or so yards away.

The other Vopo's mind was apparently made up for him, Adrienne thought, as she noticed what appeared to be some kind of a disturbance at the other end of the large field.

"What's *that* about?" she asked Galya.

"Is better not know, better not be mixed in," she whispered.

Adrienne shrugged and started to walk in Kiril Andreyev's direction.

"Please to stay near helicopter," Galya called after her. "We have no permit to be here. I heard Mongolian say field is mass grave. But not like Treptower. Not for heroes from Great Patriotic War. This is mass grave for traitors."

Adrienne stared at her.

*Like Paul Houston's friend, Stepan Brodsky?*

"Where do you think you're going?" Brenner asked Adrienne.

"To see for myself," she said flatly.

Her heels sunk into the black furrows of the freshly plowed field. It covered an area large enough for a hundred conventional graves, she thought. How many could be buried in a human dumping ground, a thousand? Two?

Dr. Andreyev, his Mongolian "shadow" a few feet behind him, was walking along a barbed-wire fence that surrounded the field. Adrienne groped in a side pocket of her bag for a slim silver object the length of a pocket comb. Avoiding the gaze of the pilots and the Vopos, but not particularly concerned about Dr. Andreyev's nurse—or was Galya his girlfriend?—Adrienne slid the outer shell of the miniature Minox back and forth, exposing the lens as she snapped photographs of the field . . . the barbed wire . . . a couple of signs that said *verböten*.

The Minox back in her bag, she was about to rejoin the others when she caught a glimpse of Dr. Andreyev's face. She was reluctant to infringe on his privacy. What changed her mind was the sight of his mouth. It was distorted by such pain that not even his dark glasses could mask it. Slipping out of her shoes so she could better navigate the pliant earth, she went over to him and touched his arm in a gesture of support.

"I have seen their barbed wire, their submachine guns," he said slowly as if conversing with a total stranger. "I have been to their detention camps and their mental wards. I have seen how they punish the living. But *this*. This is a form of vindictiveness I had never imagined. To punish the dead? To rob them of a decent burial?"

"The dead are beyond punishment," she said gently.

"What about the people who mourn them?" he countered. "A grave is for remembering. Why else do we return again and again to converse? To leave flowers? To say a silent prayer?"

*Why else, indeed?* she thought. Then he said something she would never forget.

"Now I must spend the rest of my life trying to forget this place."

In an effort to distract him, she pointed out the disturbance she'd noticed at the other end of the field. "What's happening over there?"

He shrugged. "I've no idea."

"Why don't we find out?"

As the two of them made their way back toward the fracas, Adrienne, lost in thought, was certain of one thing. Whatever his motives, her "tour guide" was no apologist for a totalitarian regime, neither East German nor Soviet. Kiril Andreyev was one of its victims.

\* \* \*

Angry words nudged Adrienne out of her somber reverie.

"Are you denying what we both know? This is a burial ground!"

The angry words came from a short muscular man dressed in laborer's clothes who was addressing a Vopo. Three other men stood next to the laborer, looking uncomfortable in their neatly pressed suits. One of the men had a protective arm around the shoulder of an old woman in black shawl and babushka.

. . . Not so old, Adrienne realized, moving closer. Just tired, bent, and weary, with deep crevices running down her parched cheeks.

"Can I help?" Dr. Andreyev asked in German, to the consternation of the Vopo.

"My name is Zind, Albert Zind," the laborer said. The man's hair was the color of sand. His blue eyes were expressionless.

"Erich and Gunther, my brothers. Our friend, Otto Dorf." He pointed them out. "Our mother. We were told my sister's body was here so we came all the way from Potsdam to visit her grave."

Kiril translated for Adrienne.

"Our papers." Albert Zind handed them to Kiril, who looked them over. "You can see they're in order. And *still* they refuse to help us."

"These people are a pack of fools," grumbled the Vopo. "They claim to have special permission to visit some grave. Where do you see graves around here? Where are the headstones? Let them visit every cemetery in Berlin for all we care," he said with feigned indifference.

"My mother is not well," Zind persisted. "The trip has been grueling. I promised her she could say a few words at her daughter's grave. Only a few words. *Then* we will leave."

Again, Kiril translated for Adrienne. For once he was grateful that Luka Rogov was dogging his footsteps. The grim authority of Rogov's military tunic, the red star emblazoned on his cap, spoke volumes to the East German Vopo.

With a friendly gesture in Rogov's direction, Kiril said,

"We insist that you allow this family to mourn. Unless, of course, you can prove to the appropriate authorities that their papers are false? If you cannot, my associate and I will file a report that you refused to follow our orders."

The Vopo turned sullen, but he backed off.

"How did you learn of this place?" Kiril asked Albert Zind.

"I'm in bridge construction. Foreman on the repair work being done on Unity. That's what they're calling Glienicker Bridge these days, at least in Potsdam," he said, making no attempt to mask his contempt.

"The bridge between Potsdam and West Berlin?"

"That's the one. A Russian crashed into the bridge recently," Zind said, looking at Kiril curiously now. "Poor bastard tried to make it across in some diplomat's limousine. Almost did, from what I heard," Zind added, making no attempt to mask his sympathy. "The minute word got out about burial arrangements, I asked a few discreet questions. That's how I knew where to find my sister. Turns out she and your Russian friend had the same idea except that Eva tried it through a place not yet closed by the wall."

This time when Kiril translated, Adrienne gasped.

Zind's mother tugged at Albert's sleeve. "But where is Eva's gravestone? You promised me, Albert!"

"She's here, mama. We don't know exactly where. I told you how it would be, remember? I kept my promise. Now you must keep yours. Say a prayer for Eva and—"

She shook her head, uncomprehending.

Kiril dropped to his knees.

Adrienne watched, fascinated, as Kiril removed a tiny gold scalpel from a chain around his neck. Watched him smooth a patch of soil with his hand and outline the shape of a headstone.

At the very top of the "headstone," Kiril carved four words in German: HERE LIES EVA ZIND.

"Eighteen years old," Albert Zind said tonelessly.

"Number 13 Hollandische Siedlung, Potsdam," said one brother.

Kiril bent to his task—tiny letters so Eva Zind's age and address would fit inside.

"Beloved daughter of Frieda. Adored sister of Albert, Gunther, and Erich," said Erich Zind.

"Beloved by Otto," said another voice, husky with unshed tears.

The mother had already dropped to her knees beside Kiril, her lips moving in silent prayer. When he finally rose, Zind's mother crossed herself and got to her feet without assistance.

Albert Zind gripped Kiril's hand. His blue eyes were no longer expressionless.

# CHAPTER 31

Drizzling water landed unceremoniously on Aleksei Andreyev's head. He wiped it away, oblivious to the rain. In the last sixteen months he had been on and under Glienicker Bridge at least a dozen times since Stepan Brodsky died there while trying to defect.

The pressure from General Nemerov had been intense. Unrelenting. Aleksei could understand why. As he'd reminded Emil von Eyssen soon after the incident, Brodsky had been a Captain in the Soviet Air Force who had worked for Aleksei. Worse, it was Aleksei who'd put Brodsky in charge of security for the Four-Power summit! So what was Brodsky's final act? Pushing a cigarette lighter into the Havel River before von Eyssen could confiscate it.

"Did you really think there was only cotton inside the lighter?" Aleksei recalled asking von Eyssen sarcastically.

No, Aleksei thought, Nemerov had every reason to be concerned that day and all the months since. He *had* to find the damnable lighter. Especially after reading Luka Rogov's report about what had happened near the Treptower Park cemetery on the way back from Waren. About his brother's strong reaction after learning that his friend Brodsky was doubtless buried in a mass grave. Would it so enrage Kiril that he'd throw caution to the wind and try to defect?

Quite apart from General Nemerov's interest in the cigarette lighter, Aleksei had spent many a sleepless night worrying about the lighter's contents. What if it contained something that might incriminate him in some way?

All of which motivated him, after several unsuccessful attempts with East German dredging equipment and operators, to bring in Soviet engineers and equipment.

They had systematically dredged the water on both sides of the bridge, then under it, then down and up the Havel River. Mud was sucked up and strained. Debris was examined. The detritus of decades, if not centuries, of dumping was sorted. Divers searched the muck by hand. And came up with nothing.

So here he was again. He had expected to be bored and irritable but, surprisingly, he found himself fascinated by the dredging. By the scooping device at the end of the boom that came up from the river looking like a giant dripping clamshell with a mouthful of mud.

A lanky man in a windbreaker stuck his head outside the door of the East German guardhouse. Aleksei barely noticed his approach. He was watching a sleek gray-green East German patrol boat pass underneath the bridge, its diesel engines belching clouds of black soot.

"What is it now, Mueller?" Aleksei asked, glancing up.

As Mueller cupped a hand to his ear, obviously straining to hear, Aleksei realized the noise from the dredging equipment and the patrol boats beneath the bridge were drowning out their voices.

"You've been working on repairing this bridge for how long, Mueller?"

"Nearly sixteen months. But it's not fair to blame me, Colonel," he said defensively. "The damn bridge was built in 1906 and nearly destroyed during the war."

Aleksei cut him off. "This isn't about blame. Is that Vopo around—the one who was on duty the night of Brodsky's attempted defection?"

"I'll send him out here right now, Colonel," Mueller said, relieved.

The door of the guardhouse flew open and banged against a stone wall. The man walking toward Aleksei in long impatient strides had a raw, seething vitality not unlike Luka's, Aleksei thought. But unlike Luka, the East German resented Russians. Pity. Men like Luka Rogov were becoming extinct.

"You wanted to see me . . ." the Vopo said, then added reluctantly, "sir?"

"I know we've been over this before, but I need you to answer a few more questions. Tell me again—Bruno, isn't it?—where you saw Stepan Brodsky's cigarette lighter go over the side. The exact spot."

Bruno's eyes went to the left-hand side of the bridge. Pointing to a space between two lower parallel iron bars just opposite a mass of newly painted steel supports, he said, "Right through there he pushed it."

"Now tell me everything you saw and heard, from the moment Brodsky got out of the second limousine and walked over to the first one."

"The limousines had stopped single file behind the horizontal striped pole. A Russian Air Force officer got out of his jeep and . . ." Bruno flushed. "I was arguing with the American diplomat—he blew smoke in my face!—when the Air Force captain butted in . . ."

Aleksei had a gift for visualizing. As Bruno talked, he pictured the first limousine moving leisurely across. The second, stalled by the angry exchange of words. He saw Brodsky's sudden move. Heard the screech of tires. The clatter of machine guns. Saw a large Mercedes smash into the side of the bridge. Pictured Brodsky's body arc through the air before he was thrown clear. Saw the limousine burst into flame. Touching the steel of the bridge with his fingertips, Aleksei pictured East German patrol boats cruising restlessly back and forth under the bridge, ready to swing into action whenever—

Under the bridge? *Under* it?

He seized Bruno's arm. "Think hard now. Since this is the spot where Brodsky lay just before the lighter went over, were any boats patrolling right about here?"

Bruno frowned. "They might've been, sure, but—"

Aleksei headed for the cobblestone square and entered the Soviet guardhouse just opposite the East German one.

Bruno scurried after him. He was curious. He was paid to be curious about the Russkies.

Inside the Soviet guardhouse, Aleksei telephoned the East Berlin KGB station, explained what he wanted, and sat down to wait.

Two hours later he was picked up by his trusted aide, Lieutenant Anatoly Barkov. On the way to their destination, Lieutenant Barkov explained what Aleksei had put in motion. The Russians had obtained from the East Germans a list of every patrol boat in the vicinity of Glienicker Bridge for two hours before and two hours after Stepan Brodsky's escape attempt. The roster of every man on every boat was obtained. There were only four such boats, with a crew of four on each boat—four Schnellboots. Sixteen men.

As Aleksei and his aide sped to the dock, the East Germans were locating the boats and sending out Vopos to question the crew members. By the time they arrived at an inlet on the Havel River where the boats were berthed and serviced, one was already in dry dock for repairs.

"I have been assured that the other three boats are on their way and should arrive shortly, sir," Barkov reported.

The two of them were intrigued by the steel-hulled vessels. Roughly thirty feet long, they had a large cabin that bristled with searchlights, loudspeakers, sirens, radar, and other electronic equipment.

Aleksei had asked for a hundred Vopos, intending to use them for turning each ship inside out as they looked for the lighter. "Where are the men?" Aleksei wondered out loud.

"On their way, Colonel. They should be here momentarily."

Which they were. The East German officer in charge assembled his men in formation, saluted the two Russians, and said to Aleksei, "My men are at your command, sir."

Standing in the bed of a nearby truck, Aleksei addressed the men in German. "You will divide into teams of 25 men each, one group for each boat. The other three are arriving as I speak. You are looking for a cigarette lighter. I cannot describe it because I have not yet seen it, but you will know it when you find it. Begin your search with the equipment attached to the cabin—searchlights, loudspeakers, sirens, radar, and other electronic equipment. Some of you will search the cabin. Others are to inspect every vent and drain on the surface of the boat, every place on the deck where a lighter could be hidden. If it is not on deck, you will search below deck. Dismissed."

Turning to the officer in charge, Aleksei said, "See that bar not far from the dockyard?"

"Yessir."

"That's where we'll be once your men find the lighter."

Just as their dessert was being served, the Vopo officer rushed in.

"We have it, Colonel!" He handed the lighter to Aleksei. "And I have a theory," he added, flushed with success. "Someone must have dropped it on the wet deck in the dark. When the vessel rolled from the strong current, the lighter slid into an uncovered drain where one of my men found it. If whoever lost it looked for the lighter in the daylight, he couldn't have found it."

"Sounds plausible," Aleksei said with a smile. He shook the officer's hand. "Please commend your man."

As Aleksei left the bar, he kept a firm grip on Brodsky's lighter. Once inside Lieutenant Barkov's vehicle, he fingered the Zippo lighter, frowning at the double-eagle emblem on one side. He spun the lighter's ridged wheel to strike the flint and ignite the device. Nothing. The wheel worked. There was a flint. Also a wick. He tried again with the same result. He studied the lighter. Opened and closed it. Turned it this way and that.

This time he pulled each working part out of the stainless steel case. Yes, there was cotton stuffing for lighter fluid that should have been able to work its way to the wick but—

Aleksei sniffed the cotton. No discernible odor of lighter fluid.

*He had it—the Holy Grail!*

Digging out the cotton stuffing with a fingernail, he found a tiny piece of microfilm in an equally tiny piece of sealed cellophane.

"How long to get this developed and some prints made?" he asked his aide.

"We can be at the station in a half-hour, sir."

"I must attend an important function at the Humboldt University Medical Clinic, Anatoly. I want you to drop me off there, then have the film and the photographs delivered. But to *me*, no one else. And I want you to process the microfilm yourself. No one else is to see it or, for that matter, know anything about it. Understood?"

"You can count on me, sir."

Aleksei smiled at the lieutenant's response. It was true. He had been counting on Lieutenant Barkov for over five years.

# CHAPTER 32

Aleksei opened the curtains of his limousine, chasing the semi-darkness from the rear seat but admitting a different kind of gloom—a colorless landscape under a gray sky that had swallowed up an earlier promise of sunshine.

His eyes kept returning to the place next to his driver—Luka Rogov's customary seat—now uncharacteristically empty.

He thought of Luka's reliability. His soothing presence. His incredible strength. Just thinking of Luka's strength gave Aleksei comfort, although he had never tried to identify the nature of that comfort.

He sat back and lit his pipe.

But as usual, along with his relaxed state of mind, memories invariably followed . . . .

Aleksei Andreyev was no more than three years old when he first encountered fear. He feared the fat boy on his block who'd grab Aleksei's toys and run off with them. The skinny girl who'd kicked him in the ankle once and left a throbbing bruise. The red-bearded man who came regularly to his family's flat, dragging huge clanking milk cans behind him. And his father—his own father!—whose booming voice and large rough hands would hoist him high in the air whenever his breath had that funny sour smell. Aleksei never wondered why such things made him feel helpless and bewildered. He took his fear for granted, as much a fact of life as the sidewalk in front of his building.

Until the day he made a double discovery. Grownups had fears too. And, wonder of wonders, he, Aleksei Andreyev, could make them afraid!

The day had started out like any other. School. Homework afterward. A visit to the home of his best friend, Ilya. The same old invitation to stay for supper. During the meal he had reached past Ilya for a platter of meat instead of asking for it as he'd been taught, and his elbow had knocked against a bowl of thick brown gravy.

Ilya's older sister, Dasha, had leaped up in a rage. "Look how you've splattered gravy all over my dress, you clumsy fool!" she sputtered.

Aleksei jerked away from her, eyes squeezed shut with terror, sure that Dasha would strike him. Nothing happened. He opened his eyes a crack, then all the way. He saw it first in the eyes of Dasha's parents, and then in hers as well. *Fear.* They kept pushing apologies at him. Dasha's mother kept saying he shouldn't tell his father. What did his father have to do with his bad table manners and the spilled gravy?

It was only when he was walking home that he realized what they were afraid of—his father. But why? Aleksei made up his mind to find out.

His father, he learned, was an early member of the *Cheka* in Moscow. Its full name was "The Extraordinary Commission for the Struggle against Counterrevolution and Sabotage"—whatever *that* meant. The *Cheka* was new to the Soviet Union, appearing almost immediately after the Great Socialist Revolution, and Aleksei's father held an important position in the organization—"high-ranking," someone told him. People spoke of it in whispers. But what did it mean?

Aleksei tried to understand what his father did but gave it up when he realized it didn't really matter. *Whatever* his father's job was, it made people like Dasha and her parents afraid. He heard two things over and over about his father. That he was a *powerful* man and that he was in *intelligence*, which meant looking into the secret activities of "counter-revolutionaries." He shook his head over that one.

But no one had to tell him about *powerful*. His father, he discovered, could have whole families arrested or sent to Siberia. Or even shot.

Once he knew this, things began to happen—he *made* them happen. Like mentioning his father's name in a roomful of people and waiting for the nervous coughing or stillness in the air that was suddenly thick with fear.

One day he made the most important discovery of all. In the face of other people's fears, Aleksei forgot his own. He began to study people more closely. With a word or a hint, he found he could always get his way, and no arguments. He got lots of presents and invitations to parties. He began to experience a secret pride—and a heady new feeling of power. He became a sort of crown prince, reigning in the dark shadow of his father.

When he was about seven years old, the presents and invitations ceased abruptly. His mother had gone to Germany with his little brother Kolya and then disappeared. His father was blamed for letting her leave the country. At first Aleksei feared for his father's personal safety but what happened turned out to be worse. Three judges from his father's own organization held a "troika"—a secret trial—and his father was branded an "Enemy of the People" even though he'd been cleared of being a "co-conspirator" and a "wrecker."

Aleksei had never particularly noticed his style of living, but he noticed its absence. No more five-room flat in Moscow filled with furniture and paintings and Oriental rugs. No more dacha in the country. Gone in the blink of an eye. One day the Andreyevs were at home. The next, they were living in a two-room flat shared by three other families in an apartment house on the outskirts of Moscow.

But physical discomfort and hunger weren't the worst of it. Aleksei Andreyev, crown prince in a secure world, experienced a raw terror that transcended his old fears. This time, it was a *knowledgeable* terror. It sprang from the fear-inducing tools he had used against others that could now be used against him! He knew informers were planted, not just in factories, but in apartment buildings like the one he, his father, and his little brother Kiril lived in. His father complained endlessly that even thieves and murderers fared better when it came to punishment than "betrayers of the revolution."

Aleksei  realized his father would never rehabilitate himself and resume his old career. His father was drinking himself into an early grave . . . On that same night, Aleksei made a solemn oath that someday he would win back the family honor. Someday, he would hold his father's post.

In the midst of making bold plans, he noticed that the prospect of such a future brought him a sense of relief. That the terror he carried with him, like a heavy knapsack on his back, didn't bear down quite so heavily.

\* \* \*

It took him over twenty years, but by the time Aleksei was in his early thirties, the terror had disappeared. The years he'd invested in the Archives Section of the Information Directorate—his "mole years," he was later to call them—had finally paid off. After being given access to the Classified Library, he set about learning its contents as no one ever had—lovingly, like a violinist with his

Stradivarius. He became an expert researcher. He stole files. He honed his ability to ferret out and file away in a steel-trap memory the secrets and misdeeds of people who were in a position to help him. As to those who might do him harm, he became adept at applying just the right combination of hints and pressure, promises and threats, to keep his potential enemies at bay.

At first, he barely survived. Over time, he prospered.

Until the day he realized his career could be crushed as swiftly as his father's had been—and by the same kind of sledgehammer.

His brother Kiril was leaving a trail of unhealthy rumors in his wake. Allusions were made to Kiril's diversionist tendencies. His unpatriotic attitude. Some of the disreputable people he hung out with.

Cursing himself for his lack of foresight, Aleksei put into immediate operation a tight surveillance program. Even so, a feeling of vulnerability continued to dog him until the day—following a chance encounter on a Moscow street—Luka Rogov, who'd served under him during the Great Patriotic War, reentered his life. Luka, the fearless, incapable of entertaining a scruple inside that sluggish brain. Luka, the human torture machine. Luka, his loyal soldier, who—when necessary—took pleasure in meting out pain to Aleksei's enemies. Over the years, they had morphed into an effective interrogation team with a conventional but effective approach: the carrot and the stick. Aleksei brought to the table a subtle mind, a patient literate reasonableness, and a carefully researched dossier on the subject of the interrogation. Luka, a symbolic presence in the interrogation room, was like a bulky piece of furniture—noticeable, but more often than not, unused.

The word got around, making it increasingly easy to deal with recalcitrant subjects. Plum security assignments came his way—most recently when Chairman Khrushchev had a good excuse to clash with General Eisenhower and cancel the summit.

In recognition of his achievements, Aleksei remained confident he was close to being rewarded with the biggest plum of all—a KGB intelligence position equivalent to the one held by his father in the *Cheka*.

Until a few months ago.

Until the night Stepan Brodsky had tried to defect and had almost pulled it off.

Aleksei's pipe had gone out. Tapping it idly against one of the limousine's jump seats, he followed the drift of cold ashes onto the rug. True, he thought, the Brodsky affair was no more than a blemish on his otherwise clean record. On the other hand, no one in intelligence could afford blemishes.

But Aleksei was a realist. He had mixed feelings about trying to get Dr. Kurt Brenner to defect. His plan, while a good one, had pitfalls. He thought of it as an intricate puzzle. So many pieces had to fall together in the right way for it to work.

Yet he had to admit that the average Soviet citizen with whom he had dealt over the years was no match for his interrogation skills.

Aleksei visualized a parade of faces: men, women, teenagers. One cowed subject after another. People who had grown used to his threats and the power of his office to make good on them.

But Dr. Kurt Brenner? A prominent American heart surgeon who was used to giving orders, not taking them? A man who had been raised in a decadent culture that nurtured independence?

Aleksei smiled. *There* was a challenge!

# CHAPTER 33

"**Z**um Wohle aller!" For the good of all!" The Direktor of the Humboldt University Medical Clinic smiled at his honored guest, Dr. Kurt Brenner of New York City, United States of America.

Glasses were raised. Champagne was passed around as, one by one, the array of doctors rose to toast Brenner's good health in German, Russian, Hungarian, Polish, Bulgarian, Romanian, and Czech.

Someone proposed a toast in honor of the ladies. Galya, seated unobtrusively near a desk in a corner of the spacious room, smiled shyly. Adrienne Brenner inclined her head in a silent "thank you." Herr Direktor himself was toasted for having arranged such an excellent breakfast in the gaily-decorated clinic cafeteria.

Dr. Brenner did not imbibe.

Breakfast and toasting finished, the doctors began positioning their chairs in a loose semi-circle around Kurt Brenner.

Kiril, his chair arranged slightly behind Adrienne's, whispered, "Now it begins. They are about to pick your husband's brain about the latest techniques in cardiology and cardiac surgery. All through the meal and the toasts afterward, they have thought of nothing else. But first, they will waste time going through the required ritual of claiming that doctors in the People's Democracies have the best of everything."

"The best of our goods . . . sounds right up your alley," Adrienne teased.

All except one doctor, Kiril thought. His mentor, Dr. Mikhail Yanin, wouldn't dream of wasting valuable time extolling the Soviet Union's inferior cardiac "achievements" when there was so much to learn from the eminent Dr. Brenner . . . and so little time in which to do it.

Dr. Yanin was on his feet. Kiril leaned forward as Yanin asked a highly technical question about artificial hearts—the agenda of the upcoming symposium in West Berlin sponsored by Medicine International.

Dr. Kurt Brenner spoke with eloquence for almost fifteen minutes.

The cardiologists from the People's Democracies was a poor followup as they segued into their ritualistic bragging . . .

"The Soviet Union's electronic monitoring system is a huge success!"

"A patient's heartbeat speeds up. A second attack seems imminent but we are ready with a new drug."

"A thousand-volt electrical charge to the chest was perfectly timed."

"So our vascular stapling machine has made suturing obsolete."

"It was a surgical breakthrough in congenital heart lesions."

"Medical helicopters swiftly dispatched to remote areas."

Kiril almost recoiled at this last outrageous claim. After his three years of forced internship in the remote areas beyond the Arctic Circle, even *one* medical rescue helicopter would have been a godsend.

A door behind Dr. Brenner opened and Aleksei Andreyev came in. Only two people noticed—Luka Rogov and Kiril Andreyev.

Rogov sat a little straighter in his chair.

Kiril's hand automatically went to his chest—as if something was banging to get out.

*The moment of truth! As soon as Dr. Brenner turns, Aleksei will see the likeness for the first time. Will he remember the so-called eye infection—my only excuse for wearing dark glasses?*

Uneasiness turned to near panic as Kiril realized that, the breakfast event being so early, he had completely forgotten to apply the lemon juice!

Brenner's back was to Aleksei as he finished responding to an ersatz claim by a cardiologist from Bulgaria. "Medicine is international," he intoned. "Great contributions come from every corner of the globe. America has much to learn from your countries. It's why I have always applauded medical exchanges"

"Colonel Andreyev!" cried the Direktor, spotting Aleksei. "We are pleased and honored that you could spare the time to join us."

The semi-circle opened as doctors turned to look and reluctantly moved their chairs.

As Kurt Brenner turned to greet Aleksei Andreyev, he steeled himself for the shock of seeing him across the chasm of sixteen years. "Colonel Andreyev," he said brightly, "Herr Doktor Direktor tells me it was your idea for this lovely breakfast and the opportunity to talk with colleagues from around the world."

Aleksei's voice stalled like the engine of a car left too long in the cold.

*How is it possible?*

After an awkward pause, his voice turned over. But even as he responded to the guest of honor, then to the director of the clinic, questions buzzed in his brain like annoying insects. . .

*How could there be such an uncanny likeness to Kiril without my being aware of it? Why didn't the Brenner file tip me off? What did I miss? Were there no file photographs?*

He frowned, trying to remember, and then realized he *had* ordered a photograph from New York. Some bungler from the Soviet News Agency must have forgotten to wire it. He shook off his annoyance just as another door opened.

Chancellor Dmitri Malik entered the room and looked at Brenner with a benign smile.

Brenner paled.

*The bastards have double-teamed me. Whatever game they're playing, it looks like I'll have the answers sooner than later.*

Taking a conveniently empty seat next to Brenner, Malik said, "I understand you served in Germany during the Great Patriotic War."

"Yes, as a matter of fact. Seventh Army. I was very low on the totem pole. A mere sergeant," Brenner said with a self-deprecating smile.

How bored you sound, Dr. Brenner, Aleksei thought, pulling out his pipe. And Mrs. Brenner? Genuinely bored. Even if she has no interest in war stories, she should be *very* interested in this one.

"I'm curious," Dr. Brenner," Malik said. "Where were you when the war ended—and when?"

"Berlin, 1945."

"I thought as much," Malik responded, as if warmed by the pleasure of reminiscence. "Odd, the things one remembers and the things one forgets. For me, the battles are a complete blank. Yet I recall with fondness some of the weapons with which we won those battles."

Aleksei got his pipe going and said cheerfully, "Come now, gentlemen, enough of this wartime reminiscing."

The relief in Brenner's eyes was so transparent Aleksei

almost felt sorry for the poor bastard.

*Do you believe, my big fish, that you have wriggled off the hook so easily?*

"But I, too, spent time in Berlin after the hostilities, serving with Chancellor Malik years before our East German comrades implored him to accept the prestigious position he currently holds."

The array of physicians, initially disinterested, were warming to the three-way conversation, intuitively sensing that there was more happening than met the eye.

"So many tragic stories," Aleksei mused. "Some eighty thousand of my Soviet comrades died fighting to rid Berlin of the Nazi scum."

Aleksei paused as Brenner reached into his pocket for a cigarette, his hand surprisingly steady.

*I'm impressed, Brenner. Let's see how long it lasts.*

"I still have vivid memories of one story in particular. We ran up against a repatriation problem after millions of my fellow citizens had been kidnapped by the Nazis. But somehow a group of orphaned Ukrainian children—refugees from one of the Nazi death camps—became unwitting pawns in an exchange of favors between a Russian officer and an American GI. By the time the children were turned over to us to be repatriated to their homeland, they were in a frightful state, having been shunted from one place to another."

Aleksei paused to shake his head regretfully. To more fully enjoy Brenner's fixed stare at a vase of flowers on a coffee table.

"But those were chaotic times so no one thought to ease the transition for these innocents," he said softly. "No one reassured them that a soldier in a Russian uniform was a far cry from a Nazi one. As they were being led away for repatriation by Red Cross volunteers, seven of the children committed suicide."

Genuine gasps throughout the room.

"They leaped into the Havel River before anyone could stop them," he continued. "Of course, you Americans could hardly criticize our well-intentioned repatriation policy," Aleksei said, his eyes boring into Brenner's. "Many of our people were able to return to their homeland with official American help."

Adrienne had had enough. "You really are too modest about what America's 'official help' consisted of, Colonel," she said with acid contempt. "My country did indeed help your country repatriate over a million refugees. The program, if I'm not mistaken, was named Operation Keelhaul. I feel compelled to add that those unfortunates were so eager to be repatriated that many of them slashed their wrists, jumped off roofs, and dove out of windows rather than return to your Soviet paradise."

*Good girl,* Aleksei thought, aware that he and Malik were the only ones in the room enjoying the heavy silence and averted eyes. He looked pointedly at Kurt Brenner as if willing the man to read his thoughts.

*Now you know what to expect should your lovely wife discover your sordid past. Your options narrow, Dr. Brenner. Defect, and you keep your dark secret. Defy me, and that secret will be exposed—and not just to your wife. To people all over the world who admire and respect you.*

The director of the clinic glanced up as the door opened. Relief in his voice, he welcomed the new arrival. "Herr Roeder! Herr Ernst Roeder, ladies and gentlemen, here to take photographs for *Neues Deutschland.*"

Polite scattered applause followed.

Aleksei happened to note Adrienne's recognition of the name but had no time to speculate about it. Luka Rogov had tapped him lightly on the shoulder, then whispered something in his ear.

"I fear my presence here has been somewhat disruptive," Aleksei apologized to the room at large. "Please continue your discussion while I attend to a private matter."

As he stood up, he gestured toward Kiril. "I feel sure my brother, Dr. Kiril Andreyev, will enjoy reciting the new oath our young physicians take before entering the profession. It should make a fitting photograph for *Neues Deutschland,* Herr Roeder, especially if you write some of your inspiring copy to accompany it."

As Luka followed him out, Aleksei heard snatches of Kiril's monotone "—work in good conscience wherever the interests of society require . . . guided in all actions by the principles of communist morality . . . remember one's responsibility before the people and the Soviet State—"

Leaving the room, Aleksei tore open the envelope Luka had just been given by Lieutenant Barkov, not knowing what to expect from the microfilm in Stepan Brodsky's cigarette lighter.

Stunned at what the print revealed.

"May 1, Andreyev, U2, Summit, Walkout, Leverage, Berlin, Nuclear"—seven words, followed by a date. In the bottom left-hand corner, he thought he saw a few more numbers and what looked like a Chinese character, but they were so tiny as to be unreadable and of no significance compared to what *was* legible.

The significance of the words and what they implied was devastating. Aleksei had assigned Stepan Brodsky to work out security arrangements. But in order to do his job effectively, he *had* to be made privy to the U2-summit plan. Knowing he'd be in Potsdam, only a half-mile from the West across Glienicker Bridge, Brodsky probably hoped to expose the state secrets of the U2 summit's demise as a bargaining chip for exfiltration out of East Germany. The key words—only seven of them!—would have enabled him to recount the entire story.

But something must have gone wrong. Why else would he have made a run for the West side of the bridge?

Was anyone else in on the plan? Kiril, perhaps?

Aleksei quickly dismissed that possibility for three

compelling reasons. The first was geographical. Kiril wouldn't be allowed anywhere near Potsdam. The second was that Luka Rogov stuck to Kiril like flypaper—and for that matter, so did his lovely girlfriend, Galina Barkova.

Aleksei didn't linger on the third reason . . . even as he felt himself slipping into the first stage of the old terror. He refused to entertain the possibility that his own brother had committed treason because it would spell the end of his career, if not his life.

Gradually, Aleksei's survival instincts kicked in. Why not foist the blame on Colonel Emil von Eyssen? After all, Brodsky's defection attempt took place in East Germany. It was von Eyssen's responsibility to secure Glienicker Bridge. It made sense.

More important, it was plausible.

As for General Nemerov, Aleksei felt sure he could somehow finesse what he reported to Nemerov about the cigarette lighter's microfilm—especially if he could sweeten the pot with Dr. Kurt Brenner's defection.

Maybe, just maybe, he could get out of this mess with his skin intact.

As was his habit, Aleksei began talking aloud as he tried to organize the few facts he had. "If there's microfilm, obviously there has to have been a camera of some kind. Who had access to one? What did it look like?"

Luka tapped his shoulder. "A flat, metal thing?" he asked.

*A miniature camera. Of course!*

"You saw somebody with one, Luka?"

"American lady keep one inside her pocket book. Is there every time I search. She take pictures only with big camera. But soon as helicopter land, me and Barkova see her use small camera for first time."

"Go back inside and bring Galina Barkova to me," Aleksei said.

The minute Galya stepped outside, the door swinging

closed behind her, Aleksei said, "Tell me everything you know about Brenner's wife using a miniature camera."

The bitch hesitated.

Aleskei glared at her. "*Now*," he snapped.

"It was when our helicopter landed on a plowed field—the mass grave where they bury traitors," Galya said, her voice hushed. "I told her not to."

"Go back inside," he said. "You have *two* people to watch from now on."

Aleksei waited a few minutes before reentering the clinic. Adrienne Brenner was engaged in what appeared to be a serious conversation with Ernst Roeder. Aleksei could not escape the thought of how the lady had recognized the mere mention of Roeder's name.

Everything clicked into place.

*What an amateur you are, Adrienne Brenner. You toss your anti-communist sentiments in my face, and then expect me to think you're here to see the sights and participate in a medical exchange program that clearly bores you? You play the part of the dutiful wife even though your husband is so flagrantly unfaithful you haven't lived with him for months? Shall I fit the pieces into my puzzle? From the microfilm to Emil von Eyssen's photographer brother-in-law to you to the CIA in a nice neat recapture of the ball that Stepan Brodsky fumbled.*

Over my dead body!

Aleksei gritted his teeth, a scissor-sharp pain making him long for numbness. He knew the signs. The old terror was accelerating.

When he managed to pull himself together, he played with the idea of pulling Luka off his brother and shadowing Ernst Roeder instead.

Much too obvious, he decided. If Roeder were alerted, he'd never make his move. Better to save Luka for a showdown in case Roeder proved to be obstinate.

He studied his most charming co-optee until she

cringed under the scrutiny. "From now on," he said *sotto voce*, "whenever Adrienne Brenner is not in her room, you will not let her out of your sight. That's an order."

* * *

It had been a few hours since Colonel Emil von Eyssen received a call from his man at the Schnellboot dock. The information was scant. Colonel Aleksei Andreyev had been on Glienicker Bridge and something had occurred— important enough for him to contact the East Berlin KGB station. A few hours later, the Vopos had recovered a cigarette lighter from one of their patrol boats and the lighter was now in Andreyev's possession.

Under von Eyssen's impatient questioning, the Vopo who surrendered the lighter to Andreyev confirmed he had been accompanied by a Soviet lieutenant, but, no, he did not get his name. Yes, Vopo personnel had conducted the search; but no, he did not know who had authorized it. Yes, the lighter had some kind of design on its metal case; but, no, he could not remember what it was.

With every answer, von Eyssen had become more frustrated. He was certain of only one thing. What he *did* know was potentially fatal.

Air Force Lieutenant Stepan Brodsky had attempted to defect. He did not succeed because of the chaotic bloodbath on the bridge. But the summit had dissolved just *before* Captain Brodsky had made a run for it—and that's when Brodsky had been spotted talking to von Eyssen's brother-in-law, Ernst Roeder. If Ernst *was* somehow complicit in the security leak, Colonel Aleksei Andreyev would find a way to lay it at von Eyssen's doorstep.

Unless he could buy Andreyev's silence?

Impossible. The man was impervious to every human feeling, even greed. He thought of the East German guard, killed on Glienicker during Brodsky's aborted escape and how Andreyev had reacted to the news with callous indifference.

Not that von Eyssen's superiors weren't equally indifferent. With the summit looming, word had come down from above. Keep the borders quiet. No incidents during the negotiations. None after they were over. None during the expected new round of talks when bold proposals by the Soviet Union would be tossed on the bargaining table for the first time.

Von Eyssen's jaw clenched as he relived the criticism that had been heaped on him by his superiors—and worse, by the likes of Aleksei Andreyev. What should he have done, allow some Soviet swine to escape and peddle his espionage wares to the West? The Soviets this, the Soviets that—and to hell with the Germans. Potsdam wasn't even in his normal jurisdiction!

How carefully, how cautiously, he had nurtured his career. No sacrifice had been too great, not even the humiliation of being patronized by inferiors. Soviet barbarians who raped, not just our women, but our country! That the Soviet Motherland *had* plundered twenty billion dollars' worth of German industry by calling it "reparations" never ceased to enrage him.

But there would be a day of reckoning. A day when Germany's leaders, East *and* West, were replaced by men of vision and courage, he brooded. He would be ready for that day, his record spotless, his career intact.

Von Eyssen rose, walked to a floor-length mirror, and stood at rigid attention. The reflection that stared back was, as always, reassuring. White-blond hair and azure-blue eyes. Tall and broad-shouldered. Neat green uniform adorned with medals. A true Aryan . . .

The man of the future.

Colonel Emil von Eyssen clicked his heels, did a smart about-face, and cleansed of fear and anger, returned to his desk.

Where a pile of photographs rested placidly. Von Eyssen forced himself to leaf through them again. A face loomed with each name, like a roll call. *This one is in no position to betray me. That one is, but would not dare. This one has no access to classified information. That one used to, but not anymore.*

And his brother-in-law?

*Damn you, Frieda!*

He could hear his sister's voice as if it were yesterday.

"My husband must have an important position in life, Emil. The kind that allows us to mingle with important people. And besides," she pouted, "Ernst happens to be very talented. He takes such beautiful photographs."

*And I gave in to her,* von Eyssen groaned.

He put through a call to his sergeant, who had just returned from tailing Roeder. "From now on," von Eyssen told him, "I want my brother-in-law under twenty-four-hour surveillance."

# CHAPTER 34

Everything was in readiness for the high point of the Humboldt University medical conference. The amphitheater was standing-room only—physicians, nurses, medical students, staff members, journalists, even some of the idly curious.

The elderly patient, unconscious on the operating table, lay between a sheet and a hypothermia mattress that had lowered his body temperature to the required coolness. Doctors, nurses, and technicians were stationed around the table. Behind them, in customary white smocks and masks, were four honored guests: Dr. Mikhail Yanin, Dr. Kiril Andreyev, nurse Galina Barkova, and Mrs. Adrienne Brenner.

A technician sat placidly at the controls of a heart-lung machine.

The chief surgeon, an East German of excellent reputation, leaned over the patient. Making an incision from collarbone to diaphragm, he sawed through breastbone, spread open the rib cage to expose a gleaming fibrous membrane laced with blood vessels—the pericardial sac.

As if on cue, at that precise moment Dr. Kurt Brenner entered the operating room from a side door. He walked to the table, held out a gloved hand for an instrument, and with a quick deft movement in what seemed a split second, cut open the pericardial sac to reveal the patient's heart. There were murmurs of approval from many in the audience, a scattered clapping of hands. A woman in a green operating smock high in the amphitheater murmured, "Bravo, Maestro."

With quiet authority, Dr. Kurt Brenner began issuing orders in German that would stop the heart and delegate its indispensable functions to the heart-lung machine.

Brenner glanced at a balloon-like device hanging above the machine—and frowned.

Kiril Andreyev wondered how many other doctors had noticed, let alone figured out why Dr. Brenner was forced to work with a bubble oxygenator rather than the more efficient disc version he probably was accustomed to.

But there was something else. If it troubled Kiril, it *had* to bother the hell out of Dr. Brenner. The technician's responses to Brenner's orders were a touch too lethargic.

Still, Kiril reassured himself, the machine *had* taken over the patient's breathing. Everything seemed to be normal.

As the operation progressed, the only sounds in the room were those of the operating team, Brenner's occasional commands, the gentle whir of an electric motor as the patient's blood and oxygen were rerouted, and the repetitive blips of an electro-cardiac monitoring machine.

Adrienne, struck by the grace and economy of her husband's movements, glanced up at the mesmerized students—and was transported back to the balcony of another operating theater the first time she had watched Kurt assume responsibility for someone's life even as he was in full command of his own. She wished his parents could have been here, especially his father. Max would have been bursting with pride.

The hypothermia mattress signaled the gradual warming of the patient's body. He was injected with a drug to neutralize the effects of the anti-coagulant in his bloodstream. An electric shock jolted the patient's heart. The lifeline between human heart and heart-lung machine was about to be severed.

There seemed to be a collective holding of breath as everyone waited for normal contractions to begin. For the patient's heart to start beating on its own.

Nothing happened.

The eyes of every doctor in the room leaped to the technician in front of the control panel.

The man looked stunned—unable to react to Brenner's urgent commands.

Someone shouldered the technician aside. One hand whipped off dark glasses. The other shot out for the backup oxygenator, then reached for a bottle of fresh fluid to wash the lines of tubing free of blood and avoid fatal clots to the brain. Kiril Andreyev went to work, pausing only once—to exchange a glance, like a firm handshake, with Dr. Kurt Brenner.

The famous American surgeon could do nothing but massage the patient's heart . . . and wait.

In less than five minutes the waiting was over, the malfunctioning heart-lung machine once again ready to take the place of the patient's heart.

But too many valuable minutes had been lost. The operating team bent over the form on the table, going through motions everyone knew were as futile as they were routine. The patient was dead.

The amphitheater began to empty as one visiting doctor after another silently left the room. Dr. Kurt Brenner stood immobile at an operating table ringed with solemn faces, the operating team's masks now lowered.

Galya made her way toward Kiril to console him on

his valiant but unsuccessful race with the clock. He had retrieved his dark glasses and was about to put them on again.

But not before she saw that there was no redness, no trace of an infection in his left eye.

*There never had been!*

Her glance moved back and forth between two faces in the room—Kiril's and Dr. Yanin's—as she recalled Dr. Yanin's little joke that morning at breakfast.

"So, Kiril! What are you—a modern version of the Prisoner of Zenda? Don't try to bring literature to life by playing the King of American surgery just because you look like the man. I would hate to part with you."

I would too, Galya thought, realizing for the first time why Kiril had looked at her in Moscow as if he'd never expected to see her again.

\* \* \*

Kurt Brenner stared at the ceiling. He had locked himself in the bedroom of his hotel suite, not even bothering to make his excuses about missing lunch. He knew his East European colleagues understood and sympathized, having been told in advance that he invariably shut himself away on the rare occasion when a patient died while under his knife even though, like today, it wasn't his fault.

So why this acute anxiety?

He wasn't quite sure, but he could make an educated guess.

In recent years he'd begun to cultivate his reputation on a broader scale, making round after round of media appearances coast to coast and abroad. Being interviewed, feted, lionized—

Unbidden, the thought of a renowned publicity-loving pianist of his acquaintance came to mind. The man had admitted approaching the stage with trepidation whenever he had neglected his practicing . . . fearful, he'd admitted, of blowing the performance.

So when Adrienne tapped gently on the bedroom door—closed even to her—and in a voice thick with genuine sympathy told him she was going for a walk, it wasn't her voice he clung to, but the awe in heart surgeon Dr. Mikhail Yanin's voice earlier in the day as he turned to his colleagues and announced: "Dr. Kurt Brenner can accomplish in forty-five minutes what it takes most surgeons two hours to attempt!"

# CHAPTER 35

Kiril chose a grouping of chairs near the hotel lobby's only row of telephone booths to the left of the bank of elevators. As he took the end chair, Luka Rogov sank heavily into the next one. Kiril had deliberately skipped lunch because of the cafeteria just off the lobby. If Rogov got hungry enough . . .

He eyed the telephone booth almost wistfully. One call and he would know where he stood.

What if Stepan's contact had moved away? What if he'd been caught?

The number Stepan had made him memorize was less than a year old, he told himself. Surely nothing could have changed in so short a time.

He leaned forward in sudden anticipation. Adrienne Brenner had just emerged from an elevator and was heading in his general direction.

But as she walked past without noticing him—intent, like everyone else in the lobby, on some urgent errand of her own—Kiril sat back again, eyes lowered in disappointment.

\* \* \*

"Yes, Colonel." Galya hung up the receiver, reached for her purse, and rushed down the corridor, propelled by a gust of nervousness. Keep in mind what this means for your future, she told herself.

*Not that I have any choice—not anymore.*

She stepped quickly into an express elevator. As soon as the door slid open, she spotted Kiril. Her first inclination was to tear across the lobby and tell him what she suspected—desperate to hear him tell her that it wasn't true. But all she had time for was a smile and a wave as she hurried through the lobby and into the street. And not a moment too soon. Adrienne Brenner had just crossed the plaza and was about to enter a ground-floor shopping arcade.

Adrienne checked her watch. Three o'clock sharp. Sauntering past a refreshment booth, she paused to watch a woman as she arranged thick meat patties on a large iron grill.

"Would you care to sample one, Mrs. Brenner?"

She turned. "Herr Roeder! How nice to see you again." She gestured at the tray. "I'm really not hungry."

"Perhaps I can tempt you with a drink?" He tilted his mug so she could see the pink liquid inside. "Weisse mit schuss. Beer and raspberry juice. It's especially popular with Berliners in the summer."

She smiled. "I'm game—even if it *is* the color of bubble gum."

They sat down at a small table. As he signaled a waitress, she saw that his hands really were enormous. Maneuvering a miniature camera had to be child's play compared to what she'd been going through.

"How do you like it?" he asked.

"Refreshing," she said. It really was.

"Do you have children, Mrs. Brenner? If so, might I suggest a souvenir of some kind?"

"No children. Just a couple of nephews. What did you have in mind?"

"Wooden toys from the Czechoslovak Socialist Republic." He led her to a toy counter and picked up a wooden figure. "Look at the labor that has gone into this. See how easily you can move the tiny limbs about?"

"Looks very flexible. How is it done, with elastic?"

But he was no longer examining the toy. His eyes scanned the arcade's long, uncrowded aisles.

"So once again, Paul Houston is poised to expose the dark side of your country's State Department," he said, his voice low.

*Not just the State Department, Herr Roeder, she thought. Our mutual friend, Paul Houston, may be CIA.*

Aloud, she said, "I gather Paul Houston has more in mind than just avenging Stepan Brodsky's death."

Roeder nodded. "Soviet-American negotiations are in the making as we speak. New concessions to the Soviet Union head the agenda. Paul Houston's revelations about the sham summit in Potsdam last year will shatter them," he said with a guarded look around. "It was Stepan Brodsky who fed him the information."

"Is that what the microfilm in Brodsky's lighter was all about?"

"It was a trade—or so Stepan hoped. But after the State Department balked, he made a last-ditch attempt to escape—an impossible gamble. Even so, he came close to beating the odds. Did Paul mention how he spent his last seconds on earth?"

"No," she said gently, remembering that Ernst Roeder had been a friend of Brodsky's.

Roeder's eyes were moist even as his hands were clenched in anger.

"Stepan dragged himself forward, inch by excruciating inch, until with one outstretched hand, he pushed his lighter over the side of Glienicker Bridge."

"Do you know why?" she asked.

"Only from what Paul told me afterward. Stepan wanted to keep the identity of a close friend from falling into the wrong hands."

Wincing at the image in her mind, she asked him about the lighter.

"An ordinary American lighter—Zippos, you call them— with an emblem on one side. Black wings of some kind."

"What happened to the friend, I wonder?"

"I have also wondered. I never knew his name. Just that he would try to buy his way out of the Soviet Union."

"How?" she asked, intrigued.

"With the microfilm in a cigarette lighter identical to Stepan's."

Microfilm as good as buried in Moscow, Paul Houston had told her in a burst of frustration . . .

Roeder's eyes made one last sweep of the arcade. "And now I think it the better part of wisdom to conclude our business."

He signaled a saleswoman at the far end of the toy counter. "You will find what you expect wedged behind the left leg of one of the figures. I cannot vouch for its quality, mind you. Even with high-speed film, there were floodlights instead of a flash. I had to shoot quickly—and with a miniature camera. Come," he said, "I will walk you out."

He handed her the wrapped package as if it were nitroglycerine.

*As if, at any moment, it might explode in his face.*

Adrienne took hold of his arm protectively.

Standing at the far end of the arcade, Galya saw the prominent East German photographer hand a package to Adrienne Brenner—the signal she'd been waiting for.

*If Mrs. Brenner meets with the photographer, Ernst Roeder, and if anything passes between them—anything at all—get word to me immediately.*

Stepping into a phone booth, careful to avert her face as Adrienne Brenner and Ernst Roeder left the arcade together, Galya pulled the booth shut, inserted a coin, and dialed.

Adrienne was talking animatedly, half-turned in Ernst Roeder's direction as they walked down the aisle of the arcade, when Roeder froze.

Luka Rogov stood in the doorway of the arcade, blocking their exit.

"Get the hell out of my way," she told Rogov. "My husband and I are honored guests. You, on the other hand, are a poor excuse for a bodyguard. The man you're *supposed* to be watching isn't even here."

Hopeless, she thought. Dr. Andreyev spoke only Russian to his "shadow." On the few occasions she'd heard Rogov expand on his vocabulary, it was delivered in cave-man English.

"Give me toys," Rogov demanded, reaching for the package.

"Go to hell, she hissed."

"Give it to him, Mrs. Brenner," Roeder urged.

Adrienne tossed the package on the floor so the goon would have to stoop to pick it up.

"You come with me." Rogov gripped Ernst Roeder's arm.

"Let go of him, damn you!"

"Please, Mrs. Brenner. It's all right, I will be all right," Roeder said.

Despite the unmistakable terror in his eyes, Adrienne knew she had no choice. She stepped aside. "I'll see you later, Herr Roeder," she promised, knowing damn well she might never see him again.

From the other side of the plaza, Galya watched Adrienne Brenner leave the arcade and head for the hotel while Luka

Rogov hustled Ernst Roeder toward a waiting limousine.

So it was the prominent photographer they wanted, not Adrienne Brenner . . .

I don't care, she told herself. If this Roeder has nothing to hide, he has nothing to worry about.

*But who doesn't have something to hide—especially from Colonel Aleksei Andreyev?*

I don't care, she repeated with uneasy defiance in a fruitless effort to convince herself.

Kiril would be alone now, she realized. For once, he was pried loose from his revolting bodyguard. She made a bee-line for the hotel.

As she stepped into the lobby, she relaxed. Kiril was right where she'd spotted him earlier—standing next to the row of telephone booths, although she couldn't tell if he was still waiting to enter the booth or if he'd just stepped out.

"Kiril," she called out with relief. "I *must* speak with you!"

"Not now, Galya, please. I have to—"

"But it's important. It can't wait."

"It will have to."

He walked out of the hotel.

She stared after him, thinking that she was nothing to him anymore. Not even someone to be courteous to.

*It's not like him to be rude or insensitive*, an inner voice reminded her.

Because he has other things on his mind, she shot back. How foolish of him, how short-sighted. She had no choice now but to make a full report. For his own good, she added quickly, taking her cue from what Colonel Andreyev had told her at the outset. Men like Kiril needed to be protected from themselves.

But as usual, her inner voice had the last word.

*Protected how, Galina Barkova—and from whom?*

# CHAPTER 36

The limousine was spacious enough to accommodate four passengers—six, if the jump seats were used. Luka Rogov, enjoying the novelty of sitting in back, sprawled comfortably across two seats.

Ernst Roeder sat as close as he could to a window on the opposite side of the vehicle.

Rogov had upturned his military cap and rested it on one large knee. Chuckling, he began rolling the toy figures around inside the cap, clearly enjoying the sound of wood against wood.

As Roeder stared out the window, a trapped-animal look in his eyes, he automatically dug into his pocket for a small bottle and slipped a pill under his tongue. Barely ten minutes later, no longer able to evade the knowledge that his breathing was much too labored to be normal, he went back to the well and pulled out his pill bottle.

Luka Rogov's burly arm whiplashed across the aisle and caught Roeder's wrist in mid-air.

Ernst Roeder recoiled as if he'd been struck by a snake.

"Medicine," he said hoarsely in Russian. "It is

only medicine."

Luka sniffed the contents of the bottle, shrugged, then dropped the bottle into his cap with the wooden figures.

Roeder sat back and closed his eyes.

He was so ashamed. He had worked hard to prepare for this moment, to meet it without fear. He had calculated the risks well in advance, even preparing himself for the prospect of a firing squad. He could have left East Germany long ago but had chosen to remain—his way of defying his own countrymen and their obscene edicts on how he should live and what he should think!

A poor weapon, his stark photographs that graced the grim pages of underground publications, and now *Das Wort* whenever he could smuggle them out. But he knew that his way of fighting back had kept his spirits up all these years.

He knew also that defiance came with an inevitable price tag. It was time to pay up.

*But with dignity, Ernst, with dignity!*

Why couldn't he stop the palpitations? Why couldn't he forget a certain month and a year—May, 1945—from his mind?

Foolish question. The answer sat on the other side of the limousine.

He forced himself to look at the shaved head. The flat Mongolian face. Slanted eyes that gleamed at the sight of helplessness, of fear.

\* \* \*

Ernst Roeder's mother had warned him well in advance, even though he was eighteen years old and knew the score. In May 1945, Russians and Mongolians were turned loose on Berlin—the last stronghold of the Third Reich. What they found were mostly old people, women, and children.

The first thing Ernst did after his mother disappeared was to blacken his sister's face with coal dust. His mother had told him how all the women were doing it to make themselves ugly to the Soviet soldiers.

But his sister hated the coal dust. Complaining that it was itchy, she kept rubbing it off. So he made her wear a pair of his trousers—the baggiest he could find—and as a further precaution, he hid her long blonde hair under a cap.

But his sister was fourteen and her figure was becoming harder to disguise. So he kept her with him constantly while he foraged for food, afraid to let her out of his sight.

He had found a vacant cellar months ago and managed to rescue a dilapidated mattress from a garbage dump, scrubbing it clean with rags. His sister slept on the mattress. He slept nearby on hard cement.

He had trained himself to be a light sleeper—to bolt upright at the sound of a slight noise—and was proud of the fact that he awoke early each morning so the two of them could go on the hunt for food, water, clothing—anything that could help them survive.

But one night, weakened from lack of decent food the last few days, he overslept. He was sleeping soundly when he heard a string of Russian curses followed by boisterous laughter. As he bolted upright, he gagged on the overpowering smell of fish, sweat and leather in time to see his sister stir in her sleep, her cap loosening a long golden strand—

They went at her like a wolf pack, tearing at her clothes, smothering her screams with their laughter.

Roeder flung himself at these savages in soldiers' uniforms, but he was knocked aside, his head smashing into concrete.

Dazed, sobbing, he kept calling his sister's name.

He was still calling it after they left, but his sister wouldn't answer.

He stayed by her side and would not let her out of his sight. Not for five days.

After that, he buried her in a corner of the cellar.

\* \* \*

Ernst Roeder removed his glasses and wiped his forehead and upper lip with the back of his hand. "Please," he said, "let me have one more pill."

Rogov ignored him.

Twenty minutes later Roeder's agitation subsided even without his medication. He had been driven to an unpretentious little house and taken up a flight of stairs and into a room that was half kitchen, half parlor. He was grateful for the overstuffed chair he'd been offered.

There was nothing threatening about Colonel Aleksei Andreyev, who sat opposite him—probably not a good sign. Andreyev's reputation preceded him, Roeder having been in his presence more than once. Even so, he thought it polite of the colonel to speak to him in colloquial German.

"—so in order to save us both time which, for me at least, is essential," the colonel was saying, "I will tell you what I already know, and you will then tell me what I do *not* know. I know that you are in the business of selling secrets to the West. I know that one of your partners-in-treason was Stepan Brodsky. I know that the two of you conspired to pass certain information to our enemies regarding the summit negotiations and that your partner was planning, for reasons not yet clear to me, to deliver what I have reason to believe was only a first installment."

He held up Stepan Brodsky's cigarette lighter.

"Through my efforts, Brodsky's lighter has just been found."

He paused.

"It has recently come to my attention, Herr Roeder,

that you were about to finalize the sale—your backup copy of microfilm—with the help of an American courier. The lovely Adrienne Brenner."

He paused. Leaned forward to scrutinize Roeder's expression.

"The microfilm you concealed in the wooden toy you passed her is being developed as we speak," he said.

Roeder looked at the man incredulously. He hadn't the faintest idea what Andreyev was talking about. He reached into his pocket, his chest pain reminding him that he no longer had any nitroglycerine.

"Who else is involved in your little enterprise? Who are your contacts? I want the name of every person who has any knowledge of this affair."

"You can trust me," Aleksei said, sounding as gently forgiving as a father confessor. "I can help you. We can help one another."

Roeder opened his mouth but no sound came out. A sudden fog had rolled into his brain and he lost his bearings in it . . .

Where to begin? How to explain that yes, he *was* involved, but not in the way Colonel Andreyev was suggesting. The microfilm in the wooden toy had nothing to do with espionage.

"You are wrong," were the only words he was able to form out of the fog.

Aleksei took hold of Roeder's arm and led him into the kitchen area, motioning for Luka to follow. He led Roeder to an open door.

"I wish I had time to play the usual cat-and-mouse games, Herr Roeder, but unfortunately you are not a man I can afford to detain too long. Not until I have something incriminating in hand. A confession would do nicely. For that I must rely on my associate, Luka Rogov."

Luka Rogov advanced like a tank edging into battle.

"Luka does his best work in a cellar. Of course if you

were to cooperate—"

*A cellar.*

Roeder screamed without sound. Gasped, choking, in a futile effort to blot out the laughter—the screams.

*Sobbing, rocking in his arms, all bloody and broken, so lovely and golden, so still—*

One oversized hand began to claw at his chest.

# CHAPTER 37

Colonel Emil von Eyssen strode up to a parked car where his sergeant was waiting.

"Which house?" he rasped—and realized the man had noticed his agitation. "My poor brother-in-law has a history of heart disease—scarlet fever," he explained. "You remember how it was in Berlin right after the war. Prolonged stress. Malnutrition. How long have they had him?"

"A quarter of an hour, not counting the time he was in the limousine. It's that house over there," his sergeant said, pointing.

"Wait here unless I call you," von Eyssen said in a tone that substituted for clenched teeth.

He headed for the house in rapid strides. Took the steps two at a time. Kicked at the front door with his boot. They have had no time, he told himself. They cannot have a confession yet.

A scowling Luka Rogov opened the door.

Von Eyssen rushed in. Ernst was on the floor, Andreyev kneeling beside him, holding his brother-in-law's wrist.

*Taking his pulse?*

Aleksei dropped Roeder's wrist and stood up. "I've been expecting you," he said. "I'm afraid there's been a regrettable accident. Your brother-in-law has had a fatal heart attack."

"Brought on by your so-called interrogation, no doubt." von Eyssen glared pointedly at Luka Rogov. "You tortured him."

"I assure you, he was not tortured," Aleksei said calmly.

"I don't believe you. Do you have any idea how young my brother-in-law was? He may have looked older—he had a history of scarlet fever—but Ernst was only in his mid-thirties. We were about to celebrate his 34th birthday. You have made my sister a widow," he said hotly.

"You're bluffing," Aleksei retorted. "The fact that you're here—and so quickly—tells me you know there's been a security leak."

"I do," von Eyssen admitted, unwilling to say more.

"What you *don't* know," Aleksei said caustically, "is that ultimately I located Stepan Brodsky's cigarette lighter. The microfilm inside was intact. The prints of the film I obtained from your late brother-in-law are on their way here. They will prove that Ernst Roeder was a traitor and a spy. That he was about to deliver a backup copy to Adrienne Brenner, who in turn intended to courier the microfilm to the CIA—information about the Four Power summit."

Stunned by Andreyev's revelations—microfilm, backup copies, Dr. Kurt Brenner's wife a courier who passed sensitive information to the CIA—von Eyssen managed to mutter, "You are mistaken. The security leak originated in your office, not mine."

Aleksei gestured to a chair. "Shall we both reserve judgment until the jury arrives?" he said snidely.

Von Eyssen's expression was one of disdain, as if to say, Why should I lend myself to this charade? But he sat down.

The doorbell rang. Aleksei stopped Luka with a glance

and went to answer it himself. He took an envelope from the uniformed messenger, and with the smugness of a poker player who raises his bet without looking at the last card dealt him, tossed the unopened envelope to von Eyssen.

Hastily tearing the envelope open, von Eyssen quickly scanned the photographs. Frowning, he went through them again slowly.

"But this is nothing," he said, genuinely puzzled as he waved the photographs in front of Aleksei's startled face. "Of what significance are a few harmless pictures of Stepan Brodsky on Glienicker Bridge? Or of a German border guard killed at the midpoint? As a matter of fact, Ernst photographed the border guard on *my* orders—a kind of consolation prize for the widow. As for the photographs of Air Force Captain Stepan Brodsky, he was Russian, not German. As I've said all along, he is *your* problem, not mine."

Aleksei grabbed the photographs out of von Eyssen's hand and studied them. His brain reeled, unable to process the knowledge that his nearly airtight theory was fallacious. That he was left with more questions than facts. Because Brodsky *had* worked for him, his traitorous actions, together with his aborted escape attempt, were indeed Aleksei's problems!

But if Roeder hadn't been spying, what in hell had he been up to? Where did Adrienne Brenner and her trusty Minox fit into the puzzle? Most important, who was Brodsky's Russian confederate?

Von Eyssen stuck his head out the window and yelled for his assistant.

"You have killed a prominent citizen of the Deutsche Demokratische Republik, my dear Colonel," von Eyssen said in a voice filled with triumph. "You murdered him in a crude attempt to cover up your incompetence and the treason of one of your own people. I will not allow you to point the finger of suspicion—"

Von Eyssen's assistant burst into the room, revolver drawn.

Aleksei continued to stare at the photographs, his expression that of a man who scrupulously follows a road map and ends up on a dead-end street.

"How many times have we Germans been encouraged to get on the hot line and call critical matters to the attention of our Soviet friends?" von Eyssen said caustically. "Rest assured that the wires between Berlin and Moscow are about to heat up. By tomorrow morning, you will be up to your neck in an investigation—your own."

"Before you do anything rash, Emil," Aleksei said—the personification of reasonableness—"there's something you should consider. You and I are in this mess together. It's in our self-interest to act accordingly. There's no getting past the fact that Stepan Brodsky almost pulled off a defection on your watch—and worse, that he managed to push a cigarette lighter with microfilm off Glienicker in order to protect the identity of god knows who. As for your brother-in-law, even if these photographs really *are* harmless, too many people in both East German and Soviet intelligence will continue to be suspicious about what may or may not have been going on between him and Adrienne Brenner."

"I hate to admit it, but you're right," von Eyssen said, scowling. "How do we get to the bottom of this?"

"We track down Brodsky's confederate, then handle it however we have to. Look, Ernst Roeder wasn't tortured. I used Luka as a threat—it's an effective interrogation technique of mine. That's why I conduct my interrogations in this house. That's why my co-optee's report to me here. But rarely have I ever had to go that far. Had I been aware of your brother-in-law's history of scarlet fever, I'd never have tried to frighten the truth out of him. My sincere apologies to your sister."

Von Eyssen nodded. "I believe you, Colonel."

"Under the circumstances, why don't you call

me 'Aleksei'?"

Von Eyssen clicked his heels and bowed slightly. "'Aleksei' it is. I'll arrange to have my brother-in-law's body picked up as soon as possible. As to our joint project, please keep me apprised. Let's go," he told his assistant.

As he was leaving the building, von Eyssen barely noticed the woman he passed on his way down the steps.

Galya stared after the imposing German officer, wondering what was going on. Something important, that much was clear. Maybe she should leave and come back later . . .

Stop procrastinating, she scolded herself. What you have to tell Colonel Andreyev is important too—and besides, he expects you. A matter of great urgency, you told him.

She came to a startled halt the minute she walked in the door. Cool, imperturbable Colonel Aleksei Andreyev pacing the room?

When she saw why, she gasped. Hand pressed to her mouth to choke off a scream, she whispered, "Is he . . . is Mr. Roeder dead?"

"What does it look like, a beauty nap?" Aleksei snapped.

Galya backed out the door cautiously. Eased her way down the steps and into the street. She'd gone half a block when she gagged, bent over, and threw up her lunch. After that, she walked at a snail's pace, unaware of distance or direction.

When she finally looked up, darkness was approaching. She found herself on a quiet residential street, deserted except for an old woman who was frowning over the flattened tire of a bicycle.

Galya sat down on an empty bench.

*Murderer. You are as guilty of killing Ernst Roeder as if you'd put a gun to his head and pulled the trigger.*

She examined her motives with ruthless unforgiving clarity, forcing herself to name what she had done, and why.

Envy, she thought bleakly. I envied Adrienne Brenner's good fortune when the woman's only "crime" had been kindness.

Jealousy. Sensing Kiril's attraction to Adrienne Brenner, she admitted for the first time that she had always known Kiril wasn't in love with her. What he felt for her was affection—no, more than affection. He brought to their relationship thoughtfulness and encouragement, a steady gentle optimism.

She let Kiril's face take form—let it hurt. In exchange for spying on her lover, for being Colonel Andreyev's most charming co-optee, she had focused only on the prospect of beautiful things, ironically immersing herself in ugliness.

*The least of what I owed you, Kiril darling, was loyalty.*

Another image began to form.

This time she squeezed her eyes shut to stop it.

But the body of Ernst Roeder sprawled on the carpet loomed . . . only it wasn't Roeder's body, it was Kiril's.

She shuddered violently, knowing she had been a breath away from delivering Kiril to Ernst Roeder's fate.

She approached the old woman who was still muttering over her disabled bicycle and pressed something into her hand. "I hope it brings you better luck," she said in faltering German.

The old woman would repeat the story endlessly to family and friends. How a Russian lady, with tears streaming down her face, made her a gift of a beautiful wrist watch made of *gold*.

# CHAPTER 38

The express elevator opened onto the 38th floor. Adrienne Brenner hurried through a deserted cocktail lounge, following the unmistakable sounds of a party. She stopped, caught by a view of the city. Her glance was drawn to a streamer of red lights blinking from the upper stem of a television tower—East Berlin's proud landmark. She could almost feel the pulse of the lights . . . like exposed heartbeats, captured and strung together. It reminded her of the amplified sound of a beating heart. Regular, rhythmic, followed by the terrifying sound of silence in an operating room and the pounding of her own heart. Poor Kurt . . .

She glanced at her watch as she hurried through the lounge and into the hotel banquet room. Every small table was full, every booth. A long table centered on a raised platform had only a couple of empty seats, the most conspicuous being the place of honor. She couldn't help wondering whether Kurt was *really* late because of his penchant for making an entrance. Even the television cameras looked impatient. As for the press—

She frowned at a small cluster of newsmen . . . and realized she'd been hoping to see Ernst Roeder in the press section.

A waiter wearing white tie and tails unceremoniously stuck a drink in her hand and walked off. Her throat was parched.

Annoyed with herself for smoking again after breaking the habit two years ago—not to mention the non-stop smoking she'd indulged in since she'd set foot in East Germany—Adrienne drank deeply. Her glass was empty for about a minute, two at the most, before a waiter refilled it.

She was wondering idly how one was supposed to distinguish the waiters from the guests since everyone was wearing a tux when she happened to look up. *Not* everyone. Dr. Andreyev, wearing his tired-looking blue suit, broke away from a conversation, made eye contact, and crossed the room toward her.

There it was again, she thought. He had a way of moving that invariably made her think of a coiled spring . . .

"Good evening," Kiril said with a faint smile.

His tone made her suddenly conscious of her evening gown—pale green, with a faint suggestion of silver. Of how weightlessly cool she felt in a fabric that enveloped her like a wave.

Returning his smile, she signaled a waiter for a refill.

"For me as well, please," Kiril told the waiter. "Where is our guest of honor?"

"Fashionably late, I'm afraid," Adrienne replied without thinking. She sighed. "I shouldn't have said that. My husband has always taken it hard on the rare occasion when a patient dies."

"Everyone in our operating theater reacts the same way, from Dr.Yanin on down," he said soberly.

She studied him for a moment. "Since Kurt shut himself in, he's had no opportunity to thank you for jumping into the breach. I'm very grateful for what you did."

He sat down. "Albeit unsuccessfully," he said, an edge in his voice as he pictured the lethargic second-rate technician . . . the outmoded bubble oxygenator . . . Once Dr. Brenner had accepted the invitation, there'd been plenty of time to order a disc version.

Their champagne arrived. They finished it off in companionable silence. "On a more pleasant note," Kiril told her, "the only thing that's left on my itinerary before you and your husband leave for West Berlin is a private goodbye. May I come to your suite later this evening?"

"Yes, of course."

"Good. Please tell him to expect me. Cigarette?"

"Why not."

He offered her one, took one himself, and tried in vain to keep the cheap East German match from sputtering and going out. He was about to try again when Aleksei entered the banquet room and scanned the center table, obviously looking for Kurt Brenner. Kiril waved Aleksei over. "Why don't you join us? I'm sure Dr. Brenner will be down soon."

"I hope you're right." Aleksei glanced around. "Quite a mob scene. Every waiter seems like he's on roller skates. Get refills for you and Mrs. Brenner, will you? I'll have vodka. Tell the waiter not to bother with a glass."

Kiril grinned. "Message received. I'll be right back with a bottle."

"No need to hurry, Little Brother," Aleksei said with a sly smile. "I've got a head start on both of you."

Adrienne giggled. "I beg to differ, Colonel." She started to weave in her chair.

Kiril caught her just in time. "Coffee for you," he said.

"I'm no spoil sport," she pouted. "Besides, it's Kurt's fault. He should be here by now."

"True enough," Aleksei said as Kiril took off after a waiter.

Aleksei sat back, preoccupied. Absently turning a

cigarette lighter over and over in one hand, he noticed Adrienne Brenner's unlit cigarette and leaned forward to light it.

She almost fell off her chair.

*An ordinary American lighter—Zippos, you call them . . . black wings of some kind. But Ernst, what on earth are they doing on Colonel Andreyev's lighter?*

When Kiril returned with the coffee, Adrienne ignored it and reached for her champagne. As Colonel Andreyev held up his bottle and the three of them shared a toast of some kind, her thoughts were so jumbled she could only marvel at his capacity to imbibe liquor without his head falling on the table! Actually, on closer examination, he *did* look bleary-eyed. But then she probably did too. As for Kiril Andreyev, she thought, he was sipping the bubbly like it was ginger ale!

Aleksei glanced at this watch, stood up on surprisingly steady feet, and announced that it was time for him to leave.

"Where to?" Kiril asked.

"The Brenner hotel suite, as it happens."

"Please tell Kurt everyone's waiting," Adrienne said.

Aleksei looked faintly amused. "I'll be sure to give him the message."

* * *

The elevator's swift descent to the 21st floor was a good omen, Aleksei thought. Act swiftly and you checkmate von Eyssen. Pull this off and no matter what happened on Glienicker Bridge, you return to Moscow in triumph instead of disgrace.

The elevator slowed. When Aleksei stepped off, Major Dmitri Malik was waiting in the foyer.

Kurt Brenner, looking refreshed and elegant in an

impeccably tailored tuxedo, opened the door to his suite much as a genial host welcomes dinner guests. Although he showed them an untroubled face, both Malik and Aleksei were trained to see below the surface, and what they saw was extreme anxiety. Both men sat down.

"Have your people gotten rid of the bugs?" Malik asked.

"Of course," Aleksei assured him as he motioned Brenner to a chair facing theirs and pushed a heavy glass ashtray to the center of the table. On his own side of the table, Aleksei placed a bottle of vodka. A connoisseur of wine, Malik limited himself to smoking. Aleksei reached across the table for the vodka, though in deference to his superior he used a glass.

"What's this all about?" Brenner asked with a combination of impatience and hauteur, determined not to let them see even a hint of fear. "The phony invitation. The use of your names. The allusion to 1945 and the Ukrainian kids. Frankly, I'm beginning to wonder if the malfunction of the heart-lung machine was no accident. I wouldn't put it past the two of you. And what's this 'Chancellor' business, Dmitri?"

"Ah, Doc, Doc," Malik sighed, warming to the business at hand. "Let's just say that my administrative position at the oldest university in Germany—East *or* West—is a convenient platform from which I can oversee goals important to the national security of both the Motherland and, hopefully, the East German government. Suffice to say, I continue to be KGB and I still outrank Colonel Andreyev. But while I readily admit that what we're about to propose was his idea, I should add that I approve wholeheartedly of the steps he's taken."

Making an effort to look nonchalant, Brenner said, "What ideas, gentlemen? What steps?"

Malik indicated a small briefcase which Aleksei had placed on the floor near his chair. "Colonel, please show Doc the 'artifact' we've been saving these many years."

Aleksei put out his cigarette, opened the briefcase, and removed a large square box that dangled an electrical cord. Placing the box on the coffee table, Aleksei plugged the cord into the nearest outlet.

Brenner's heart sank. He recognized the wire recorder. It was a World War II predecessor of today's newer tape version. "God in heaven," he whispered as if he were alone in the room, realizing that Malik and Andreyev must have recorded him when he sold out the Ukrainian children.

Unless they were bluffing. Even if they weren't, maybe he'd been careful not to incriminate himself. Or maybe a wire recording this primitive could not survive the last fifteen years.

As if Malik were a mind-reader, he said, "No, Doc, we are not bluffing. And yes, a fifteen-year-old wire recording can indeed pass the test of time." Smiling broadly, he stood up.

But instead of leaving, Malik leaned against the doorway with folded arms—as if, after all those years, he couldn't resist witnessing Brenner's frantic response to the blackmail.

Aleksei tossed back his glass of vodka in a single gulp, activated the recorder with the spool of wire . . . and released the past.

When it was over, Malik left the suite, as if he'd lost interest in what was to follow.

The first words that spilled from Brenner's mouth were, "Name your price, Colonel."

"Name your price," Aleksei repeated, parroting Brenner. "Save your money, *Doc*. We have something else in mind. We want you to defect to the Soviet Union."

Brenner shot to his feet. The idea that he would agree to spend the rest of his life in some squalid Communist dictatorship was so far removed from his rational zone of reference that he could only stare.

Aleksei shifted gears immediately, recognizing his

mistake. *All stick and no carrot . . .*

"Your reputation precedes you, Dr. Brenner," he said, feeding admiration in his voice. "You're a humanitarian. Think how your considerable talents would be a boon to us. Think of the challenge! And let's not forget your financial difficulties of late," he added, managing to sound both pragmatic and solicitous.

"You're delusional!" Brenner said, incredulous. "You expect me to leave my country for good, just like—like switching off a light bulb?"

"It need not be forever," Aleksei said, recalling Kiril's suggestion about turning this particular issue into a bargaining chip.

"You want me to desert my institute for, what—a couple of years? You want me to abandon my parents? My wife?"

*Back to the stick.*

"As to your charming wife, Adrienne, only a few hours ago she committed a serious crime against the German Democratic Republic, possibly against my country as well. I'm in a position to have her detained for taking photographs of a national security nature. Rest assured that I *will* detain her if you refuse my terms."

"Terms? What terms?" Brenner asked shrilly. "You lose nothing. I give up everything!"

Aleksei smiled. "You capitalists believe in negotiating, do you not? Lend the Motherland a few years of your life. In return, I guarantee to keep your reputation intact so that ultimately you can reclaim everything you have lost. Refuse us—" he paused while he practically obliterated the remnants of his last cigarette, "and I promise you the consequences will be permanent."

As he headed for the door, Aleksei couldn't resist one last jab. Resting one hand on the doorknob, he said, "They tell me you are an imaginative man in the operating room, Dr. Brenner. Imagine this, then. Picture your colleagues, your family, your friends—everyone who admires those capable hands of yours for their capacity to save lives. Now picture those same people unable to look at your hands without seeing a permanent stain—the blood of innocent children."

His superior having left the scene, Andreyev ignored the glass and drank from the bottle of vodka.

"The clock is ticking, Dr. Brenner. Don't keep me waiting too long. Don't keep the press and the television cameras waiting."

# CHAPTER 39

Kurt Brenner stared at his image in the bathroom mirror. "I am Dr. Kurt Brenner," he asserted, as if someone were challenging that fact. "I am not—I *will* not—be intimidated."

His image, haggard-looking, was unconvinced.

"They *cannot* destroy my career."

The image said they could.

"They'll never get away with it! In a showdown, people will believe *me*, not them."

The image looked doubtful.

His glance shifted to the coffee table in the next room, empty now except for a heavy glass ashtray. He strode over to it and sent the ashtray to the floor in a cloud of ashes.

Brenner sat down at the table and slowed his breathing, something he did just before a particularly complex operation. He thought of it as his "sniper mode"—a perfect, nearly impregnable state of calm.

A World War II "artifact" and a sixteen-year-old conversation—who would take it seriously? Who would take the word of the KGB over the word—the vehement denial—of a prominent American heart surgeon?

*Who wouldn't take them seriously? These people have proof. Facts!*

Brenner thought of his own reverence for facts. How they kicked in the minute he stepped into an operating theater.

*Fact.* A clogged line in a heart-lung machine sends blood clots to the brain.

*Fact.* A patient five or six minutes off the machine will turn into a vegetable.

*Fact.* Every patient I operate on depends on *my* skills, *my* ability to choose without hesitation between life and death alternatives.

Now, ensnared in the worst crisis of his life, Brenner was caught between the unpalatable and the unthinkable. Defect to the Soviet Union? Ridiculous. See his past exposed, his career in a shambles? Never!

In the end, as in every major crisis in his life, he succumbed to the inevitable: the famous Dr. Kurt Brenner temper. What ignited the explosion was Andreyev's smug parting remark.

*"Picture your colleagues, your family, your friends, unable to look at your hands without seeing a permanent stain—the blood of innocent children."*

Brenner could picture it all too well. *His* hands, shaking as if he were some pathetic alcoholic with the DTs. How ironic, he thought with a tight smile. It was Andreyev's last-minute threat that had galvanized him.

Seizing the telephone, he spoke rapid German to the operator. The last thing he told her was to see that the message was delivered promptly to Colonel Aleksei Andreyev, 38th floor, banquet room. Slamming down the phone, he began tossing things into a suitcase.

\* \* \*

Shortly after Aleksei had rejoined the party and taken a seat at the table with Adrienne Brenner and his brother, a messenger handed him an envelope. He opened it, scanned it, and, without comment, handed it to Kiril.

Kiril never got past the first sentence. He had trouble masking his response.

*Dr. Brenner was leaving. Now.*

As he turned his chair slightly away to make sure Adrienne couldn't read the note over his shoulder, he realized it was unnecessary. She looked . . . spacey. Too much champagne on an empty stomach.

He read the rest of Brenner's note quickly. The tragic outcome of yesterday's operation had left Brenner "too despondent to cope with the remaining events of the conference—so much so that he planned to cancel next week's Medicine International symposium in West Berlin as well. Would Colonel Aleksei Andreyev please make arrangements for an immediate flight to Zurich so that he and his wife could join his parents there?"

"Let me see what I can do," Kiril said to his grim-faced brother in Russian. He hailed a waiter and ordered a gin and tonic with a twist of lime. "Brenner's drink of choice," he told Aleksei. "Perhaps a sympathetic talk with another physician will change his mind. Can you stall things a little longer?"

"Why not?" Aleksei said, straddling between cold fury and bleak despair as he reached for his now half-empty bottle of vodka.

Kiril took the down elevator to the 21st floor, stopping first to pick something up in his own room before heading to the Brenner suite.

He found Kurt Brenner in the bedroom, one suitcase packed, and another half empty. "Given the stress you must be under, Dr. Brenner," Kiril said evenly, "I thought you might need this."

He held up the gin and tonic.

"I won't need it much longer," Brenner snapped, continuing to pack. "If you're here to change my mind, you're wasting your time."

Kiril put the drink down on the coffee table in the other room. Without another word, he entered the bathroom, flicked on the light, and closed the door.

At the sound of running water, Brenner called out, "Don't bother trying to drown out our voices. Malik already made sure your brother debugged this place."

When the water in the sink turned brown, Kiril submerged his head one more time, toweled it dry, and stepped into the bedroom. Brenner, who was in the process of folding a sports jacket, looked up—and gaped.

"Don't be alarmed," Kiril said. "I know it must be a shock, our strong resemblance."

"How on earth could I have missed it?" Brenner murmured, as if talking to himself. "I thought your hair was as brown as those dark glasses you never seemed to take off— Ah, yes, an eye infection according to your girlfriend," he said drily, recalling Adrienne's confusion at the beach. "A non-existent infection, I gather?"

"Yes. Even Galya has no idea it isn't real."

"What else isn't real?" Brenner said snidely.

"Unlike yours, my hair really is dark brown. Before I left Moscow, I bleached it white, then used a brown rinse—a near-perfect color match. Look, call it coincidence, call it fate. All I know is that from the moment I saw your photograph, I knew I had a crack at the highest stakes in the world."

"What stakes, money? You want money when your KGB brother sneers at it?"

"I'm not after money either—but for different reasons than my brother Aleksei. I've been observing you closely ever since you stepped off the plane, Dr. Brenner. The way you walk. How you light a cigarette. The way your voice sounds when you—"

Brenner took a startled step back. "You're part of this outrageous defection plot, aren't you? What's next? *You* taking my place in front of the television cameras?"

It was Kiril's turn to look startled. "Haven't you paid any attention to what I've been saying? What I've been showing you and your wife ever since we met?" he said, exasperated. "The *last* thing I want is for you to defect. Everything I said and did was calculated to make you resist my brother's blackmail."

Brenner sat down on the edge of the bed. "I think I'll have that drink now, if you don't mind."

Kiril got it for him. "Look, I have no idea what Malik and my brother have on you. But whatever it is, it can't be worth the price they're asking."

"Then you'll help me?" Brenner said eagerly. "You'll stop them from revealing what they know?"

"I have no way to do that. Ironically, it's you who can help *me*. I'd planned to approach you later tonight before you left in the morning but—"

Brenner shot him a look of suspicion.

"Let me explain. I met with a man this afternoon who's agreed to help me defect—he has experience arranging such matters. Except for one thing. I need to borrow a passport. Yours, Dr. Brenner,"

Kiril pressed on doggedly, seeing that Brenner was about to refuse.

Brenner could only shake his head. "Preposterous" was too tame a word to describe his reaction. The idea that he would *loan* this Russian physician his American passport left him momentarily speechless.

"Look, as your tour guide I'll be in the limousine that takes you to the airport. Here's how it works. The East German Vopos check passports only once—at the departure area—after which passengers are handed boarding passes. Your pass and your ticket is all you'll need to board the Swiss Air flight to Zurich." He drew in a deep breath.

"Since you won't need your passport after that, you could easily slip it to me right before we part company. That way my contact can get me out of East Germany."

"And if something goes wrong?" Brenner asked, stringing him along because his instinct for survival had just kicked in . . . "What if I get tossed into some Commie jail? What's the penalty for helping people defect? Ten years? Twenty?"

"Why should the airport authorities deviate from established procedure?" Kiril countered. "And once you reach Zurich, let alone the United States, no one could touch you."

"Did you know your brother has some trumped-up charge against my wife in his bag of tricks?"

Kiril frowned. "I didn't know. Maybe he's bluffing. Has it occurred to you he could be bluffing about everything, including the blackmail?"

"It's no bluff," Brenner admitted. "They have proof. They showed it to me just now. I was very young . . . But your goddamn country—"

"Don't expect me to make excuses for people like Malik and my brother Aleskei," Kiril said with a tinge of bitterness. "I've been locked in a chamber of horrors my whole life. Did I say I was after the highest stakes in the world? What's more precious than a man's freedom? You take yours for granted. I expected that and it's right that you should, it's healthy."

"You sound just like my wife," Brenner retorted.

Kiril winced. Brenner hadn't meant it as a compliment. He made one last stab. "If I had been born in a free country, I would feel sympathy—no, empathy is the better word. I would want to help a man like me to break free of his chains if I could."

"You make a powerful case, Dr. Andreyev," Brenner said, aiming for sympathy—the correct word for *me*, he thought grimly. "I suspect anyone who grows up in America would have difficulty making real to himself what it's like to live in a dictatorship. It's no walk in the park, god knows. Maybe I *will* lend you my passport. It depends."

It was an eternity—it was a full thirty seconds—before Kiril could bring himself to ask, "Depends on what?"

"On whether you can convince me I won't be in any real danger of getting caught. My wife tells me that Mongolian thug seldom lets you out of his sight. You even share the same room. How were you planning to deal with him?"

"Infused diazepam—valium."

"Administered when?"

"When my 'shadow' is asleep. He'll stay that way for at least four hours. I have some diazepam in my room. And I'm sure I don't have to prove to another doctor just how fast the infused diazepam will kick in," Kiril said eagerly.

"It's a damned effective drug, all right. Next question. What happens if you run into trouble between here and the border? Were you able to smuggle in a gun?"

"No. They search us too well for that."

"I take it you have an alternative?"

Kiril smiled. "Morphine sulphate. I picked up a bottle of it, along with a hypodermic needle, in the clinic this morning."

"Powerful stuff. Your English is surprisingly good, Dr. Andreyev. Your American slang is even more impressive."

"What's the question?"

"Are you good enough to impersonate an American?"

"I've had long years of practice. They can't jam all the foreign radio broadcasts. Sometimes they don't even try."

"Your plan won't work."

Kiril felt as if he were on a roller coaster—up and down up and down He closed his eyes. "Why not?"

"Our hair. How can both of us walk out of here with white hair?"

"Oh, that," he said with a flood of relief. "What do you think I was doing in your bathroom? Washing the brown out of my hair."

"But do you have enough? What if you run out?"

"I won't. I had the foresight to fill an extra bottle with brown rinse. More than I'll ever need."

Brenner stood up, one hand gripping the iron bedpost for support, his decision made. "I have to go," he said.

"So what's the plan? You refuse to succumb to my brother's blackmail and insist on leaving tonight or—"

"Not quite. As soon as I finish packing, my plan is to see a man about a trade—mutually beneficial, of course," Brenner said softly. "Colonel Aleksei Andreyev hands off his damning evidence against me in return for my equally damning evidence about his brother's defection plan. In exchange for my silence about diazepam, morphine sulphate, and brown hair rinse, he'll hand over a primitive tape recorder and a spool of wire. The authorities here will never believe that Colonel Andreyev wasn't in on his own brother's escape plan. Brothers help each other."

Brenner's words were tumbling out one after another, as if he couldn't wait to get out of a room that threatened to suffocate him.

"You people don't operate on proof over here," Brenner said, avoiding eye contact. "All your intelligence apparatchiks need are suspicious circumstances. He's smart, your brother. He'll agree to *my* terms now."

"You know your man, all right. My brother Aleksei will frame me for something that can't possibly reflect on him. Then he'll have me shot."

"You're exaggerating. He's your own brother! You'd say anything to stop me."

And *do* anything.

Kiril caught Brenner off balance with a single blow.

# CHAPTER 40

The man with brown hair, lying on the four-poster in the bedroom of the Brenner suite, wore a shabby blue suit and dark glasses.

The man bending over him wore a dress shirt, a black bow toe, and a tuxedo. His hair was white.

The white-haired man straightened up, went into the bedroom, and examined himself in the floor-length mirror. His lips curved into a practiced smile—contemptuous, amused. With an impatient gesture, he brushed away a few rebellious strands of hair that had fallen onto his forehead before stepping back for a final appraisal.

Closing Adrienne Brenner's suitcase, still on the bed, he put the other suitcase in the closet. A gown and a bathrobe hung there, along with a raincoat and a woman's cape. He put on the raincoat, took the cape, and picked up Adrienne's suitcase.

He was about to shut the bedroom door when he spotted the glass on the bureau. Not much gin and tonic left, but the twist of lime was still there. He squeezed a few drops of lime juice into the half-sprawled man's left eye, once again adjusted the dark glasses on the comatose face, and did one last check No more brown spots on the neck. A small spatter of the rinse had washed off easily.

He picked up the telephone and dialed, bracing himself for the tense voice on the other end. "Sorry it took me so long," he told Aleksei in Russian. "I know I said I'd call right back, but things got a little unpleasant . . . No, nothing like that. Brenner's initial panic is over."

Kiril continued in Russian. " . . . Get ahold of yourself, Aleksei. You sound 'drunk as a skunk,' as the Americans say. Yes, he's agreed to everything. However, he has one precondition. Hold on. Brenner wants to tell you himself."

Kiril held the phone against his chest, wondering if Aleksei could hear the rapid beating of his heart. After a few seconds, he lifted the receiver as a string of American slang expressions flashed through his mind. "You win, Colonel," Kiril said in English, his voice more sonorous, and more than a little belligerent. "But get this straight. Any blackmail threats you people concocted against my wife are out of bounds. I'm taking Adrienne to Zurich out of harm's way. . . .Of course I'll be back! I can't afford not to, can I? It won't be forever, you said . . . . Right."

A pregnant pause.

"One more thing, Colonel. That 'unpleasantness' your brother alluded to just now? Forgive my crudeness, but it seems that ever since he laid eyes on my wife, he wanted to get into her pants. He's about to find out what I think of that offensive notion."

Hanging up before Aleksei had a chance to reply, Kiril grabbed suitcase and cape and rushed down an empty corridor to his room. After stuffing a few items into the suitcase, he hurriedly dumped the brown hair rinse bottle into a waste basket in the bathroom, along with the diazepam and the syringe, then covered the contents with soiled towels.

For a long moment, Kiril closed his eyes. The next thing

he knew, he was walking with brisk authority down the hallway toward an elevator in the characteristic stride he'd zeroed in on the moment Dr. Kurt Brenner had stepped off a plane in East Berlin.

When he realized that he'd begun to swing the suitcase as if it were a tennis racket, he felt a surge of adrenalin.

*Maybe, just maybe, I can pull this off!*

\* \* \*

Aleksei had left the table he'd shared with his brother and Adrienne Brenner and was huddled with the press contingent in a lounge just outside the banquet room. When Adrienne's husband headed for the table, Aleksei cast a suspicious glance at the suitcase in his hand.

"My wife's things. She's no part of this. Adrienne is not going anywhere near the Soviet Union. Given her political sentiments, I could barely get her to East Berlin," he said waspishly.

Aleksei made his way back toward the table out of earshot of the press, teetering slightly, as if he were crossing the deck of a sailboat.

"Where's my brother?" he asked.

"In the master bedroom—out cold on the bed. I trust you won't take it personally."

"I *always* take family matters personally but not in the way you mean. I picked up on my brother's attraction to your wife. Nor do I rule out the possibility that it was mutual," Aleksei added, unable to resist chipping away at Brenner's pride after all the trouble the bastard had put him through. "Romance aside, Dr. Brenner," he said, his words slightly slurred, "what will you tell your wife about your forced separation?"

"I'll think of something."

"Indeed. Is my brother badly hurt?"

"He'll wake up with an aching jaw and a good-sized lump on his cranium where his head hit the bedpost. Does that disturb you?"

"Actually, it pleases me." Aleksei downed a slug of vodka like it was water. "Kiril's independent nature has always needed a few hard knocks."

"I presume you have a limousine waiting?"

"A limousine to take you and your lovely wife to the airport, where you'll board an executive jet for Zurich. The same plane will return you and me to Moscow in the morning."

"Then let's get to it." He headed for the table where Adrienne Brenner sat leaning back in her chair.

Aleksei's hand shot out, stopping him in his tracks.

"I have my own precondition, Dr. Brenner. A group of extremely curious newsmen are waiting impatiently in the lounge. They're expecting to hear something out of the ordinary. Naturally, I cannot disappoint them. As soon as I invite them in, you will announce your intention to defect to the Soviet Union. *Then* you may escort your wife to Zurich."

"So that after I leave, it will be difficult for me to change my mind."

"Can you blame me? But you also benefit. Your parents are already in Zurich. Think of how your decision to take a—shall we call it a sabbatical?—in Moscow will soften the blow for them. By the time you reach Zurich, they'll have had time to absorb what happened. I will arrange everything. We have friends in all the key Western cities who will make sure the press is alerted."

"The ultimate argument, Colonel. The hostage game. And I'm not even on Soviet soil yet." Arching a contemptuous eyebrow, he said, "Very well. Let's get this over with."

"One last piece of advice. Your announcement can be as brief as you like. Just make sure it lacks the flavor of coercion. Keep in mind that a decision to defect is not made on the spur of the moment between cocktails and dinner."

"I'll do my best. Now if you'll give me a moment alone with my obviously inebriated wife . . ." Without waiting for an answer, he moved to the table and took Adrienne's hands in his.

She looked up at him. "Where've you been? Honestly, Kurt, making an entrance is one thing but . . . uh oh, I think I'm tipsy."

Gently, he pulled her to her feet. "I know you are, dear, and I'm sorry. We'll leave in about five minutes. Will you do something for me in the meantime?" he asked as he draped the cape around her shoulders.

She nodded, embarrassed by the state she was in. Disarmed by his uncharacteristic solicitude.

Noticing her suitcase in his hand, she said, "Where's yours?"

"Later. I have an announcement to make to some newsmen— something you won't *begin* to understand. But as soon as we board the plane, I'll explain. Until then I don't want these people to see your reaction. Mind waiting for me in the lounge outside? The press is about to come bursting in. The minute I finish dealing with them, we'll take the elevator down and a limo will take us to the airport. Okay?"

"Okay."

"Shall I call the newsmen in, Dr. Brenner?" Aleksei asked.

"How about a simultaneous transition? You open the doors for the press while I move my wife outside to that bench near the bank of elevators. She avoids pandemonium, you avoid distraction."

"Tit for tat. How American! Fine by me," Aleksei said with a shrug.

As Adrienne Brenner was escorted out, Aleksei waved the press in, cautioning Brenner to hold off while the lights and television cameras got ready to swing into action. That done, he signaled Brenner to mount the platform.

"Ladies and gentlemen," said the distinguished-looking white-haired gentleman, microphone in hand, "I think I have spoiled your dinner, or at least delayed it unconscionably, for which I deeply apologize. In that spirit, my announcement will be brief."

A good beginning, Aleksei mused.

"I have kept you waiting because I was in the throes of a difficult decision," he continued.

And paused to take a deep, almost labored, breath. "To better serve the humanitarian goals to which my professional life has been devoted, I have decided to practice medicine in the Soviet Union. For how long," he added quickly, "I am not yet certain. I'm sure you realize that a decision to defect, even for an indeterminate period of time, is not something one makes between cocktails and dinner."

Aleksei positively beamed.

"Suffice to say, my decision is the culmination of a great deal of soul-searching."

He stepped off the platform, fought his way onto the main floor of the banquet room, and was swept along by a frenetic tide of people. At least the tide was moving inexorably toward the exit.

Poor Adrienne was being engulfed by a rush of eager faces and unintelligible questions. Just before he got to her, a reporter flashed his press credentials in her face, and asked if she planned to join her husband in Moscow.

"No comment," she said, her expression dazed. "Please, I have nothing to say."

Seizing her arm, he propelled her to the bank of elevators—and got lucky. An elevator door slid open and the car was empty. He pressed a button and down they went.

*Not so lucky.* The elevator had slowed instead of going all the way down. Could they possibly be stopping on the same floor that housed what had euphemistically become known as "the Brenner Suite"?

* * *

Galya leaned against the elevator car, disheveled and in obvious distress.

*I must say goodbye to Adrienne Brenner before it's too late!*

The inner command had broken through her lethargy after she'd learned of the Brenners' imminent departure for Zurich. From her room on the same floor, she had managed to navigate the corridor, hoping against hope that they hadn't finished packing yet. If they had, maybe she could still catch them before they left the hotel.

She pressed the down button. The elevator hissed to a stop. The door opened.

A woman was inside, a man behind her, but Galya saw only Adrienne Brenner. Turning to her, she impulsively took hold of Adrienne's hands.

"You will please to forgive," she murmured. "I have answered your so wonderful kindness with insults. I am so ashamed."

Adrienne's eyes welled up. She pulled Galya into her arms, the two of them swaying slightly.

She half-turned as she heard the man's voice.

"My wife and I will never forget your many kindnesses, Galina Barkova, when you and *Kiril Andreyev* were our tour guides."

Galya froze at the sound of his words, his voice . . .

She looked into Kiril's face, then the white hair—

*Dear god in heaven, don't let me give him away! If Adrienne Brenner doesn't seem to recognize it's Kiril and not her husband, then neither does Colonel Andreyev . . .*

"Whatever you do, wherever you go, *Dr. Brenner*," she said softly, forcing the words past a barrier of pain because

240

she knew she would never see him again, "may it be with good luck and good fortune."

"You're very kind." Kiril reached for her hand and gently pulled her close—close enough to whisper against her forehead, "Goodbye, Galya dear. I will never forget you."

# CHAPTER 41

Galya was on the bed in her room when a voice cut into her thoughts.

"I think your services will soon be needed elsewhere, Galina Barkova."

Colonel Andreyev stood in her doorway.

"My brother is unconscious in the Brenner suite. I'll let him fill you in on the embarrassing details when he wakes up."

She stood up. "I'll go at once. What happened to him?"

"Can't you forget about your lover for two seconds?" he snapped. "This is a time for celebration."

One look at his bloodshot eyes and Galya realized that the Colonel had been celebrating to excess.

"Dr. Kurt Brenner has defected," he said smugly. "He just went public at a press conference. He's coming over to us as soon as he deposits his annoying wife in Zurich."

"Congratulations, Colonel!"

Her enthusiasm was forced. Her smile was not.

*And when this intelligence "coup" blows up in your face, may your superiors take it out on your hide.*

Minutes later, Galya was bending over the inert figure on the couch in the Brenner suite.

*Bravo, Kiril! You seem to have thought of everything, even down to the redness in Dr. Brenner's left eye.*

She opened Brenner's shirt. Sure enough, she found the thin scar she had lightly followed with her fingertip on the beach. As she rebuttoned the shirt, her hand shook a little as she realized it was Kiril's shirt.

*Get on with it.*

Straightening the tie, she raised Brenner's head and pressed both eyelids open. The pupils had shrunk to the size of pinpricks. She wondered what drug Kiril had used. Wondered how long it would last.

As she passed by the bedroom she glanced at the open closet door. She saw a few garments inside.

She saw a patch of beige.

A lovely gown the color of rich cream . . .

So you've left me a gift, after all, Adrienne Brenner. What an odd trick of fate that I no longer want it.

On the way back to her own room, she stopped outside Kiril's. The door was unlocked. The sight of the cheap suitcase, lying empty on his bed, was hard to bear.

Worse was a closet, because it *wasn't* empty. She touched the things he had left behind. A robe. A few shirts and a pair of shoes. The new gray trousers they had picked out together on the day before they had left Moscow for East Berlin.

*At least I've been spared the hardest thing of all. He never knew what I did. What I became.*

She took a last lingering look in case something incriminating had been left behind. In case Dr. Kurt Brenner woke up ahead of schedule.

Nothing.

She checked out the bathroom—a more purposeful examination this time . . .

Nothing on the metal shelf above the sink. Something

in the medicine cabinet maybe—a razor?

As she moved closer for a better look, her foot knocked over a waste basket. Stooping automatically to right it, she spotted an empty bottle—

A syringe had spilled onto the floor. Perfect.

*But did she have the courage to go through with it?*

*Her hand tightened on the syringe.*

Leaving the bathroom, she passed a long mirror over the four-poster bed and caught a glimpse of her reflection.

*Drab black dress that complemented the dark circles under her eyes. Hair pulled back, giving her the pinched dry look of a spinster—*

*No!*

She rushed down the corridor and reentered the Brenner suite.

A few minutes later, she stood once more in front of the long mirror, only this time she wore a cream-colored floor-length gown, her lustrous blonde hair swept down around her shoulders.

A glass of champagne in her hand, she tried to drink away her regrets, her desolation, her abject terror.

It took a while—an eternity—before all three disappeared.

It took what she herself set in motion as she walked about the room until she was quite breathless, head held high, arms slightly apart, stealing glimpses of herself in the mirror whenever she passed it.

Ending with a graceful pirouette.

She smiled one last time, indifferent to the tears because *this* time, her smile was right and true.

Then she returned to her own room.

* * *

*How still he is.*

Kiril should have revived by now, Aleksei thought.

Could someone remain unconscious for three hours from a simple blow on the head—even a concussion?

And where the hell was Galina Barkova?

He leaned over Kiril's body to press his fingertips along the back of his scalp.

He found the lump. Of course there was a lump! Why would Brenner lie about something like that?

There was no reason to be uneasy, he told himself, knowing damn well he'd been uneasy since he had first laid eyes on Kurt Brenner.

Uneasy, but not apprehensive. There was nothing unique about the strong resemblance between Kiril and Kurt Brenner. The Index was full of people who resembled one another. In some cases the men or women in question were virtually identical.

He shrugged off his anxiety. It was a trick of nature, nothing more.

But his "something-is-missing" feeling, liberated from the mental turmoil and stress of a long tension-filled day, persisted.

*A clever man could turn a trick of nature to his advantage.*

Could his brother be *that* clever?

Certainly Brenner would have had no conceivable reason to drug Kiril—

He forced himself to complete the sentence.

—but Kiril would have had damn good reason to drug Brenner.

*Why didn't the possibility occur to me sooner?*

But he knew why. Too many distractions. The aftermath of Stepan Brodsky's attempted defection on the bridge. Intense pressure from General Nemerov about the microfilm in Brodsky's cigarette lighter. Organizing a time-consuming search for the lighter only to discover a security leak spelled out in seven ominous words. A false assumption that Ernst Roeder was in league with Adrienne Brenner, culminating in Roeder's fatal heart attack. Talking a venomous Colonel Emil von Eyssen into joining forces for their mutual preservation.

What he'd had to cope with in a very short span of time would have distracted anyone, he thought, willing himself to remain calm.

He stared at the form on the bed, thinking that the hair looked peculiar. He pulled at a few strands, wishing he could pull Kiril's brain into consciousness. Instead, he chose hairs at random.

No wig. The hair was real! It was also slightly damp.

He removed Kiril's dark glasses, remembering that he was supposed to have had some sort of eye infection—the left eye? He lifted the lid.

Of course the eye was infected!

He turned to Luka with obvious relief. "See if Galina Barkova is back in her room."

"Barkova woman asleep," Luka said.

"Really? When did you check her room?"

"One hour ago, maybe two."

"Wake her, please, and bring her to me."

Luka was back in five minutes. "She won't wake up," he reported, his brow furrowed. "Not even when I shake her."

Aleksei shot to his feet and rushed down the hall.

She was stretched out on the bed, fully clothed in a gown of some kind. "Galina?" he said sharply.

His voice trailed off as he noticed the belt of a black dress tied tightly around her upper arm. A syringe dangled from her forearm.

"*Why?*" he cried out.

But he knew why.

His own words came back to haunt him. When he'd tapped his "most charming co-optee" to spy on her lover, he'd spelled out what he was after.

*There are things a woman can see—and sense—more easily than a man.*

Had she sensed something that he had not? Come to

think of it, what was the matter of "great urgency" she'd wanted to speak to him about while he was bartering with von Eyssen and, in a fit of temper, had sent her packing?

Aleksei had never sobered up so fast after so much vodka.

There are only *two* possibilities, he thought in a wave of panic. If it's Kiril on the couch, Brenner will be back. If it's Brenner, Kiril has defected.

He knew what would happen once the real Kurt Brenner was safely back in the United States. Brenner's outrage and victimhood would drive him to display his psychological and physical bruises, confirming what the world had seen on its television screens—a clever impersonation by Kiril Andreyev, brother of KGB Colonel Aleksei Andreyev.

A successful defection in full view of a banquet-hall of East Germans, then broadcast around the world. The embarrassment of the century!

He glanced at his watch. Too late to stop the plane. They were already in Zurich.

*Think! If ever I need my wits about me, it's now. When I release Brenner tomorrow—*

"When," he said aloud, "or if?"

What if he claimed that Dr. Kurt Brenner had changed his mind about taking his wife to Zurich? That he'd decided to go directly to Moscow from East Berlin? Who could prove otherwise? Who knew for certain that it wasn't Dr. Kurt Brenner who'd announced his defection for all the world to hear?

That would leave Kiril as the only loose end. He'd deal with that later.

Aleksei grabbed the telephone from the night table and gave the operator a Zurich telephone number. When he was through talking, he replaced the receiver cautiously.

"We still have a chance," he told Luka shakily. "We may yet survive."

# CHAPTER 42

On the flight from Schönefeld Airfield to Zurich, the executive jet suddenly shuddered as it banked steeply. The cabin seemed to roll precariously over on its side.

"We'll be running into severe turbulence over the mountains," the pilot announced.

The ultimate irony, Kiril brooded. *I am going to die even as I escape from communism.*

Beside him, Adrienne Brenner moaned, still on the edge of air-sickness from a surfeit of champagne. The promised explanation had never materialized. She had barely opened her eyes the whole time. Better that way.

The sky cleared abruptly, then turned calm. The plane shifted direction.

"Zurich," he told her. "We're going down."

Adrienne nodded. Her eyes, opening for a moment, fell closed again.

Kiril stared out the window, his blank expression masking inner turmoil.

*I am forty years old. I have no work, no money, no friends. I don't even own the clothes on my back. Yet I have never felt so young. So confident of the future.*

Future? He had never had the luxury of thinking about his future, let alone planning one. All the days were his now, he thought, realizing that he would need time to get used to the idea. What should he do with that precious new commodity, time?

*Dream without restraint. Make plans. Change them if it pleases me. Buy an automobile. Travel with anticipation, not fear. What's the American expression that sums it all up? No holds barred!*

He stole a glance at Adrienne Brenner. Free to fall in love, he thought. However much he cared for Galya, he had never allowed himself to slip into a deeply emotional commitment. In the Soviet Union, to have a loved one—a family—was to forge your own chains. What kind of man plots escape when he's locked in the grip of the hostage system?

He tensed with the sudden thud of the plane's wheels on the runway, the vibrations coursing through his body—and nearly bolted from his seat. He had to grip both its arms as he counted the seconds. Taxiing . . . slowing . . . turning . . .

Stopping.

Someone slid open a door. He forgot about Adrienne Brenner's suitcase, about helping her out of the window seat, standing aside so she could exit first.

He was moving toward the open door when he became aware of a noisy cluster of people who waited at the bottom of the aircraft's steps.

But all he saw was pavement. All he felt was the desire to fall on his knees and kiss the ground. The instant his foot made contact with the tarmac all he felt was a sweet solemn wonder, coupled with an overwhelming exuberance.

*I made it, Stepan! Anna! Kolya! I'm here!*

"Look this way, please, Dr. Brenner."

A flashbulb went off in his face. Then an unbroken

series of them, popping like firecrackers, reducing his eyesight to white glare. Raising his arm like a shield, he blinked to clear his vision.

"Is it true you're defecting to the Soviet Union?"

"Are you here to say goodbye to your parents?"

"What about your wife? Does she stay or go?"

"When do you leave for Moscow?"

"What's behind the defection?"

"Was your family aware of your plans?"

"What *are* your plans, Dr. Brenner?"

The questions pitched at him were mostly in rapid-fire English, only a few in German. None in Russian.

He waited. Adrienne Brenner had joined him and stood groggily at his side.

As soon as the voices began to subside, Kiril said, "I wish to make a statement." He took a cautious few steps away from the plane. "But not here. Is there someplace we could go?"

"Right this way, Dr. Brenner, Mrs. Brenner. It's a short walk to the quarantine section of the terminal. You won't have to go through customs or immigration yet," an American reporter said, a hint of disapproval crossing her face. "Your mother and father are in a bad way about your defection," she told him. "They have refused to make a statement until they've had a chance to talk to you."

"Where are they?"

"Somewhere in the terminal. No one knew exactly what time your plane was due—or, for that matter, whether you'd even show up. I'm pretty sure your parents are still here. Should I find them and bring them to the VIP lounge? There's a private room inside."

"Please. I'd be extremely grateful."

"No problem," the reporter said, sensing the man's acute distress; the sharpness no longer in her tone. "No one will disturb you in the lounge."

By the time they reached the private room, Kiril's

thoughts were in turmoil. For the first time, he realized how difficult it would be to give a full explanation to Dr. Brenner's parents. Should he tell them that a Soviet KGB colonel had a hold on their son because of some allegedly despicable act he'd committed during World War II? That only when Kurt Brenner had threatened to turn him over to the KGB had Kiril knocked him out and switched places with him?

But *not* to explain was futile, he thought. The truth would surface soon enough when the real Dr. Brenner stepped off a plane tomorrow. The only thing he could do for Brenner's parents was tell them the truth face to face—and in private.

He thought of how, in desperation, he had used Adrienne Brenner. He owed her the truth as well.

Steeling himself for what was to come, he steered a still-woozy Adrienne Brenner into the VIP lounge. The American reporter had just passed some Swiss francs to a couple of bored VIP lounge attendants. As soon as they gave her a key, she handed it to Kiril.

"Your private room," she said.

He gripped her hand. "I can't thank you enough for your kindness."

"Good luck, Dr. Brenner," she said, and was surprised to realize that she meant it.

How incongruous we must look in this dingy little room of an airport in the middle of the night, Kiril thought. You in your beautiful green gown, Adrienne Brenner, *me* in bowtie and tuxedo . . .

And because he had been forced to deceive her and knew it was far too late to earn this woman's love, he reached out and drew her into his arms.

It was all he meant to do. But suddenly he was kissing her with a punishing violence, an unquenchable thirst—

Adrienne broke free, breathing in gasps, the back of one hand pressed against her mouth. "Where's Kurt? Where's my husband?"

"Forgive me. I had no right—"

"What's the meaning of this masquerade? Where *is* he?"

"Still in East Berlin. I never intended this to happen, but your husband left me no choice. At the moment, he's probably still unconscious from a harmless drug."

"What did you hope to gain, damn you?"

But even as she asked the question, things began to fall into place.

"My freedom," he told her simply.

"And Kurt's?"

"He's safe enough. In a few minutes I'll reveal my true identity and expose my brother's attempt to coerce your husband into defecting. Don't worry. He'll be allowed to leave East Berlin. Neither the Soviets nor the East Germans would dare to forcibly detain a man of his prominence— especially after all the publicity."

"I don't understand. Why would the Soviets want to detain Kurt in the first place?"

"Not for his surgical skills, certainly. He's the victim of Moscow-style propaganda," Kiril said bitterly. "One of my KGB brother's jobs involves defections. He was blackmailing your husband—something to do with when he was in Germany during the war. He was very young."

"You had no right—"

"I had *every* right," Kiril bristled. "It's called self-defense. Your husband threatened to trade his knowledge of my defection plan for the blackmail Aleksei was holding over his head."

He turned away from her. "I'm free," he said, turning away from her. "By tomorrow, your husband will be too."

"You could be wrong about that," Adrienne said slowly. "You must have been under a great deal of stress. You were making split-second decisions. Hoping to keep me in the dark. Figuring out what to say to the press. Wondering and worrying about whether you could pull this off."

*All true,* he thought. "What are you getting at?" he said tensely.

"Something I hope doesn't occur to your KGB brother. What if he *doesn't* let Kurt go? If Dr. Kurt Brenner's own wife was fooled—and no one knows him better than I do—why not the rest of the world?"

"But—"

"I know what you're thinking. I had so much champagne I couldn't see straight—literally. But only a handful of people knew about that—mostly East German butlers in tuxedos. If my husband is kept in a semi-drugged state and paraded in front of the cameras—not too close, just close enough to make it look good—it's conceivable that KGB apparatchiks like your brother could get away with it. Over time, they might even trust Kurt with a microphone and a rehearsed speech."

She closed her eyes briefly, as if she could picture the scene. "Drugs and blackmail are a lethal combination," she said grimly.

Kiril spread his hands in a gesture of futility. "You're right, of course. The only thing I can do is hope that Aleksei isn't as clever as you."

*And hope even more that Brenner's parents realize that I never intended to harm their son—that he forced my hand.*

A knock on the door.

"What will you tell them?" Adrienne whispered.

"What I lost the courage to tell *you*," *he admitted,* "even after I was safely on the plane."

The press, held in check by the American reporter, buzzed with impatience.

Dr. Max Brenner, grim and ashen, helped his wife enter the lounge's private room. Pausing to clasp Adrienne's shoulder for a moment, he closed the four of them inside.

Anna Brenner took her daughter-in-law's hands in hers. "I cannot find words to express how sorry I am that my son has shamed you."

"Don't even try," Adrienne whispered, squeezing Anna's hands tightly.

Adrienne remained standing by the door, near-paralyzed by the decisions she knew she would have to make before she left this room.

Max Brenner held his wife's arm—a useless restraint.

Shrugging it off, Anna Brenner made no effort to restrain her tears as she crossed the room toward her son. She moved slowly, her gait unsteady, not stopping even when she heard Adrienne burst into tears.

Kiril, having braced himself for this sad encounter, felt on the edge of tears himself. But as Anna Brenner approached him, he realized that he should have anticipated more than sadness. What he saw in the set of her mouth was a smoldering anger bordering on rage.

"Tell me to my face," she said.

He heard the trace of an accent. Her voice, in sharp contrast to her anger, was anguished.

For a moment he lowered his eyes to gather his own strength.

In the next moment he was staring at a gold charm bracelet on her wrist—a tiny thermometer, a reflex hammer, a stethoscope, a head-mirror, each charm suspended from the bracelet by a gold link—

*Except for one link with nothing hanging from it!*

For a split second, Kiril felt as if a burst of electricity had coursed through his body—the second he knew with certainty that the link had once held the miniature gold scalpel he still wore around his neck.

*A charm that held long-suppressed memories for them both. . . .*

"Tell me how you can do this, Kurt. And then, tell me why."

He looked into the face of the mother he had said goodbye to when he was four and had loved all his life. A face forever with him, forever lost.

"Are you going to tell me or not?"

He saw her mouth move, that was all. He had lost every sense but one. He stood like a statue, hungrily drinking in the sight of her.

"You are going to do this?" Her expression bordered on hatred.

And even though he knew the hatred was meant for Kurt Brenner, he accepted it as penance for the wrong he had done her.

*Oh Anna, Anna. To have spent a lifetime of pain and guilt grieving over a hostage child not old enough to understand why you never came home. But when I was older, when I learned of Kolya's injury, I knew you had a chance to raise him in a free country. And now you are suffering because, thanks to me, you think the beneficiary of that bitter sacrifice chooses to make his home in the Soviet Union. How can you endure it?*

He saw no forgiveness in her eyes.

His eyes filled with tears. He forgave her instantly.

*Did you think I would hate you for leaving me behind? I have had but one lifelong obsession—to find you again. To tell you that what you did was right. To set you free of a guilt you never should have had to bear.*

*But now the Soviets may learn that Kurt Brenner is Kolya Andreyev, citizen of the U.S.S.R., and they may never let him go. Forgive me for what I am about to say to the press. Then give me twenty-four hours and I will bring Kolya back to you. If I can . . .*

Before Anna Brenner could say another word, Kiril walked past Adrienne and opened the door.

Reporters poured into the room, jockeying for position.

"Ladies and gentlemen," he said, "my statement will be brief. I plan to practice heart surgery in the Soviet Union. My decision has been a long time in coming. It is final. I came here tonight because I want no doubt in anyone's mind that the announcement I made in East Berlin several hours ago was true. There was no coercion. You asked about my immediate plans. They are to get back on the plane that brought me here so that I may begin my new life in Moscow."

The reporters gave way as soon as they saw Anna Brenner descend on him like an avenging angel.

She slapped Kiril's face so hard he staggered from the blow.

A reporter mumbled, "The slap heard round the world . . . "

A wilted Max Brenner looked as if he were on the verge of collapsing.

Adrienne, her mind whirling, leaned against the wall, watching with horror as the scene played out before her.

Kiril's head was reeling from the impact—from the terrible irony—as flashbulbs popped, recording Anna Brenner's blow for a readership of millions. Cameras panned for reaction shots of a family in chaos.

And retreat. Max and Anna Brenner were leaving.

Adrienne hadn't moved. "Ladies and gentlemen, listen to me! Will someone please listen to me?" she shouted over the din. "I have a statement of my own."

The commotion in the room collapsed into silence as Kiril walked over to her.

"You can't stop me," she said.

He grabbed her arm and pulled her aside before anyone could react. "Say one more word and you throw away the only chance I have of rescuing your husband."

"Rescuing him? You're going back to East Berlin after what he—"

"I must. But it has to be as Kurt Brenner, not Kiril Andreyev. If he and I don't get out within twenty-four hours, make your statement then. Tell the world your husband was being blackmailed for something he did a long time ago. That he's being held by the Soviets against his will."

Kiril removed the charm from around his neck and pressed it into Adrienne's hand. "Convince them I was an impostor, and then give this to your mother-in-law. She'll be able to back up your story."

After a brief hesitation, he handed her a cigarette lighter. "And if I don't come back, give this to American intelligence."

*The cigarette lighter again!*

Stunned, Adrienne realized there was no way she could quickly process what was going on. "Kurt, wait," she called out.

Handing him the lighter, she turned to the reporters. "I've decided to accompany my husband to East Berlin and, if necessary, to Moscow. I hope to persuade him to change his mind. No more questions please," she said as the flashbulbs resumed, holding a hand over her eyes to deflect the light.

Taking Kiril's arm—ever the dutiful wife, she thought wryly, she steered him toward the executive jet.

She was still squeezing the tiny gold scalpel when something lurking in her subconscious surfaced. In the private room when her mother-in-law had clasped her hands and Adrienne, overwhelmed by emotion, had squeezed back—hard—she had felt a slight bruising sensation from the charms on Anna's bracelet.

The bracelet Anna never took off. The bracelet that was missing a single charm, she'd told Adrienne years ago— and then told her what the charm was.

She had a flash-image of Kiril as he bent in the dirt to carve the shape of a tombstone—tiny letters inside for some grieving family.

His carving tool? A miniature gold scalpel.

She whirled around to face him. "God in heaven, Anna Brenner is your mother! And Kurt must be—"

"My brother Kolya."

# CHAPTER 43

M ax Brenner sat up, awakened by a dull thud. "Anna?"
"Sorry. I dropped my shoe."

"You can't sleep?"

"It's hardly surprising."

He turned on the light and went to sit beside her on the other bed while she finished dressing. "It's two o'clock in the morning. We have an early plane."

"There are other planes to New York. We'll catch a later flight."

"Let me go with you. The streets will be empty."

"Zurich is an old friend, Max. I want to be alone with her."

"Then take a doctor's advice," he said gently. "So much pent-up emotion. Cry if you can."

She touched his cheek. "I'm all cried out."

She finished dressing and slipped out the door.

*Zurich is an old friend.*

It was a long walk down the hill from the Dolder Grand Hotel to the center of the city, but Anna knew she wouldn't notice the distance.

She never had. How many times had she walked up and down this hill and along these streets just to pass the time? To make the waiting easier?

Because Zurich had been the mid-point—a bridge that straddled Berlin and New York. Germany and America.

It had been hard, the waiting in Berlin, because there had been so much to wait for.

For fear to be abated with every passing day by the growing conviction that she was safe from the long arm of Soviet retribution. For the visits of the young American surgeon she had met in Berlin, who had assisted in Kolya's operation. For the surgeon to complete the last days of his two-year training program under the greatest heart surgeon in Germany, perhaps in all of Europe.

Then it was on to Zurich and more waiting.

For papers to come through which "proved" she was a native-born German. More papers which "documented" that the young surgeon was the father of her three-year-old son, Kolya. And, finally, for two American passports. One for Anna Petrovsky, the other for Kurt Brenner.

The day they set sail for the United States, the captain had married Anna Petrovsky to Max Brenner, the doctor whose surgical skills had helped save her son's life. The man who had given her son an opportunity to live that life to the fullest.

Kurt had never fully achieved that goal, she thought. His spectacular achievements—and they *were* spectacular— had always been marred by a need for approval and a taste for flattery.

He'd been flattered by his first invitation to a widely publicized medical exchange in the Soviet Union—had accepted without telling her in stubborn defiance of her request that he never set foot in the U.S.S.R. She had made him back down by the sheer force of her will, making it unnecessary to tell him things she thought he was better off not knowing.

"You're unreasonable," he'd said to her then—and many more times since. "What have the communists ever done to you that you should detest them so?"

Nothing special, she thought now. Nothing the communists haven't done to countless others.

Through the years, she had persisted in her refusal to enlighten him—a mistake, she realized now.

Worse than a mistake. A monstrous injustice.

*But for you, Kolya, I would have returned to the Soviet Union. But for you I would not have abandoned your brother, Kiril. I would not have left him with a sister who was an Enemy of the People and in no position to protect him.*

As snow began to fall, Anna trudged up the hill to the hotel, tortured by the thought that she had never made inquiries about what had become of her middle son, Kiril. Max had convinced her that any attempt to make contact would have been painful, possibly futile—and worse, it might have endangered Kiril's life. Max had been right, of course. But that was a long time ago.

By the time Anna had re-climbed the hill, she'd made her decision.

It would be unsettling to set foot on German soil after narrowly escaping the Nazis so many years ago, but the truth about her son's lineage was long overdue.

What better time, what better place, than tomorrow's Medicine International symposium in West Berlin?

# CHAPTER 44

As Kiril and Adrienne approached the executive jet that would return them to East Berlin, they were met by the pilot, who apologized profusely. There was a mechanical problem. One of the red wing lights was not illuminating and a short circuit indicator was appearing on the instrument panel. Dr. and Mrs. Brenner were welcome to board and wait with the pilot for the problem to be diagnosed and corrected, after which the Zurich airport would clear the plane for takeoff.

Kiril and Adrienne climbed the jet's staircase, practically fell into some seats, and were soon asleep. Several hours later, the pilot gently nudged Kiril. The problem had been diagnosed as a burned-out circuit breaker, the part unavailable until now. The red wing light was functioning, the short circuit indicator normal. All that remained before departure was for the Brenners to fasten their seat belts.

"Will you *please* tell me your plan?" Adrienne implored as soon as their plane took off.

"I'll tell you this much," Kiril said evenly. "If anything goes wrong, you'll wish you had stayed in Zurich."

Lost in their own thoughts, neither one spoke for the rest of the flight.

At the sound of wheels jolting onto the runway, Kiril and Adrienne undid their seat belts. The plane rolled to a stop near an empty office building adjoining the terminal, and they prepared to disembark.

As he helped Adrienne out of the plane, Kiril could see an East German staff car that looked like an American Crown Victoria waiting for them on the tarmac.

Luka Rogov was in the driver's seat.

Aleksei, rumpled and red-eyed from lack of sleep, surveyed them silently.

The office they entered, obviously having once belonged to some clerk, smelled of empty beer bottles. Papers were all over the desk and floors. Wastebaskets were overflowing. File cabinet drawers yawned open, as if they'd been ransacked. Paper clips, staplers, unopened mail—the detritus of a once-busy place—was everywhere.

As the others stood around surveying the mess, Kiril began clearing debris off the chairs, making space for the four of them to sit.

He pulled out a chair for Adrienne.

She sat down and cleared her throat. "Where is my husband, Colonel Andreyev?"

"So you know." Aleksei sounded weary. "I found out barely an hour ago. Your husband is in good hands. He's recovering from the effects of a large dose of Valium."

He turned to Kiril. "You played your part to perfection," he said in Russian. "I know what you did in Zurich—what you told the Western press. Dr. Brenner told me about the elaborate preparations you made to defect. What I *don't* know is why you came back."

"I'll tell you as long as we include Mrs. Brenner in the conversation by speaking English."

"Aren't we chivalrous," Aleksei said drily—but in English.

"Actually, it was Adrienne Brenner who realized

something which hadn't occurred to me when I took her husband's place. I'd just assumed you and your KGB pals would capitulate in the wake of all that publicity. That you'd send her husband back on the next plane. But, as she pointed out, I had managed to fool *her*—his own wife—so how hard could it be for you to convince a worldwide audience that her husband's defection was real? Dr. Brenner was in your custody. All you had to do was keep feeding him drugs and parade him before the cameras every once in a while."

Aleksei smiled. "My compliments, Mrs. Brenner. You are a very discerning woman."

"Perhaps you should compliment *me* for knowing what Dr. Brenner's ultimate fate will be. You will take him to Moscow where he'll be installed in some nondescript cardiac hospital—if he's lucky. More likely, he'll disappear in the Gulag."

"Consider yourself complimented as well, Little Brother. But I still can't grasp why you came back."

"Once I realized what I'd inadvertently set in motion, I had no choice but to return," Kiril continued as if he hadn't been interrupted. "And since I'm under no illusions about what's going to happen to me—"

Adrienne gasped. "You've traded your life for Kurt's?"

Ignoring her outburst, Kiril said, "Just so you know, I explained most of the story to his parents in Zurich last night shortly before we left. They're expecting their son in Zurich tomorrow. You have no choice but to let him go. I've no idea what the blackmail was about—something that happened a long time ago when he was in the army. But whatever Brenner was so desperate to hide, it can't be enough to hold him here. If it ever was," Kiril added caustically.

*Take the bait, Aleksei. Buy into the idea that I'm a self-sacrificing fool. That I've given up all hope of surviving.*

"It's about time you and Mrs. Brenner are made privy

to a sordid story," Aleksei said irritably. "Chancellor Malik and I dropped hints of it at that Humboldt University Medical Clinic breakfast, but you had no way of knowing we were talking about Dr. Brenner."

"Hints of what?" Adrienne asked cautiously.

"Of helpless, half-starved orphaned children who, after surviving a Nazi death camp, were rescued by the Red Cross and turned over to American servicemen. The Americans took over the care and feeding—literally—of these kids, hiding them until they could be placed in a DP camp and eventually sent to America. Your husband—for strictly self-serving reasons, I might add—betrayed them. As the Russians led these children across Glienicker Bridge into East Berlin, they chose death over Soviet custody."

Adrienne was visibly shocked. Kiril's face had turned ashen.

Aleksei pounded the final nail into Kurt Brenner's coffin. "I know all this because I was there. So was Chancellor Malik. We recorded it."

Aleksei learned forward to scrutinize Kiril's face.

"Let me get something straight. In spite of the fact that Brenner was about to betray you and knowing full well I'd have had you shot, you came back here ready to sacrifice your freedom for his?"

"I did."

"You hypocrite!" Aleksei exclaimed. "So much for a man who's spent most of his life condemning altruism."

Adrienne groaned inwardly. She felt as if she were trapped in a nightmare.

The nightmare turned surreal when she and Kiril were reunited with a groggy, disheveled-looking Kurt Brenner—a man who was usually buttoned-down neat. Next to him stood Kiril Andreyev, stunning in a tuxedo that nearly blotted out memories of his tired blue suit. To complete the absurdity, Kurt's hair was still dark brown, Kiril's completely white.

Aleksei snapped Adrienne back to reality.

"Once our aircraft is fueled and serviced—there seems to be some problem with a wing-tip safety light—all of us will leave for Moscow," he announced. "You two are surprisingly docile," Aleksei said, his eyes shifting from Brenner to Adrienne. "Getting resigned to a lengthy sojourn in Moscow? I hope you understand my position, Mrs. Brenner. I cannot possibly let you leave now."

Adrienne shrugged. "My place is with my husband."

"I'm not going anywhere," Brenner shouted as Luka moved to stand behind him.

"Where's Galya? Isn't she going back with us?" Kiril asked.

Aleksei touched Kiril's shoulder in a genuine gesture of sympathy. "She's dead, Kiril. She committed suicide right after you left for Zurich."

Adrienne's eyes filled with tears.

"No need to grieve, Mrs. Brenner," Aleksei said thinly. "Our Miss Barkova was working for me. She was spying on you as well as Kiril. Who do you think let me know when Herr Roeder passed you that incriminating package? You behaved like a well-trained homing pigeon, my dear, leading me straight to—"

"You tortured him to death, didn't you?" Adrienne lashed out.

"As it happens, I didn't. For what it's worth, Herr Roeder died of heart failure—a vestige of scarlet fever when he was a child. There was a great deal of it going around at the time."

He turned to Kiril. "Galina Barkova's body is being loaded into the plane's cargo hold as we speak—the least I can do. Don't blame yourself. Her unrequited love wasn't quite what it seemed. She was spying on you for the last two years in exchange for a few trinkets." He paused. "She didn't give you away in the end though, did she?"

Eyes closed, Kiril pushed back in his seat. He'd been

virtually certain Galya had been co-opted—but with misgivings. Would she have committed suicide because he was leaving the country and in no position to take her with him? That may have been part of it, he reasoned, but guilt was more likely the greater part. He'd seen it too often in the camps. People clinging to life as they scrambled to survive just one more day. Another. Still another . . .

Checking his watch, Aleksei did a quick mental calculation. "It's about time for Dr. Anna Brenner's speech at Medicine International's symposium in West Berlin. I suggest we listen while we wait for our plane to be ready. A comrade in West Berlin tells me she has some harsh things to say about you, Dr. Brenner."

Aleksei nodded to Luka, who turned on a radio and fiddled with the dials until the radio coughed. Static muffled the background noise.

The symposium had begun.

Kiril and Adrienne leaned forward in their chairs, straining to hear. Aleksei was paying close attention. Brenner, looking mildly curious, had a pretty fair idea what his mother was about to say about his alleged defection. Luka, blank-faced, sat in the corner.

A Master of Ceremonies' preliminary remarks signaled the start of the symposium, his mellow voice announcing the presence of an unscheduled but much respected speaker, Dr. Anna Brenner, mother of the esteemed heart surgeon Dr. Kurt Brenner, who had just told the world of his defection to the Soviet Union.

"I am here to speak the truth about my sons," Anna Brenner said. "I chose to speak at Medicine International because my son, Kurt Brenner, is a peer of many in this audience. Until the mid-1920s when I married Max Brenner and became a German citizen, I resided in the Soviet Union. My name at that time was Anna Andreyev. My eldest son was, and perhaps still is, Aleksei Andreyev. My second son was Kiril. My youngest son, the eminent

American heart surgeon Dr. Kurt Brenner, is about to learn that he was born—not in America—but in the Soviet Union. His name was Nikolai 'Kolya' Andreyev."

Aleksei's body turned to stone.

He noticed that neither Kiril nor Adrienne Brenner seemed surprised.

*They must have learned about this in Zurich.*

"—and it was because of a near-tragic accident that I received permission to take Kolya to Germany in hopes of saving the child's life. I lost my eldest son Aleksei— politically, you might say—to his father and ultimately to the Communist Party. And once I made the painful decision to raise Kolya in a free country, I lost my son Kiril. Any attempt to communicate with him would have placed him in grave danger because of who I was—an Enemy of the People.

So this is what I wish to say by way of farewell to my son, Kurt, who has just defected to the Union of Soviet Socialist Republics."

\* \* \*

The close of Anna Brenner's speech brought silence in West Berlin as a distinguished gathering of doctors, scientists, and politicians absorbed her shattering words.

In a small office at the East Berlin airport, three men and a woman looked at each other, pondering their new relationship.

*You!* Aleksei's eyes were fixed on the radio, as if Anna Brenner awaited his reaction.

Kiril's mouth was twisted with the violence of his emotion.

Kurt Brenner's near-hysterical laughter rose above a raucous mix of voices and static. "The Brothers Andreyev! It's more like the Brothers Karamazov," he said disdainfully, looking from Kiril to Aleksei as one would look at a couple of bastards who had abruptly sprouted on an impeccable family tree.

Aleksei's hardened features melted into feigned amiability. "Little Kolya, is it?" he said, turning to Brenner. "And all these years I thought you were dead. My father—excuse me, I should say *our* father—never considered the possibility that German records could be forged. That citizenship could be so easily obtained. So the doctors gave you a forty percent chance of recovery? You certainly *have* recovered. Prospered, too. Time to share the wealth, Kolya—not literally, of course. Your operating skills will most certainly put our current heart surgeons to shame. But it's your defection that has great propaganda value."

"Dear God, the man is serious," Brenner muttered, groping for Adrienne's hand.

"Have you no sense of humor?" Aleksei mocked. "Has your soft American life bred it out of you? The joke is on our dear mother. Three sons, and the only one who merits her undying devotion—her precious Kiril—is the very one who tricked her and delivered you back into my hands. And now, madam,"—his glance shifted to the radio—"Mother Russia has all three of your sons. How you must be suffering!"

The static yielded to the animated voice of the Master of Ceremonies.

"But the biggest surprise, ladies and gentlemen, is how the woman whose revelations set off the tumult you hear is bearing up. The mother of Dr. Kurt Brenner is waiting, microphone in hand, for people to quiet down, ready to answer all those painful probing questions many of you are eager to ask. Yet Anna Brenner is the very picture of that old cliché—calm, cool, and collected. In point of fact, she looks relieved—"

Aleksei shot to his feet and snapped off the radio.

It was dusk when the phone rang. Aleksei picked it up.

"Well?" he asked, and waited for an answer. "Good." He hung up. "Time to go," he announced unceremoniously.

Kurt Brenner was terrified to the point of immobility. He was silent as Luka Rogov twisted one arm behind his back and pushed him out the door. Adrienne and Kiril followed, heading for the waiting staff car.

Unwilling to risk losing his prize possessions, Aleksei ordered Luka to put Brenner in the front passenger seat, and then get under the steering wheel next to him. Aleksei himself sat behind Brenner. Telling Adrienne to sit in the middle of the back seat, he left the seat in back of Luka for Kiril.

As soon as Luka cranked the ignition, turned on his lights, and headed for the executive jet that would take them to Moscow, Aleksei was visibly relieved—though guardedly so.

Adrienne reached for Kiril's hand, puzzled when he brushed off her overture.

Minutes into the ride—in a motion too swift for anyone to integrate—Kiril slipped one hand under his tuxedo jacket and removed a letter opener from his belt. He'd spotted it while he was clearing off the chairs in the clerk's office.

Leaning forward, he placed the metal blade on the left side of Luka Rogov's thick neck.

Aleksei blanched.

"This blade is resting on Rogov's carotid artery, Aleksei," he said. "If I were to push it just an inch or so, there will be a gusher of blood that even Dr. Kurt Brenner would be unable to stop. Your alter ego will be exsanguinated. Tell him what that means, Kurt."

Brenner turned and had the pleasure of seeing Aleksei Andreyev's terrified expression. "It's true, Colonel," Brenner said with authority. "If Kiril cuts or punctures this man's carotid artery, he's finished."

Kiril had always sensed that Rogov was an irreplaceable part of the psychological netherworld that Aleksei inhabited. That in some primal undefinable way, Aleksei would do almost anything to keep Rogov safe. He was relieved to find that, so far at least, he had been correct.

"Do whatever Kiril tells you, Luka," Aleksei said. He couldn't resist adding, "We will have our time soon."

"Drive to the furthest and darkest part of the tarmac and stop when I tell you," Kiril told Rogov. "Aleksei, I want you to unholster your revolver—slowly—and hand it to Mrs. Brenner butt first."

To underscore his orders, Kiril lightly scratched Luka's neck with the letter opener. A tiny droplet of blood dribbled out.

"Kurt, please tell our brother Aleksei whether Rogov is bleeding and whether the cut is serious."

"Yes about the blood, no about the serious," Brenner said—and on his own added, "Not yet."

Adrienne held Aleksei's revolver by the butt, resting it in her lap.

"Mrs. Brenner," Kiril said, "do you know what the hammer on a revolver is—the piece just above your thumb?"

Adrienne almost smiled. "I've seen enough movies. You want me to pull the hammer back?"

"Yes. Then put the end of the gun's barrel into Aleksei's side. If he so much as burps, I want you to pull the trigger. Can you do that?"

Her answer came slowly. "The hammer, yes. I've just done it. The rest? Maybe. I'm not sure."

*Half a loaf. Well, Aleksei can't be sure either.*

"Sit on your hands, Aleksei," Kiril said.

Aleksei did as he was told.

By now Rogov had driven at least two miles deep into the airport. The tarmac was enveloped in darkness, the car's headlights providing the only light. Before them were dense stands of trees. To the left there appeared to be a dirt trail, maybe an old logging road.

"Aleksei, tell Rogov to stop slowly, turn off his bright

lights, and turn on the parking lights."

Both men complied.

Kiril slowly moved his free right hand to Adrienne's, took Aleksei's revolver from her, and put it at the back of Luka's head while replacing the letter opener in his belt.

"Kurt," Kiril said, "Rogov's revolver is holstered on his right side, next to you. See it? I want you to open the holster, remove the weapon, pull back the hammer, and step out of the car. Then go around to the door behind you, open it, and press the barrel against our KGB brother's head. Can you do that?"

"With pleasure," Brenner responded with undisguised enthusiasm.

"Kurt, step back so Aleksei has room to get out of the car. He will walk about ten feet—backwards. As you walk backwards *behind* him, aim at the lumbar spine. If he makes any sudden moves, put two bullets in his spine."

"My pleasure," Brenner said—and had to admit that the mere thought of crippling the sonofabitch was delicious.

"Mrs. Brenner," Kiril said, "get out of the car through the r*ight* door and step about ten feet away."

She did.

Kiril spoke to Luka Rogov in Russian. "I am about to get out of the car. The gun in my hand will be aimed at your head. If you make any move I don't like, I will blow your head off and then do the same to Colonel Andreyev. Nod if you understand."

Rogov, his bushy eyebrows creased in a frown, nodded.

"I'm not finished, Luka. Once you're out of the car, you will walk backwards until I tell you to stop."

Rogov nodded again, left the car, and started walking backwards.

"Now stop and turn around," Kiril told him.

"No, don't. Don't kill him! He can't harm you now!" Aleksei cried out.

"Listen to me, Rogov," Kiril said, ignoring Aleksei's

anguished plea. "I want you to remove your tie, your belt, the straps that hold your equipment, the shoelaces from your boots—all of it. You too, Aleksei."

As soon as they were done, Kiril asked Adrienne to collect whatever items would effectively bind their hands and feet.

Walking Luka to roughly ten feet from where Brenner guarded Aleksei, Kiril told both men to drop their trousers.

Luka just stared at him, not comprehending.

Not so Aleksei. Realizing they weren't about to die after all, he made a crude joke.

"Explain what I want—what Rogov must do next—and why, Aleksei."

He did, and they did.

Kurt Brenner was amazed that such a simple expedient virtually froze the two Russians in place. Unable to walk, let alone run, all they could do was hop like kangaroos!

Kiril signaled Adrienne to bring him what she'd sorted. There were more than enough sturdy items to secure both Aleksei and Luka Rogov.

Kiril tied up Rogov, Brenner doing the same with Aleksei.

"What now?" Brenner asked cheerfully.

"My original plan, of course," Kiril replied, making no effort to lower his voice. "We'll hijack the executive jet and fly to Tempelhof Airport in West Berlin."

Kiril had no such intention—but no way yet to let the Brenners know what he really planned to do.

With a touch of alarm, he realized that he was slipping into a state of deep fatigue, every last ounce of adrenalin draining out of him . . .

So much had happened without respite. Knocking Brenner out and taking his place. Fear that Adrienne Brenner would realize who he was. His exhilaration when the plane landed him in Zurich. The painful discovery that his long-sought freedom was illusory. The stunning realization that he'd found his mother but simultaneously caused her unbearable pain. The bleak resolve to go back for his brother. The disgust he'd felt when he learned what Aleksei had been holding over Kurt Brenner's head. The desperate hope, as he and Adrienne returned to East Berlin, that he could come up with a workable escape plan.

"Before you truss me up like some pig," Aleksei said, "why don't we brothers share a last cigarette. After all, before long one of us will be dead. You, if we catch your merry threesome. Me, if we don't."

Kiril took a crushed pack of cheap Russian cigarettes out of his pocket, offered one to Aleksei, and without thinking used his lighter. When it failed to spark he tried again—and only then noticed Aleksei staring at the lighter, his expression half-shock, half-knowing.

"So *you* were the source of the microfilm," he said. "It was *you* who gave it to Stepan Brodsky. *You* who was his backup. And inches from my face is the last surviving copy of the microfilm that would prove you are guilty of treason, you—"

Kiril shrugged. "Now there really are no more secrets between us."

"Let's finish up here," he told Brenner.

As soon as Aleksei and Rogov were tied and gagged, Kiril took Brenner and Adrienne thirty feet away. "My original idea was to hijack the executive jet once Aleksei got us on board. It would have been hard but it might have worked. Without Aleksei, it's impossible."

"What *can* we do?" Brenner asked.

"We have at least four hours lead time, maybe more, before someone finds them or before they manage to free themselves and get to a telephone or a radio."

"Then let's end it here and now."

"What's the matter with you, Kurt?" Adrienne snapped. "We should stand by while you blow their brains out?"

"Don't worry about Aleksei's plane," Kiril said in an effort to defuse the tension. "In the meantime, we'll figure out a way to get to Potsdam."

"You have friends in Potsdam?" Brenner asked.

"I think so."

Kiril was remembering a handshake. A look of profound gratitude in a man's eyes. Letters carved in dirt by a miniature scalpel.

Adrienne smiled. She was remembering it too.

And thanks to a strong retentive memory, Kiril thought he could recall an address . . .

"For now," Kiril told them, we have to hide out until it gets dark tomorrow night."

"Why"? Brenner pressed.

"Because Aleksei will be looking for this automobile."

# CHAPTER 45

They made good time. It was almost dawn when they arrived at the outskirts of Potsdam in the powerful ZIN-110.

Knowing they had to get off the road soon before Aleksei sounded a quiet alarm, Kiril had pushed the automobile so hard it overheated twice and their petrol was almost gone.

He pointed out other factors in their favor. Aleksei would have to concoct some story about why he was looking for them—something that would take him off the hook for losing them in the first place. Which meant a large-scale search—lots of people in lots of places—was unlikely.

As the sun rose, they spotted a farmhouse deep off the road. "We have to chance it," Kiril told them.

He drove down the road and parked behind a barn. The farmhouse was two stories of gray fieldstone with the top floor boarded up. The place looked abandoned. No farm animals. No outbuildings apart from the barn and a dilapidated shed.

But a plot of rich black soil in the back was plowed. Kiril smiled.

"We're in luck," he whispered as he moved to a window and looked inside. "A man and a woman. Retired farmers, probably. Too old to be put into a collectivization program."

He took out his handkerchief. "Put your dollars and jewelry in this."

"All of it?" Brenner asked. "Shouldn't we save something for your pals in Potsdam?"

"If they help us it won't be for money."

Brenner looked skeptical but he emptied his pockets.

Adrienne unwrapped her scarf and handed Kiril a wad of greenbacks and a handful of jewelry.

Her gold-and-diamond wedding band included, Brenner noticed.

"Do we all go in?" he asked.

Kiril shook his head. "I'll come back for you."

In a few minutes he returned with food, water, and no jewelry.

"They were farmers. Owned a lot of land here. After the war, the East Germans seized most of it while the Russians took off with whatever animals and equipment they had left. 'Reparations' they called it," Kiril said with disgust. "They've managed to eke out a living by cultivating the small plot in back and husbanding a few animals. We're to hide the car in their barn. We're leaving it for them, along with our money and jewelry. Their hope is to bribe their way out of East Germany. As soon as it's dark, we'll walk up to the house so they can help us get out of here safely."

"Can we trust them?" Brenner asked.

"Maybe. Maybe not. But I can tell you this much. They detest communists."

As soon as the three of them settled down in the barn, fatigue began to overtake Kiril. He started to doze on the hay-covered floor.

Adrienne shivered. The draft from under the barn door made her long for the cape she'd left behind in East Berlin.

"Cold?" Brenner whispered.

Without waiting for an answer, he covered her body with his.

"Kurt, don't."

"He's asleep."

"How do you know?"

"Listen to his breathing. Then listen to mine . . ."

"What if he wakes up?"

"What if we're all dead tomorrow or the day after? I want you, Adrienne."

*But I don't want you. Not now. Not ever again.*

"Damn it, Kurt," she hissed, trying to edge him off her body without making noise.

"You're my wife. Ever heard of conjugal rights?"

As he bent to kiss her, she turned her head abruptly in the opposite direction—and saw that Kiril Andreyev was no longer lying flat on the floor of the barn. Were his eyes open?

. . . Did it matter even if they were? She knew Kiril wouldn't feel free to intervene. Not when he had yet to call her "Adrienne" instead of "Mrs. Brenner."

She struggled to free herself.

But her resistance had become a challenge. The more she fought each wordless demand on her flesh, the more she was convinced that Kiril's eyes were wide open.

She jammed hers shut and concentrated on her first glimpse of him at an airport terminal. The look on his face as he crossed a banquet room to meet her. She pictured the morning his shadow had fallen across her body and blotted out the sun. His tortured expression as he kissed her passionately in the privacy of an airport lounge in Zurich—

Despite the hay, the floor was cold against her back, the night air colder. Neither were cold enough to bank the liquid heat that rushed into her limbs.

*Oh no*, she thought, realizing too late that the images of Kiril had betrayed her senses. Wanting *him*, not the man who was forcibly entering her body. Her fingers dug into the hay, her body arching, pushing past her protesting mind, greedily reaching for the unreachable and, with a shudder, finding it.

Afterward she lay on the cold ground, eyes open to the sky.

*Kiril*, she whispered, but only in her mind.

She wept as silently as she had fought.

* * *

It was dawn when the farmer rapped his knuckles on the barn door.

"You can change clothes in the house while I'm getting the bicycles," he told them.

The room they entered was all wood—floor, ceiling, walls, furniture. But no firewood to spare, Adrienne realized. The stone fireplace was pristine. The place smelled of raw potatoes. An old woman, indifferent to their presence, was slicing the potatoes at a pitted sink. Adrienne turned her back and slipped into the clothes Kiril handed her. The hem of the long dress—a faded yellow—stopped just below her knees, the fabric straining under her arms and over her breasts. "I have my own scarf," she told Kiril, turning around—then smiled mirthlessly even as Kiril shook his head.

*A designer scarf from Bloomingdale's? Yes indeed, Adrienne.*

She folded a square of rough yellow cotton and tied it, babushka-style, on her head.

"Good fit, even if they're slightly threadbare," Brenner remarked as he examined the trousers he'd just pulled on.

Kiril wore a similar pair—coarse serge, wide and gathered at the waist.

Both he and Brenner put on formless grey caps.

"Ready?" he asked, holding the back door open.

A tall dignified man with thick steel-gray hair waited outside. He looked more like a businessman than a farmer, Kiril thought. Three bicycles leaned against the back of the house, their scrawny tires and tinny-looking bodies giving them the look of pre-war relics. The old man rattled off a few sentences in German and went back into the house.

"He wished us good luck," he told Adrienne. "He said this is a good hour to enter the town because people will be leaving work."

"Let's hope he meant it," Brenner said drily.

"They need the money. The jewelry's worth a lot on the black market. They won't turn us in," Kiril reassured him.

But will *you?* Adrienne wondered silently as a man on a motorbike with slicked-back hair and no helmet fixed them with a curious stare as he passed.

Will *you* turn us in? she asked a shabbily clothed family who examined them closely before pedaling off in the opposite direction.

*Will you be the ones?* she wondered, her question aimed at a couple of Vopos who stood just inside the Potsdam city limits while she tried to ignore a sign too prominent to miss:

UNDYING FRIENDSHIP AND ALLIANCE
WITH THE SOVIET UNION!

*Don't turn us in,* she pleaded whenever Kurt or Kiril paused to ask directions, leaving her to envy them their flawless German.

They walked their bicycles down narrow cobblestone streets, every face, every frown, looming as a potential threat. Even the unbroken gray stucco on both sides of the street seemed less like rows of connecting houses than solid impregnable walls.

Only when gray stucco gave way to red brick did

Adrienne's fear give way to hope. She saw signs of a cheerful Dutch influence in the high rounded tops of the attached houses. In the black shutters with their white trim.

It was she who spotted the sign on an iron post: Hollandische Siedlung.

She who spotted number "13."

When Kiril pulled the bell cord, she slipped her hand into his. The tightness of his answering grip became a substitute for breathing.

The door opened. A pair of expressionless blue eyes looked them over, curiously at first, then intently.

"Come in. Quickly!" Albert Zind said.

Adrienne was stunned. Not because she thought Albert Zind and his family wouldn't help them. After taking his measure in East Berlin, she had felt sure that he would.

What she *hadn't* expected was that he spoke English!

As soon as all three of them were inside, the door was closed and bolted behind them.

# CHAPTER 46

Albert Zind sat in the cab of an ancient truck parked on the middle of the bridge. It was a huge 1942 Studebaker, one of thousands sent by the United States to the Soviet Union during World War II.

It had four sets of double wheels in the rear, and two more up front. It could carry up to 2½ tons of cargo, had heavy springs and shock absorbers, and boasted a powerful diesel engine. The height of the Studebaker's sides was increased by six horizontal slats around all three sides, making the cargo area roughly six feet high. The height of the bed's sides were increased even more by U-shaped struts that could be fitted to them. A tarpaulin, if tossed over the top, would completely enclose the rear of the truck.

Zind had built an armoire-like structure in the bed of the truck just behind the cab for storing tools and other supplies. The vehicle's front and rear bumpers were massive. And though not fast, the truck was a veritable juggernaut when rolling. Its front windshield could be raised, removing any impediment to the driver's line of sight in inclement weather. The glass window in the rear was roughly four feet wide and two feet high.

For a man like Zind, who was in the construction business, it was the ideal vehicle to own.

For a tough-guy type like his Vopo "pal" Bruno, who drove Zind and his crew on and off the bridge every day, it was pure pleasure—an opportunity to change seats with Zind, get behind the wheel of the powerful '42 Studebaker, and drive!

Seemingly absorbed in thought, Zind was acutely aware of what was going on. Bruno had tried—unsuccessfully—to start the engine. Three times the diesel motor almost caught. Three times it died. Bruno was well aware that if he continued to crank the heavy-duty battery, he would kill whatever power the truck still had.

Shooting a sideways glance in Albert Zind's direction, Bruno said, "Cat got your tongue, Zind?"

"Just wondering what the foreman will say when he finds out I pulled the crew off an hour early."

Bruno shrugged. "Who could work in all this rain? Those twenty guys in the back of the Studebaker are already soaked. You're a foreman same as me, Zind. Foremen are supposed to take care of their men, am I right?" he said good-naturedly.

"The problem is that *my* foreman is nervous about completing the repair job on this bridge," Zind said. "He's being pressed, so naturally he's in a big hurry to get it done. Glienicker Bridge handles way too much traffic—particularly going from East to West."

*There has to be some way to take advantage of that.*

This time when Bruno hit the starter, the engine struggled to life and turned over—barely. Bruno revved it for a few minutes until the battery was charged, then left the bridge and pulled to a stop at the cobblestone square between the East German and Soviet guard houses. Yanking the hand brake, Bruno killed the diesel engine and got out of the truck.

"You better check that battery, Zind," he chided.

"Will do."

"See you Wednesday. Tomorrow I'm off duty," Bruno reminded him.

"Wednesday it is," Zind acknowledged as he slid behind the wheel.

The bridge crew scrambled off the back of the truck and lined up for the headcount.

The "headcount" triggered a reminder of its own . . . How the Wall was being haphazardly thrown together, and what desperate East Germans were doing to escape. During the past several weeks, some would-be defectors were leaping from windows and rooftops to freedom even as other windows and doors were being bricked up, other rooftops sealed, entire buildings demolished.

Sewers were one way out, Zind mused, but there was a price tag attached—the risk of drowning from a sudden rainfall, like today. Or suffocating from accumulated gas. Or being blocked by iron grates and manhole covers that had been welded shut.

Elsewhere throughout Germany, the East and West had always been separated by fences and barriers, he thought. Checkpoints and guard shacks. Barbed wire and land mines. Scrutiny by watchtowers that were manned by Vopos with machine guns. Swimming across a lake or a river even in darkness was problematical.

Yet according to the grapevine, a handful of would-be defectors had made it out not long ago. The student who'd buried his fiancée in a trunkful of clothes. Two heavily-clothed families, eleven kids between them, who'd flattened themselves under a refrigerated truckload of frozen meat. Some electrician who had scurried hand-over-hand across a disconnected high-tension cable. Four East German soldiers who'd bulled their way through fences and mines in an old armored Cadillac.

Such incidents were unique, unrepeatable—ideas that worked only once because the border patrols hadn't anticipated them.

The Zind brothers, Erich and Gunther, climbed into the front seat. "Crew's all counted," Gunther said to Albert.

"Come up with any ideas?" Erich asked him.

"Not yet.".

He headed for the marshalling yard. When he pulled up, his foreman was pacing outside the engineering office.

"I know, I know," Albert grumbled as he and his brothers emerged from the truck. "We just cost you an hour out of your schedule. But everyone is soaked to the skin."

"That's not the worst of it," Mueller groaned. "Those new steel supports I ordered? They're being delivered on Wednesday. Day after tomorrow."

"So?"

"So I need to be on the bridge when they get here! But they want me in Berlin that day so they can grill me about the delays on repairing this godforsaken bridge. How can I be in two places at once?"

"What are you worried about? I'm an engineer too. I'll handle it."

Mueller was visibly relieved. "Then do," he said.

As Albert and his brothers waited in the rain for the bus ride home, a torrent of water rushed down the gutter heading for the sewer—prompting Albert's thoughts to turn to tunneling. A lot of tunnels would be built—eventually. But not yet. *Lousy timing*, he thought as he replayed what Kiril had told them last night . . .

*Any minute now this whole town can be subjected to a house-by-house search by Vopos—maybe even Russians. We're running out of time.*

\* \* \*

That Monday evening as everyone sat around the dining room table, Albert raised a troubling question. "Is it time to relocate the three of you?"

"Where to?" Kurt Brenner asked.

"A place far from the border until I can come up with a plan."

"No," Kiril said with quiet emphasis. "The time is now. The place is Glienicker Bridge."

Albert's eyes narrowed. "Why do you think you'll have better luck than your dead friend?" he asked solemnly.

"I'm not irresponsible, Albert," Kiril said, not taking offense. "It's just that we're too close to run. We're only *meters* from West Germany. But run deeper into East Germany? I'm convinced that the risk is much worse. Is there any chance we could pose as members of your construction crew?"

"Not with the share-the-work policy," Erich said.

"Which means what?" Brenner asked.

"A labor pool. Albert has to choose a different crew every morning. It's for security reasons. The idea is to keep everyone off balance. Make it harder for anyone to plan an escape attempt in advance—like hiding under the truck after a head count," he said drily.

Albert stood up. "There *is* a way to switch crew members," he said as the room went quiet. "Kiril and the Brenners could take the place of Erich, Gunther and our friend Otto Dorf. My foreman expects delivery of new bridge supports the day after tomorrow. But Mueller has to be in Berlin. I promised I'd take up the slack—get the new supports to the bridge early in the morning. Do whatever engineering work comes up until he gets back." He cracked a smile. "But when we finish work, I won't leave the truck at the marshalling yard like I usually do. I'll take it to Otto's uncle's warehouse. We'll build a false wall in the tool cabinet, creating a hidden space about six feet wide by three feet deep to hide all three of you—close enough to the middle of the bridge to make a run for it."

Kiril knew why Adrienne looked alarmed. Brenner was claustrophobic.

Would he be able to keep from panicking?

# CHAPTER 47

"Let's run though it one more time," Albert said as they ate breakfast Tuesday morning. "Today and tonight, the three of you sit tight here. Wednesday, we'll hide you behind the false wall in the cabinet while I drive the truck to the yard to pick up the bridge supports."

Brenner's jaw tightened.

"Once we're loaded and the crew is on the truck, Erich and Gunther will ride with their backs against the cabinet—"

"Why?" Brenner cut in.

"An excess of caution. We want to be sure no one else goes near it. Not a single member of the crew, and no one else. *No one.*"

Erich and Gunther nodded.

"Agreed," Otto chimed in.

"What about the tear gas on the bridge?" Erich wondered out loud.

Brenner paled. "Tear gas? You people must be crazy!"

"Not a problem," Albert said calmly. "When we get to the bridge, the truck will appear to be empty. Even though the

Vopos routinely spray front to back and top to bottom to smoke out anyone who's hiding, we'll have already sealed the compartment where the three of you will be standing."

"Bottom line, Kurt, no gas will seep in," Adrienne said impatiently.

"So all three of us are on the bridge," Kiril said. "Then what?"

"We create a diversion. Maybe a fire from the hot rivets. Maybe a fight. Someone could fall into the river." Albert shrugged. "We'll figure out something plausible to distract the guards. It's only about ten yards."

"That's one helluva lot of 'maybes,'" Brenner said frostily. "This brilliant plan has more holes than a slab of Swiss cheese."

Adrienne could only roll her eyes at Kurt's unseemly outburst.

As she started to help Frieda Zind scrape remnants of sausage and scrambled eggs from the breakfast plates, she was rewarded with a tentative smile on that ravaged face.

"Level with me," Kiril said as Albert stood up to leave. "Even if we do escape, aren't you and your family in jeopardy?"

"We knew the risk when we took you in."

"I guess what I'm really asking is whether there's a way we can do this without your being exposed."

"You know there isn't. Sure, we might be arrested and interrogated, maybe beat up some. But it's capitalism that'll save us."

Kiril and Adrienne were stunned. Instead of just cracking a smile, Albert actually grinned.

"For years, the East German regime has done a brisk business with West Berlin swapping relatives and friends," Albert explained. "We don't have either. What we *do* have is something that's in short supply in West Berlin—skilled workers. In our case, a structural engineer and a couple of iron workers."

"And in return, East Germany gets what?" Kiril asked.

"Consumer goods that are practically unobtainable in this so-called worker's paradise. Coffee, butter, spare parts, electronic equipment. As for our Soviet comrades taking it out on us for helping you, there's one thing we can count on. It won't be a *Soviet* affair because everything we're doing takes place here in East Germany. So if you make it out—and I think your chances are excellent—the regime won't want any publicity about a single defection, let alone three, two of them Americans."

"So it's on to the Dorf family's warehouse," Albert said cheerfully.

"Hold on a minute," Kiril said, following Albert and his brothers out the front door. "I just thought of something—"

The door swung shut.

Brenner headed for the stairway leading to the bedrooms.

Adrienne put out a hand to stop him. "You've been acting like a snob ever since we got here, Kurt."

"Don't lecture me," he snapped.

"Even Mrs. Zind, who doesn't speak English, is nervous just being in the same room. Your attitude jumps the language barrier like an Olympic pole vaulter," she said coldly. "Can't you show a little gratitude?"

"I thanked the older brother for what they're all doing."

"I know the German word for 'thank you'. You said it once, maybe twice. The point is *how* you said it. Like a condescending employer to the hired help. And by the way, the older brother has a name. It's Albert."

"You're coming unstrung."

"And you're in denial. If the accommodations here are too modest, you can always return to that affluent Brenner hotel suite in East Berlin."

"You have an irritating sense of humor."

"And you have a callous side to your nature that's even worse than I suspected. You can be affable to people in New York who, if you needed them, would slam their collective doors in your face. Yet you're barely civil to a family who took us in without question and are trying, at great personal risk, to save our lives."

"I think you're enjoying this little melodrama, Adrienne," he said slowly. "It's just your style. All these people you can feel sorry for and identify with."

"It's maddening how your mood shifts. You seemed so different when things fell apart in East Berlin while we listened to Anna—"

"Are you serious? I *didn't* defect. So what does she do? Unload on our family history! If it weren't for her, I'd have been home by now."

Adrienne plunged ahead. "Maybe not. Aleksei Andreyev had no intention of releasing you. But he was so stunned by Anna's revelation that he was caught off guard. That gave you and Kiril time to disarm and disable Andreyev and his so-called shadow. The way the two of you worked together in perfect harmony . . ."

She looked away for a moment. "For the first time," she said softly, "I sensed—"

"What, that we were brothers? Don't remind me," Brenner said with an expression of distaste just as Kiril walked back inside.

"You shouldn't have come to Kurt's rescue, Kiril," Adrienne said. "You sacrificed your freedom for the bastard and he resents you for it."

"You're wrong. I don't believe in sacrifice," Kiril said evenly. "I did it for Anna. I'd never have taken the risk if I hadn't thought we had a decent chance of escaping. We still do."

"And if they catch you now, what will it mean, a labor camp? A firing squad?"

He didn't answer.

"A firing squad," she said, closing her eyes in a vain effort to hold back the tears. She reached for him and drew him into her arms.

"You're still my wife, damn you," Brenner hissed, fury in his eyes. "'My place is with my husband,'" he mimicked. "That's the noble little sentiment you shared with that mob of journalists when you and this—this stand-in—were about to return to East Berlin."

"I was stalling for time."

"Are you forgetting about the night when you were cold and I—"

"That was rape."

"It may have started out that way," he admitted, "but that's not the way it ended. Or am I being too crude?"

Resisting the impulse to slap the smugness off his face, she said, "I'm not crude enough to tell you *why* it ended the way it did. Just so you know, Kurt, I'm locking you out of the room we've been sharing for appearance's sake so that your 'stand-in' and I can go to bed."

Turning their backs on him, she and Kiril walked upstairs hand in hand.

# CHAPTER 48

It was Tuesday evening. Everyone sat at the kitchen table while Albert and his brothers pored over a large topographical map of Potsdam and the surrounding area.

Gunther pointed to what looked like a small earthen bowl about 200 meters across and surrounded by a heavily treed area. The hint of a dirt trail ran to the bowl from the blacktop road about a mile away. The blacktop led to the Havel River. Glienicker Bridge was a half-mile beyond.

"What are we looking at?" Kiril asked.

"An old cobalt mine," Erich said. "Been closed for years ever since the war. It was owned by the British."

"The Brits left all their equipment there," Gunther said. "Then our Soviet comrades carted most of it off it to Mother Russia in 1946."

"We have a new plan," Albert announced, "but we'll need an additional day. We'll hide the three of you in the mine until we're ready to move on it."

"So what's new about your plan?" Brenner said impatiently.

"Yesterday I had battery trouble. Back at the yard last

night I saw that a fan belt was loose."

He looked at Adrienne. "The fan belt drives the generator, which, in turn, charges the battery."

She nodded.

"I tightened the belt last night so there'd be no problem with the battery today," Albert continued. "Tomorrow—Wednesday—the Vopo who drives us on and off the bridge returns to work. I have an okay relationship with him. I'll have already picked up the bridge supports at the yard. The Vopo will remember the fan belt problem we had last Monday. I mention that I had the same problem again on Tuesday but the battery seems all right now. I'll check it again later, I tell him. I have all day."

Albert paused. "When no one's looking," he said grimly, "I open the hood and disconnect the fan belt. Sometime earlier that day, Gunther will have put a metal bar under a front tire. There should be enough leftover juice in the battery to start the truck—which means we'll immediately run over the metal bar. My Vopo driver will stop short. Can't be too careful. After all, there are tools lying all over the bridge. If we risk a flat tire, the truck would have to stay parked on the bridge all night. Can't have that! I'll have to look under the tire. But I *won't* until Bruno turns off the engine. I get out of the truck, return with the bar. The Vopo pushes the ignition. Nothing. Engine won't start. Now I look at the fan belt. Disconnected—imagine that! Needs a special pry-bar to be reinstalled, but I can't get one until early tomorrow morning. Can't recharge the battery until then."

"I love this part," Erich said. "Bruno goes into panic mode. *What, and leave the truck on the bridge until tomorrow? My superiors would never allow it!*"

"So we mobilize guards and crew members to push the truck on the slight downward slope of the bridge and into the cobblestone square," Albert said, picking up the thread. "The guards return to their posts in the middle of the bridge. The crew lines up for headcount. The East German and Soviet guards rush out of their guard houses. Can't leave the truck blocking the mouth of the bridge— blocking most of it, anyway. So they find some chains and use their cars to tow the truck behind the East German guard house."

"We're back to a bunch of 'maybes,' are we?" Brenner said with disdain. "*Maybe* you'll be able to disconnect the fan belt. *Maybe* you'll get the driver to stop so you can get under the truck. *Maybe* someone in charge will be unwilling to leave the truck on the bridge overnight. *Maybe* some men will push it downhill. *Maybe* they'll have chains. *Maybe* the truck can be towed around the corner in back of the East German guardhouse."

Everyone in the room looked grim.

"There's no other way," Albert said.

Kiril, Adrienne, and Brenner spent the rest of Tuesday evening mulling over their own thoughts.

Kiril relived the years he had spent making plan after plan to defect from the Soviet Union.

Adrienne thought of the sham her marriage had become, wondering if Kurt's love for her had been illusory from the start—and why she had no doubts at all that Kiril's feelings for her were real.

Kurt Brenner's mind was focused on more pragmatic matters. How to ditch the Brothers Zind before he practically suffocated to death in their six-feet-wide, three-feet-deep tool cabinet. Once he'd managed that, he would figure out how to make it to West Berlin on his own.

\* \* \*

Late in the evening, the Zinds returned home. The tool cabinet false wall part of the plan had been executed flawlessly. The Studebaker was now parked behind the East German guardhouse with a disconnected fan belt. Construction on the truck cab and the cabinet was complete. "There's more," Albert told them. "In a little while we'll take you to the old mine area. A few structures are still standing. They'll provide some shelter. You'll spend the rest of tonight there."

Kiril noticed that Brenner had gone into alert.

"Before sunrise tomorrow—Thursday—you'll make your way close to the guard houses at the mouth of the bridge. As you hide nearby, you'll see the Studebaker parked in the back of the East German guardhouse. While it's still dark," Albert reminded them. "The three of you will enter the flatbed's hidden compartment. After sunrise, I'll show up to reconnect the fan belt, collect the bridge supports at the marshalling yard, return to load the work crew, and sit next to my East German Vopo pal while he drives us even closer to the middle of the bridge. You won't be squeezed in that small compartment for more than a few hours," he said, glancing pointedly at Kurt Brenner.

And was puzzled by Brenner's expression. He seemed inattentive.

"Now we get to the tricky part," Albert continued. "As we all know, there's no way around it. So listen carefully because timing is everything from here on. I'm talking freedom or recapture. Life or death."

Nobody moved. It seemed as if nobody breathed, Adrienne thought.

"Before we came home tonight," Albert said, "we loosened the glass window in the back of the cab and replaced the back wall of the cabinet with sturdy painted cardboard. We also unscrewed the wood slats between the truck bed and the cab. They're being held by bolts without nuts."

Albert saw that Kiril was the only one who understood what was coming.

"The instant the work crew is off the flatbed and

grouped behind it, Gunther will whistle as if it's time to start work. Several things happen close together now. From the outside, Erich opens the driver's door. I shove the Vopo out of the cab and jump outta the passenger's side while Kiril—"

"Pushes out the cardboard wall, slides the six slats away, shoves the window into the cab, slips under the steering wheel, pushes the starter and engages the gears, and drives like hell to the West," Kiril said vehemently.

He had a frightening flash image of Stepan Brodsky having done the same thing—until he realized that Stepan had commandeered his diplomat friend's limousine *not from* the middle of the bridge, but way back at the guard houses. With East German and Soviet firepower covering both the guard houses and the watch towers, the odds of his friend making it across had been near impossible, he thought bleakly.

# CHAPTER 49

Kiril, Adrienne, and Brenner entered a ramshackle Quonset hut. Debris was everywhere. Missing windows, twisted metal, empty file cabinets, upturned furniture.

Knowing none of them would get any much-needed sleep if Kurt pulled another attempted-rape scene, Adrienne deliberately kept Kiril between them, bedding down with some heavy blankets that the Zinds had left for them.

All three of them slept in their clothes, removing only their shoes.

The day's events had taken a heavy emotional toll.

Kiril wondered whether he—whether all three of them— would live to see another night. Even though he was utterly fatigued, he forced himself to stay awake until he heard the rhythmical breathing of the others. Minutes later, he fell into a deep sleep.

When he awakened, he had a long moment of disorientation . . . Sunrise, he reminded himself. Thursday.

Adrienne was still asleep, her face in repose. He turned in the direction of Kurt Brenner.

*Gone.*

"Adrienne," Kiril whispered, gently shaking her awake. "Your husband's not here."

* * *

Kurt Brenner had feigned sleep until Adrienne and Kiril's regular breathing told him they really *were* asleep. Carrying his shoes, he moved soundlessly through the Quonset hut. He knew that the dirt trail they'd walked down with the Zinds the night before would take him to the blacktop road—and from there to the Havel River.

Outside, he slipped into his shoes and, keeping off the trail, moved cautiously parallel to it through dense underbrush. He headed for the road with only a sliver of moon for light. Once he got there, he began to follow it while still keeping himself hidden in the underbrush.

Dawn was about to break when he stopped to rest. His plan was to reach the river in early daylight, then hide nearby until the fracas on the bridge started later in the morning. Then under cover of the ensuing chaos, he would swim for the west side of the Havel River—he was a powerful swimmer—and put an end to this long, drawn-out nightmare.

As Brenner crawled on his belly through the underbrush, obscured by foliage, he kept Glienicker Bridge and the Havel River in sight.

A watchtower Vopo noticed what appeared to be movement. Unsure if he could trust his eyesight because dawn had not yet broken, the Vopo looked away. But when he quickly looked in the same direction again, the movement under the foliage was even closer to the river.

# CHAPTER 50

V on Eyssen was halfway out the door when the buzzer rang on his desk. He frowned with annoyance, hoping whoever it was wouldn't make him late for his appointment with a Soviet major general who didn't like to be kept waiting.

"It's some captain from the Potsdam checkpoint," his secretary apologized. "He insists on speaking with you."

*Potsdam? The major general will have to wait.*

"Put him through."

"We've got him!" The voice from Potsdam was triumphant. "We've got the Russian spy. The one you're looking for."

"Kiril Andreyev? You're certain?"

"It's him, all right. I just checked out the latest bulletin. No question that it's him."

"What about the American couple?"

"Andreyev was alone."

"Did you search him yet?" von Eyssen asked, trying to keep the concern out of his voice.

"No."

"Do it the second we get off the phone."

"Yessir."

"Have the Russians been informed?" von Eyssen asked cautiously.

"They must have been. That's how it always works with defectors."

*Too bad. What will Colonel Aleksei Andreyev do when they contact him? Make a run for Glienicker Bridge, of course. If Andreyev gets hold of his brother's lighter first, he'll destroy it and then I'll be back where I started—his word against mine.*

"You want me to search him before the Russians take him, Colonel?"

"Take him? Take him where?"

"I don't really know," the captain said. "That's what happens every time with defectors. Our Russian comrades get them first. Then us."

"Listen to me, Captain. I don't care what you have to do, but search Kiril Andreyev before the Russians grab him. I want whatever you find. And the Russians are not to know, goddammit! Do you understand?"

The usually unflappable Colonel Emil von Eyssen smashed the phone down, sweat oozing from his armpits. Staring off into space, he wondered if he dared go anywhere near the damn bridge after what had happened with Stepan Brodsky last year. Any more trouble in the vicinity of Glienicker could prove to be a personal disaster, with severe criticism being the mildest punishment. On the other hand, if he were to get his hands on the lighter first, von Eyssen could prove that a Soviet—the brother of Colonel Aleksei Andreyevich Andreyev—was the traitor, not an East German citizen.

Not his late brother-in-law, Ernst Roeder.

\* \* \*

"Out!" the East German captain ordered.

Those who were sitting shot to their feet. Everyone left.

Except Kurt Brenner, handcuffed to a radiator, who wasn't going anywhere soon.

After the captain finished a quick but thorough body search, he picked up the telephone and called von Eyssen.

"Kiril Andreyev has nothing in his pockets. Nothing on him—period. Should I do a cavity search?"

"Don't be a fool," von Eyssen snapped. "Even someone as clever as Kiril Andreyev wouldn't hide a Zippo cigarette lighter up his ass," he said, and hung up.

Brenner was stunned. So this Kraut, confused by his dark hair, had searched him looking for something important—a cigarette lighter. And apparently the captain had good reason to think the real Kiril Andreyev had the lighter.

Brenner felt an insane desire to laugh in the man's face—just as a very sane idea came to him.

His instinct for survival hadn't deserted him after all, he thought with an inner smile as he pictured a Studebaker truck just on the other side of the wall from where he sat.

# CHAPTER 51

During Brenner's odyssey, Kiril and Adrienne had reached Albert Zind's truck and secreted themselves in the tool cabinet's small compartment.

It was close to dawn. Albert would soon be coming for the truck, Kiril thought. He heard Adrienne take a deep breath, then let the air out slowly. "How are you doing?" he whispered.

"There's barely enough air for breathing and all I can think of is how desperately I want a cigarette."

"I know what you mean. Legs getting tired?"

"Terribly. I think they'll hold up."

"Lean against me instead of the wall when you want to shift position. It will relieve some of the pressure."

"Kiril?"

He closed his eyes.

"Why don't you answer?"

"I wanted to hear you say it again"

"Kiril," she said softly.

"We'd better stop talking the minute we hear voices outside."

"There's something I want you to know in case anything else goes wrong," she said. "I agreed to accompany Kurt to East Berlin because—"

"Don't explain. It was obvious from the beginning that you weren't some apolitical wife along for the sightseeing. The questions you asked, the notes you took."

Kiril closed his eyes, his mind on Stepan now. On their twin cigarette lighters. On the microfilm inside. He thought of their naïveté that the information would prove to be so valuable the CIA would help Stepan defect and somehow exfiltrate Kiril to get their hands on it.

*And here I am, Stepan, not far from the place where you struggled to push your lighter over the side—your final protective act.*

*Your end and, perhaps, my beginning. Thank you, my friend, my fellow exile.*

*My true brother.*

As Kiril held the lighter in one hand, his fingers automatically moving back and forth over it like a talisman, Adrienne reached for his hand. Her forefinger followed the outline of outstretched wings.

"What do they stand for?" she asked.

"The black wings? Somewhere in his travels, Stepan picked up a pair of American Zippo lighters and attached the emblems himself. They represent your American eagle. It was our symbol of hope. I've read your *Declaration of Independence* many times. Is it really the freest place on earth, the United States of America?" he asked wistfully.

Shifting her body, she leaned against his, needing a contact more personal than words.

"It's still the freest place on earth," she whispered. "And if we want to get there, now is the time to worry about what's happened to Kurt. What he might be up to."

"You really believe he'd betray us?"

Before she could answer they heard footsteps. A clanging noise. Someone puttering around at the front of the cab. The driver's door opening. The ignition being cranked. The engine turning over. They winced in unison at the thud of the driver's door slamming shut.

Albert . . . the battery.

The truck was ready.

# CHAPTER 52

"I don't understand," von Eyssen said in German as he paced back and forth in the East German guard house. "Why would you give the cigarette lighter to Dr. Brenner?"

"I told you. For safekeeping. He's an American, after all." Brenner's emotions were on the edge of crumbling despite his pose of nonchalance. He took a long drag on his cigarette. "Brenner's escape plan involved less risk than mine. Why is that so difficult to grasp?"

"What plan? What risk? How did you get here from the airport? Where have you been? Who helped you? Where *are* Brenner and his wife?"

Brenner smiled enigmatically.

"What was your plan? Swim for the other side?" von Eyssen said slowly. "You of all people should have known better. You know what's out there. You'd probably be dead now instead of sitting here toying with me. A bullet in the back. Loss of blood from some underwater barbed wire. Maybe ripped apart by one of the dogs on a patrol boat—"

Von Eyssen couldn't contain his fury. "God damn it, Andreyev, where is Dr. Kurt Brenner?"

"*And* his wife? I'll tell you. But only if you let me walk across that bridge. I go free. You get the Americans and the cigarette lighter."

*And proof of what Aleksei and the Russkies were up to at the summit.*

"Shall we stop playing games, Colonel?" Brenner said, feeding impatience into his voice. "You think I don't know what's at stake for you here? Letting me cross that bridge gets you a lot and costs you nothing. I'll vanish into the West. The Americans are your problem. But you'd better decide. Brenner and his wife are almost out of your grasp."

Von Eyssen made a lightning-quick calculation. If he acted fast, not only would the Russians be embarrassed, not only would Stepan Brodsky's attempted escape finally be laid at the doorstep of both Andreyevs, but *he* would get the credit. The cherry on the cake? Von Eyssen's superiors would be delighted.

"Now or never, Colonel," Brenner snapped.

"How do you want to do this?" von Eyssen asked, acutely aware that Aleksei Andreyev was on his way. "Do you really think I'll let you walk across that bridge, then wait patiently for a postcard from Paris?"

"Do you take me for a fool? We're wasting time. My brother Aleksei will be here soon. You and I will walk side-by-side to the middle of the bridge. We stop about fifteen feet from the West Berlin side."

"With my revolver in your ribs, don't forget," von Eyssen snarled. "Get on with it, man!"

"Think of it as a three-step scenario. I tell you where Brenner and his wife are. You verify it *instantly*. I cross the dividing line."

*And into West Berlin.*

"Instantly?" von Eyssen said, incredulous.

"Instantly," Brenner repeated. It was true enough.

"Let's go." Von Eyssen practically pushed Brenner out the door.

As soon as they began walking, he waved the bridge guards aside.

They were halfway to the middle when a Soviet limousine skidded into the square on the rain-soaked cobblestones at the mouth of the bridge. Out leaped Aleksei Andreyev, followed by Luka Rogov. As von Eyssen and Brenner walked toward the middle of the bridge, Aleksei and Luka froze in place.

Hearing the car, von Eyssen said under his breath, "We're going to turn around slowly, our backs to the West."

They turned.

"Now start walking backward very slowly," von Eyssen ordered.

As soon as he saw the two men start to turn, Aleksei grasped what von Eyssen was up to. He'd made a deal. Set Kiril free in return for Kurt and Adrienne Brenner's hiding place—and, most important, for the microfilm in the cigarette lighter.

*Stupid, stupid, stupid. Kiril will lie—who wouldn't? And whatever else he is, von Eyssen isn't stupid. What's he up to? One thing is certain. They must be stopped.*

Von Eyssen and Brenner continued to walk carefully backward.

Aleksei and Luka ran toward them, slipping and sliding on the wet pavement, Aleksei cursing under his breath at their slow progress.

As they closed the distance, von Eyssen said, "They're only a few yards away, Dr. Andreyev. It's now or never. Either you tell me where the Brenners are or I'll blow your brains out."

"They're in the truck," Brenner told him.

"Truck? What truck? Where?"

"They're hiding in the Studebaker behind the guardhouse."

Von Eyssen smiled. "Just in time," he said as Andreyev and the Mongolian reached them. He raised his revolver and shot Brenner in the right eye.

Kurt Brenner's body sank to the pavement.

"You fool!" Aleksei yelled as sirens blared and guards rushed to the bridge. "With Kiril dead, we've lost our only lead to the cigarette lighter!"

Von Eyssen smiled inwardly.

*If you only knew how close you are to it.*

Aloud, he said innocently, "You always said there was no love lost between you and your brother. Is that really why you're so angry?"

"Frustrated, not angry. I'd have put Kiril before a firing squad once the dust settled," Aleksei said, nudging Brenner's head with the toe of his boot.

They saw it simultaneously—dark brown stains seeping into a puddle under Brenner's head. A small patch of white hair slowly growing larger in the water.

"You idiot! You stupid Kraut!" Aleksei screamed. "You just shot the wrong man! You killed a famous American heart surgeon who just told the world he intended to defect to the Soviet Union!"

Aleksei knelt down, oblivious to the muddy water seeping into his pants. Seizing Brenner's head with both hands, ignoring the ghastly hole in one eye, he pulled at a patch of hair. Another. Another.

*White, all white!*

"Look! Look at his hair, you moron. It's *you* who's going before a firing squad!" he screamed.

"You think so?" von Eyssen said, leveling his revolver at Aleksei's chest.

Luka Rogov dropped von Eyssen with one shot to the head.

Utter chaos erupted.

Guards running. Voices screaming. Sirens wailing.

And lying amidst it all, the hollow-eyed corpse of Dr. Kurt Brenner.

* * *

*Gunshots.*

From the flatbed's compartment Kiril and Adrienne had heard the commotion.

"What's going on?" Adrienne whispered.

"I don't know. But it's time to leave."

"Do we have a chance?"

"A chance, yes. Can we make it from here? Maybe."

*Ironic,* he thought. *I'm as far back from the middle of the bridge as Stepan was.*

Ripping the cardboard away, he exposed the six slats and the rear of the cab. Sliding the slats away, he kicked out the cab's window and slid under the wheel as Adrienne jumped into the passenger seat.

*The Zinds had done their work well.*

Kiril engaged the Studebaker's gears, swung round the guardhouse and, slipping and sliding through the cobblestone square, headed for the mouth of the bridge, pressing the truck's air horn as if his life depended on it. Which, in fact, it did.

The unearthly sound of the air horn on the bridge stopped everyone in their tracks. There was no way people could miss that oncoming behemoth of a truck in the distance.

Everyone sprinted to the sides to avoid it.

Everyone except a stunned Aleksei Andreyev and a puzzled Luka Rogov. They stood frozen in place as if, by the sheer force of their combined will, they could stop the juggernaut hurtling toward them.

Confused by the chaos on the bridge, the watchtower guards held their fire. A signal from Aleksei would have instantly sent a torrent of machine gun bullets to drench the bridge with death.

Aleksei, recognizing what was happening, signaled Luka to move away from the middle of the roadway.

Kiril had just passed the mouth of the bridge.

*A straight run to the middle, then West Berlin and freedom!*

"Crawl under the dashboard—now, Adrienne!" he shouted as he floored the accelerator. His brother had just signaled the watchtowers to fire.

Aleksei was nearly halfway to the middle of Glienicker when the watchtowers, joined now by some of the soldiers and guards on the bridge, opened up with everything they had. Most of the rounds missed because of the truck's speed.

But Kiril knew how vulnerable they were, just as Stepan had been. The tires, he thought—as one of the truck's eight rear tires blew.

The Studebaker slowed but didn't stop. Kiril kept to the middle of the blacktop road.

*West Berlin just ahead.*

Off to the right, Kiril spotted Aleksei and Luka Rogov. Seconds before he had to decide, he hesitated.

*Monsters. They deserve to die!*

At the last second, he swerved away.

But Luka Rogov stepped into the middle of the road, aiming his submachine gun at the Studebaker as if it were some huge animal he could bring down.

Kiril had no choice but to run him over.

Bullets raked into the right side of the truck. The cab's front left tire blew. Through the driver's door, Kiril took a 30-caliber round in his thigh.

Seconds later, Kiril and Adrienne burst into West Berlin.

# EPILOGUE

When Dr. Kiril Andreyev qualified to practice medicine in New York City, he and his parents took over the Dr. Kurt Brenner Medical Center for Underprivileged Juveniles. Despite the many wrongs Kurt had committed, continuation of the Center's work would rightly commemorate his many contributions to helping young heart patients.

Adrienne Andreyev turned over her husband Kiril's microfilm to Paul Houston, who still claimed he was employed by the Department of State.

Two years later, with the help of unknown persons somehow connected with Houston, the entire Zind family was ransomed out of East Germany and settled in West Berlin.

No one ever learned what became of KGB Colonel Aleksei Andreyev.

In 1992, a year after German reunification, Dr. Kiril Andreyev returned to Berlin. A search of *Stasi* records had revealed that Stepan Brodsky had not been buried in Treptower Park's mass grave after all.

Kiril had tracked down Stepan's younger sister, a

longtime anti-communist, who knew of Kiril through her brother. He persuaded her to allow disinterment of Stepan's remains from a family plot near Frankfurt.

Air Force Captain Stepan Brodsky was reburied in Kensico Cemetery, Hamlet of Valhalla, County of Westchester, State of New York.

*United States of America.*

# EYE FOR AN EYE: A NOVEL OF REVENGE

With scalding suspense and a plot ripped out of the headlines, *Eye for an Eye* explores urban violence and retribution.

Karen Newman is a smart savvy executive whose sole contact with violence is abstract, and whose soft-on-crime inclinations are in striking contrast to her hard-headed business acumen.

Until violence strikes a much-loved member of her family and sends her life spinning out of control.

Confronted with the spectacle of street gangs and sadistic young killers free to kill again, an increasingly enraged Karen finds herself the object of recruitment efforts by people who promise "vigilante justice." Mildly curious, she takes the first tentative step, cynically anticipating a bunch of bat-swinging amateurs — and is caught off guard by the professionalism she encounters.

Despite her initial reluctance, Karen finds herself seduced by what she sees and hears firsthand. Gradually, she is drawn into the inner circle of a fascinating, chillingly organized group. Its name: VICTIMS ANONYMOUS. Its structure: secret cells in far-flung major American cities.

Its motto: *Vengeance is mine.*

Knowing her particular business expertise is needed to catapult a growing organization into a national phenomenon — a force to be reckoned with — Karen tries to convince herself that Victims Anonymous is a *force for good.* In the face of mounting evidence that the police and the courts are increasingly unable to cope with violent crime, she no longer needs much convincing.

She makes the ultimate commitment.

It does not waiver until she crosses swords with a man who shares that commitment — a passion for justice that equals her own. A man she must deceive before he can bring the entire edifice crashing down upon the heads of everyone and everything she cares about.

*Eye for an Eye* is the story of a gutsy woman's personal struggle to balance genuine compassion for the abandoned victims of a collapsing criminal justice system with a dangerous romance and a growing conviction that vigilantism, however well intended, is a magnet for evil.

\* \* \*

**Nelson DeMille,** best-selling author of *The Panther*, has said that:

> "*Eye for an Eye* is a serious and disturbing look at street gangs, urban violence, and the criminal justice system. It is also a story about the uniquely American response to crime—vigilantism.
>
> *Eye for an Eye* is not so much about America as it is a book of America; a story that grows

organically out of the ongoing American obsession with law and order. Erika Holzer, an attorney, understands the system, and more importantly she understands the society she and the rest of us live in. She has created a plot from what could be, and often is, any newspaper headline, and carried it a step further, a step many of us would not take but think about in our darkest moments.

Holzer's characters are vividly created, impassioned, and interestingly flawed so that we relate to them and believe they exist. The writing is sharp and terse, moves at a fast pace, and the dialogue is snappy and to the point.

**Highly recommended. A sort of American *Clockwork Orange*.**

# PROLOGUE

Reflections. The diamond at her throat, flashing splinters of orange. The crystal chandelier, out of range of her roaring fire but dancing with candlelight.

Her tight grip on the telephone?

Reflection of a holiday mood gone sour . . .

"Karen, for God's sake," she protested into the phone. "What are you trying to do, scare me to death? Tonight of all nights," she said, willing her voice to turn calm.

"Utter privacy is a mixed blessing, isn't it?"

"I love it now," she lied. "After three years, even a city dweller gets used to the Westchester woods."

But she never had.

"So much crime, these days. It worries me. I was reading—"

"On the West Side of Manhattan, maybe," she cut in, "not out here."

But she'd been reading about it, too. Burglars from New York and NewJersey heading for the suburbs. Looking for bigger game. Burglars with wheels . . . and what else, guns? Knives?

"Sarah, your alarm system—"

"My security blanket, you mean," she admitted drily. "We had it upgraded while you were away. Goes off in the police station now. The cops are on the scene in five minutes tops. Hold on while I check the roast."

On the way to the kitchen, she glanced in the mirror. The full treatment, she thought, pleased with *this* reflection, at least. Black satin lounging pajamas. Slippers with stiletto-thin heels. Blonde hair looking sleek, straight, and sexy, just the way Mark liked it.

*All's well in the dinner department,* she thought, sniffing and prodding, practically sailing back to the living room, her festive mood restored.

"Listen, killjoy," she said, cocking an ear to the phone, "no more raining on my parade, okay? You're supposed to say—"

"Happy anniversary, I know. Don't mind me, dear. Tonight will be very special."

"Starting with my table. Wish you could see it!"

"As exquisite as that? Draw me a picture."

"My centerpiece would knock your socks off. Mark's too, I hope. Masses of tiger lilies, the most glorious shade of orange—"

"In a black vase, of course."

"Darn right."

"What else?"

"Candlelight, crystal, and the good china." She smiled. "Artfully arranged on a lace tablecloth—that wispy silvery one, remember? Goes with the glasses."

She touched the delicate rim of a smoky, long-stemmed champagne glass. Ran a finger along the intricate pattern of a sterling-silver knife. Picked up the knife just to enjoy the weight of it in her hand.

"I even liberated a couple of place settings from the safe-deposit box—"

She could have bitten her tongue.

"Since when do you keep your sterling in the bank? Have there been any burglaries near you, Sarah?"

"Don't be silly. People around here play it safe, that's all."

*People around here don't want their sterling—not to mention their jewelry—carted off in a pillowcase while they're out to dinner.*

"What are you sighing about?" she asked.

"I just wish Mark didn't take these night classes."

"Mark doesn't *take* them. They're assigned. Besides, I've never minded." Another lie. "Don't start, Karen. You're making me jumpy all over again."

"Don't blame *me*. You were always jumpy on Halloween."

"And you're a big help. Hold on again, okay? I had a hard time getting the fire started and it's looking a bit feeble."

Lie number three. She was having a hard time holding her temper. She took her impatience out on a log that her robust fire didn't need, teetering on the damn heels as she struggled with the iron tongs, hair rippling around her shoulders.

*Like liquid gold, Mark would say.*

The tongs back in place, she gave the radio dial a defiant twist, then said into the phone, "Mood music."

"I can hear the lyrics all the way down here. So could your neighbors if you had any."

"Wise guy. Don't worry, I switch to Brahms the minute Mark walks in the door."

"When *is* he walking in?"

"Best guess? Half an hour. Why don't we play catch-up while we're waiting? Tell me about your presentation. Bet you snared the account."

"Before I even took off my coat."

"They don't pay you enough, you know that? When I think—"

"Boo, mommy, boo!"

She whirled around, almost dropping the phone, then laughed at the small masked figure in the doorway above.

"Only ghosts say 'boo,' darling."

"Oink, oink."

"Thata girl. Now off to bed, Miss Piggy."

"Rhyme, rhyme, you owe me a dime!"

"Stop stalling, Susie. Tell you what. You get *three* dimes for three rhymes under the pillow by morning—*if* you're in bed by the count of five. Ready? One . . . two . . . three . . ."

She retrieved the phone. "Susie is still keyed up. Lots of little trick-or-treaters made house calls."

"Ghost and hobgoblin time . . ."

"You're dating yourself, kiddo. These days, it's characters out of *Star Wars* and the *Muppets*. Me, I'm nostalgic. I prefer ghosts and hobgoblins."

"Isn't that your doorbell?"

"What's on the other end of that line, Karen, an amplifier?"

"Why would Mark ring? Could he have forgotten his keys?"

"Not likely. Probably some last-minute trick-or-treaters. No home-by-eight in the suburbs. Be right back."

She pressed her face to frosted glass and grinned, feeling like a kid again as she picked out the slightly distorted shapes. Kids draped in sheets, clustered around one little Muppet in green. All of them were holding tight to their goody bags.

"Would you believe old-fashioned ghosts outside my door?" she chuckled into the phone. "Takes me all the way back."

"Sarah, maybe you better—"

"Oh, and one modern touch," she said. "An adorable little Muppet frog. Hang in there while I distribute the loot. Homemade candied apples this year, if you please!"

She held a silver platter of apples in one hand. With the other, she turned a key. A chip of light next to the doorknob went from unblinking red to bright yellow. She opened the door.

They pushed in on her so that she teetered precariously, almost dropping the platter. "Hey you little roughnecks," she scolded, "I was about to hand you—"

Except for the frog, they weren't so little, she thought. She counted seven ghosts as they fanned out into the foyer . . . the dining area . . . the living room.

She opened her mouth to yell at them—

And was cut off by a howl. They were howling and whooping!

A brown hand flipped the radio dial, turning up the volume.

She took an automatic step backward as a ghost moved in on her. A denim sleeve shot out from under a sheet, tilting the silver platter. The candied apples went flying.

"What do you think you're doing?" she gasped when she saw where he was headed.

*He was piling up her silverware.*

"Put it back, damn you!"

But he didn't. Then one of them, a ghost like the others but with a black hood, approached her table—her exquisite table—and she didn't move to stop him because he had picked up a knife. A vicious yank of the tablecloth sent her crystal and china to the stone floor with a splintering crash. An overturned vase spilled water, drowning the flame of a candle.

Black Hood advanced on her—

But stopped short while the frog took his picture.

She could almost feel him smiling under his mask as he stood there holding the knife as he waited for the picture to develop. Instant results from an Instamatic . . .

Her head swayed to the crazy rhythm. Ghosts wearing sneakers and running shoes. Thick denim legs, weaving and bobbing. Hands that grabbed, ripped out, piled up, tore through, smashed aside—

And stopped, they kept stopping while a frog took

their picture.

*Insanity!*

She snapped out of it with a jolt. Inching sideways, step by invisible step, she moved in the direction of the front door. She was almost there when Black Hood let out a yell. She lunged.

Her heels caught in the doormat as her hand snaked out, missing the alarm's panic button by an inch.

She went down.

Two of them dragged her toward the mess in the dining room. Water seeping into black satin . . . fabric tearing—and flesh. Her thigh scraping across broken glass.

The howling started up again, turned piercing—

And brought her, thrashing, to her feet.

*Susie!*

It was less a thought than a silent cry of panic that leapt to her eyes. That sent her glance up three steps to the doorway on the left. Had Black Hood noticed, damn him? He was coming over!

"Jewelry," she told him. "Up there. The bedroom to the right. My jewels. My husband's. Just open the—"

He cut her off with an imperious wave. Two of them went up without waiting for her to tell them where it was. But they'd stopped howling. And they'd gone in the opposite direction from Susie's bedroom.

When they came out of the master bedroom with a pillowcase, she forced herself to turn away.

A few others disappeared into her kitchen and came out gnawing on a chicken breast. What turned her legs to rubber was that they'd let her see their faces.

Black Hood walked over to her. She backed away slowly. She knew what the bastard

had noticed *this* time . . . the diamond pendant that had been her engagement ring. It rose and fell with her ragged pulse. She had a flash-memory of telling Mark that, as much as she loved her engagement ring, it was too many carats to wear safely in public. With a rush of bitterness at the irony, she reached for the clasp. "Take it, it's very valuable," she told Black Hood. "Take your loot and get the hell out of my house."

Her hands were still fumbling with the clasp when he ripped her blouse open to the waist.

They came at her like a wolf pack.

Her only weapon was a silent litany . . .

*Susie, Susie. Dear God, let me be quiet for Susie.*

Her arms were grabbed from behind.

*Susie—*

Her legs were yanked up, stripped, pulled apart.

*Susie, Susie!*

Her body was slammed against the wet stone floor.

As their leader whipped off his face mask, Sarah stared into utter vacancy . . . and shuddered at the thin slash of a mouth. And because she dared not scream, dared not risk awakening her child, she gave in to tears.

His mouth twisted as his hand shot out, knocking her senseless.

Not quite senseless. She felt the tearing pain of forced penetration.

She felt it again . . . again—oh God, again and again! How much more could she endure?

"Hey, lookee, a natural blonde!"

They were gloating, howling, whooping over her, while someone kept yelling at them to stop—the frog?

She half raised her head in time with a flash of his camera.

More flashing, more howling, she was on the verge of howling herself, she was on the brink of unconsciousness—

She was yanked back by a squeal of laughter and an "oink oink."

"Kermit! Mommy, it's Kermit the Frog!"

Her scream went off like a delayed siren.

When Karen heard the scream, the telephone clattered to the rug, a strangely muffled sound.

She snatched it up again. "Sarah, in God's name, tell me what's happening!"

No voice to answer her. Only the sound of raucous disco and some weird repetitive howling. But she'd heard Susie's voice babbling about a frog and a—a hermit?

She yelled Susie's name into the phone. She yelled for Sarah.

She heard Sarah's voice, heard her rage—

"No, don't—not on my wedding anniversary! You've got the diamond, damn you to hell! What more do you—"

*A scream—agonized.*

She heard her own scream as she dropped the phone again.

*Hang up. Get help.*

But how would she get Sarah back?!

She heard the baby crying—so clear, so close to the phone.

"Somebody turn the fuckin' brat off!"

*Sobbing—deep-voiced. Sarah? Please God, Sarah?*

"We better get outta here!"

"Shut your face and take your fuckin' pictures."

"Hey, anybody want some roast piggy?"

"Put those tongs down! Don't hurt my baby!"

"Leave them alone! Don't hurt them!"

"Shut your face, I tole ya! Wipe those prints, asshole."

"Mommy, Mommy!"

"It's all right, darling. Mommy's coming. It's all right."

*Sarah . . . so close she could almost reach through the wire and touch her.*

"Sarah."

It had come out a whisper.

"Sarahhhhhhhhhhhhh! "

"Check out the phone! Hey, boss, we got us a motherfuckin' snoop!"

"Sonofabitch . . ."

"—be afraid, Susie darling, it will be all—"

The sound that came through the phone stopped her in mid-scream. Dry, rasping—

She stared at the receiver.

*What had she heard?*

"Did you hear that, bitch? You get yourself a fuckin' earful?"

What she heard next were sharp repetitive cries, a kind of whooping, like Indians on the warpath.

Then a click.

She was calm when she got the Bedford police on the line. She would have stayed calm if they hadn't kept badgering her, wasting precious minutes with their questions. Who's this calling? Where you calling from? Manhattan? How come you called in the emergency? Over and over they kept at it until she had to scream at them to shut them up, she couldn't stop screaming.

"I'm her mother!"

# ACKNOWLEDGMENTS

Kai Bowen — "The Computermeister" — has been helping me (and my husband) with hardware and software computer service and advice for years, both in person and remotely. Kai is very accessible, reasonably priced, and no problem I have ever had has stumped him. (See www.thecomputermeister.com). Any possible errors in *Freedom Bridge's* German phrases are mine, not Kai's.)

Judith Sansweet (www.proofreadnz.co.nz) put my text through the fires of professional proofreading as she polished the manuscript for print and digital publishing. I learned a great deal from Judith during the always delicate matter of editing an author's writing, knowledge which I intend never to forget! (Deviations from the *Chicago Manual of Style* and Strunk's *Elements of Style* reflect the author's preferences and are entirely my doing, not Judith's.)

Rita Samols (www.jejune@mail.com), reading Freedom Bridge for pleasure, made considerably useful comments about the manuscript, for which I am very grateful.

To Tabatha Haddix, a fellow novelist (www.tlhaddix. com), my thanks for graciously, and with good cheer, altering my scheduling and consults with *Streetlight Graphics* numerous times.

Glendon Haddix of *Streetlight Graphics* has been an unmitigated pleasure to work with from Day One. His talent and subtlety, from book cover to graphics, and his ability to divine exactly what I wanted before I was fully able to express it, has been invaluable.

My gratitude to Robert Bidinotto, bestselling author of *Hunter*. Robert is a *very* old and valued friend who, over the years, has had unstinting praise for my novels. Thanks to his posting on P.J. Media entitled "10 Reasons You Should Skip Traditional Publishers and Self-Publish Ebooks," I—and lots of other fiction writers—did just that. Perhaps Robert's generosity can best be expressed by what he wrote me a few years ago: "It gives me great pleasure to help great writers!"

In my earlier novel, *Eye for an Eye*, my acknowledgment to my husband, Hank Holzer, reads: "To my first editor and best friend." Even though he has asked me to keep it that simple this time around, I cannot oblige. *Freedom Bridge* is enriched throughout with Hank's historical research and some dramatic turning points.

Oh, and he's still my first editor and best friend!

# BOOKS BY THE AUTHOR

*Eye for an Eye**

*Double Crossing*

*Ayn Rand: My Fiction-Writing Teacher*

*Fake Warriors: Identifying, Exposing, and
Punishing Those Who Falsify Their Military Service*
(with Henry Mark Holzer) (Second Edition)

*Fake Warriors: Identifying, Exposing, and
Punishing Those Who Falsify Their Military Service*
(with Henry Mark Holzer) (First Edition)

*"Aid and Comfort": Jane Fonda in North Vietnam*
(with Henry Mark Holzer)

---

\*   A Paramount feature film based on *Eye for an Eye,*
starring Sally Field and Kiefer Sutherland and directed by
John Schlesinger.

# ABOUT THE AUTHOR

E rika Holzer received her B.S. from Cornell University and her law degree from New York University.

For several years following her admission to the New York bar, she practiced constitutional and appellate law with Henry Mark Holzer. Their clients included Soviet dissidents and defectors, and other lawyers for whom they prepared appellate briefs and Petitions for Certiorari for the Supreme Court of the United States.

One of the Holzer firm's clients (and later friend) was the novelist, Ayn Rand. Because of Rand's literary influence, Erika Holzer switched careers from law to writing.

With Henry Mark Holzer, she co-authored *"Aid and Comfort": Jane Fonda in North Vietnam*, proving that Jane Fonda's trip to Hanoi during the Vietnam War, and her activities there, constituted constitutional treason.

Again with Henry Mark Holzer, Erika co-authored *Fake Warriors: Identifying, Exposing, and Punishing Those Who Falsify Their Military Service.*

Her other non-fiction writing consists of essays, articles, reviews, political and legal commentary.

In addition, Erika is author of the book *Ayn Rand: My Fiction-Writing Teacher: A novelist's mentor-protégé relationship with the author of Atlas Shrugged.*

Holzer's most recent short story, *Eyewitness*, appears in *Scout & Engineer*, available on Kindle and most other eBook readers and through www.amazon.com.

Author Nelson DeMille has said about Erika Holzer's novel, *Eye for an Eye*, that it is "a serious and disturbing look at street gangs, urban violence, the criminal justice system, and vigilantism. Erika Holzer, an attorney, has created a plot from what could be any newspaper headline and carried it a step further. Her characters are vividly created, impassioned, and interestingly flawed so that we relate to them. Highly recommended. A sort of American *Clockwork Orange*."

Holzer's *Eye for an Eye* became a Paramount Pictures feature film starring Sally Field and Kiefer Sutherland.

Erika Holzer can be contacted at
erika.holzer@erikaholzer.com and
through www.erikaholzer.com.

www.ingramcontent.com/pod-product-compliance
Lightning Source LLC
Chambersburg PA
CBHW020334180626
46812CB00001B/195